WORLDS OF WONDER

A desperate, jittery crew on a spaceship hurtling toward the outer edge of the galaxy . . . A great scientist revolutionizing the mind of man with the simple statement of a shocking new truth . . . Men and robots in a bizarre contest for control of the universe . . . The fantastic story of man's exploration of the stars . . . The incredible drama of the human body and the great chain of life around us . . . And much, much more. . . .

They say that everything King Midas touched turned to gold. Isaac Asimov is the Midas of modern writing and here, freshly minted, is an Asimov treasury of his greatest work—from his first 100 books!

"Asimov's genius begins with his ability to understand and retain almost everything he has ever read, to recall the most demanding material readily and in exact detail . . . and then to put it into straightforward, crystalline prose."

—*The Boston Globe*

OPUS 100

ISAAC ASIMOV

A DELL BOOK

ACKNOWLEDGMENTS

The author wishes to thank the following for permission to quote all
or part of the works listed:

Abelard-Schuman Limited: *Only a Trillion. The Chemicals of Life.*
Copyright 1954 by Isaac Asimov. *The Wellsprings of Life.* © 1960
by Isaac Asimov.
American Institute of Physics: "An Uncompromising View," book
review from February 1969 issue of *The Physics Teacher.* Copy-
right © 1968 American Association of Physics Teachers.
Analog: Science Fact-Science Fiction: "Thiotimoline and the Space
Age." Copyright © 1960 by Street & Smith Publications, Inc.
Astonishing Stories: "The Calistan Menace." Copyright 1940 by
Fictioneers, Inc. Copyright © renewed 1967 by Isaac Asimov.
"Superneutron." Copyright 1941 by Fictioneers, Inc. Copyright ©
renewed 1968 by Isaac Asimov.
Astounding Science Fiction: "Liar!" Copyright 1941 by Street &
Smith Publications, Inc. Copyright © renewed 1968 by Isaac
Asimov. "Runaround." Copyright 1942 by Street & Smith Publi-

To Time and Circumstance,
which have been kind to me.

CONTENTS

OPUS
100

INTRODUCTION

FRANKLY, I never planned it this way. I never planned anything at all in my writing career. I don't even have an agent to do my planning for me. I just worked along, from day to day, as the spirit moved me, rather like the cheerful idiot I seem to be, and everything broke right.

To begin with, I have never quite recovered from the rather incredulous relief I feel that people are willing to pay me for what I write. If they didn't pay me, I would still write, of course, for I wrote for years and years before it occurred to me to submit anything for publication. However, if I wrote for non-pay as an adult, my friends and family would view me as some kind of nut. (Come to think of it, they do, anyway.)

On October 21, 1938, when I was eighteen, I made my first professional sale—a 6400-word short story, entitled "Marooned Off Vesta," for which I received $64.00. The price of one cent a word was what I commanded in those days and sometimes I commanded even less. The story appeared in the March, 1939, issue of *Amazing Stories,* an issue which was on sale in January of that year, just a couple weeks after my nineteenth birthday,

I had the fugitive thought, even then, that I might succeed in writing and selling other science-fiction stories, but my expectations were rather moderate to begin with. After all, I had a college education to finish, a chemical career to launch, and a life to live. Writing was merely an amusement, and the most I could honestly hope for were a few dollars to help pay my college tuition.

For eleven years I continued to sell science-fiction stories to the magazines and to gain a certain minor fame among that very small (but infinitely wonderful) segment of the population known as "science-fiction fandom." And it *did* help me with my college tuition. Indeed, it helped me right through to my Ph.D. in chemistry which I received from Columbia University on June 1, 1948 (I was delayed by World War II).

Then, on January 19, 1950, my first book appeared—just two and a half weeks after my thirtieth birthday. It was *Pebble in the Sky* (Doubleday, 1950). I received some small reviews that were, for the most part, mildly favorable, and I felt much more like a professional writer than I had ever felt before.

But it was still only science fiction and I still reached only science-fiction fandom. Even a real hardbound opus, a regular *book,* couldn't make me think of myself as, primarily, a writer. After all, I had just begun a teaching career as Instructor in Biochemistry at Boston University School of Medicine (on June 1, 1949—for those who must have exact statistics) and there was no question in my mind that my true calling lay in the classroom and the laboratory. Writing was only my avocation.

It was a curious avocation, though, since I was in no position to "take it or leave it." I had been writing ever since I was eleven—I would have started sooner, I think, if I could have laid my hands on a nickel copybook—whenever opportunities were in the least favorable. Even when I was in the army, I cajoled the post librarian (a most sympathetic lady) into letting me stay inside when it was closed so that I could write in peace. I not only managed to write a story under those conditions; I sold it.

And here I was in the early 1950's, attaining professional status in 1951, and yet still scribbling away at all times, evenings and weekends. I was beginning to realize consciously what I must surely have known unconsciously all along. Let's face it: I was that serious distortion of the human condition—the compulsive writer.

My "avocation" continued to grow and by the end of 1957, I could no longer kid myself into thinking I wrote "on the side." Writing was all I really wanted to do. What's more, by the close of 1957, I had published a total of twenty-four books, and six of them were *not* science fiction or, indeed, any kind of fiction. I was beginning to write books on science. ("Straight" science, I am forced to call it, so that it is clearly distinguished from science fiction.) I could scarcely consider twoscore books in eight years a mere sideline. Especially since my writing income was now two and one-half times my school income.

In 1958, then, I abandoned teaching altogether and began to devote myself entirely to writing. And if I needed anything to tell me that I had made the right decision, it was the feeling of absolute delight that washed over me as I did so.

With the thought that now I could bang, bang, bang away at my typewriter for ten hours at a time every day if I wished (and I bought an electric typewriter to lower the rate of approach of physical exhaustion), a little bug bit me. I was turning out books at an increasing rate (in 1957 five of them had been published) and, being very number conscious, I couldn't help but do a little figuring. Could I live long enough to publish a hundred books?

Somewhat wistfully, I mentioned the possibility to my wife, who promptly found herself out of sympathy with that as a tenable ambition. Being the wife of a compulsive writer is a fate worse than death anyway, since your husband is physically home and mentally absent most of the time, and that is the worst possible combination. The thought that I would set myself a hundred-book goal and get worse and worse as I strove to reach it was too much for her.

She said to me, "Someday, Isaac, when you feel your life drawing to a close, you'll think back on how you spent it at the typewriter and you'll feel sorry you missed all the pleasures you might have experienced. You'll regret all the years you wasted just so that you could write a hundred books, and it will be too late!"

I'm afraid I was not impressed. I've listened very carefully to people describing the glories of their vacations and I don't see that it's a patch to what I feel when I am clicking away, smooth and harmoniously, at my typewriter. So I said to her, "Listen, if you're at my bedside when I'm about to read that Big Galley Proof in the Sky, you just bend close and get my last words because they're going to be, 'Only a hundred?' "

I don't suppose I was entirely serious, but if I can hang on just a little while longer, till I complete what needs to be done to prepare this manuscript, the whole question will become academic.

For this, you see, is My Hundredth Book.

The idea for this precise book arose at a luncheon at

Locke-Ober's here in Boston on September 28, 1968. With me were Austin Olney, Walter Lorraine, and Mary K. Harmon of Houghton Mifflin. I was about to have my ninety-second book published and the question arose as to how many other books I had in press. As I began to tick them off, we all realized that My Hundredth Book was upon me.

Various suggestions were made and finally someone (I think Austin) suggested that I make it a completely personal book in which I rattled on and on about myself and my writings, with selections from books, articles, and stories where those were appropriate.

I thought about it briefly, and said, "Any writer who is a monster of vanity and egocentricity—like myself, for instance—would love to write a book like that. But who would buy it?"

"You let us worry about that, Isaac," said Austin.

All right, then. I intend to have a lot of fun and as for you, Houghton Mifflin—worry!

PART 1
ASTRONOMY

AS YOU MAY KNOW (and as any writer must *know) there is a disease called "writer's block" which is pitiful to see. A block writer can go days, months, years, without ever being able to satisfy an unbearable craving to write. He may stare for hours at a time at a blank sheet of paper in the typewriter; or he may type and tear, type and tear endlessly; or he may visit a psychiatrist to ask for the return of his compulsion neurosis.*

So far, thank goodness, I have managed to escape this plague.

I do not attribute my escape to any superior intelligence or virtue on my part at all. I attribute it entirely to the lucky circumstance that I can write with equal readiness in a number of different branches of science, and in some fields that are far removed from science—to say nothing of fiction.

The result is that when, far off on the distant horizon, the faintest twinge of weariness with what I am doing makes itself felt, I merely pull the sheet out of the typewriter, adjust it neatly on Pile A, pull the top sheet off Pile B, and carry on with something else which may be so different in nature that I am once again overcome with total eagerness.

Consequently, if I have the liberty of selecting from my own material at will, I warn you that it will be a potpourri indeed. And I'll start with astronomy.

I have never really taken a single formal course in astronomy in college, but astronomy is the science for a science-fiction writer. I picked up quite a bit in my omnivorous reading, and have kept on picking up quite a bit to this very day. This reflects itself in what I write and I suppose some future candidate for his master's degree can set a new record for research-topic inconsequentiality by study-

ing my output in chronological progression and deducing the state of my educational advancement therefrom.

I shall save him part of his trouble right here by considering my treatment of the satellites of Jupiter at various stages in my career.

The satellites of Jupiter appear in the earliest piece of writing I ever published professionally, which makes it a good subject to start with anyway.

No, it didn't appear in "Marooned Off Vesta," which I mentioned earlier as my first published story. That was first published, but third written. The first written was never published (its title was "Cosmic Corkscrew," if you're curious) and no longer exists. The second written was "The Callistan Menace."

I wrote "The Callistan Menace" in July, 1938, and it appeared, eventually, in the April, 1940, issue of Astonishing Stories, two years after "Marooned Off Vesta," though it had been written a month earlier.

I wouldn't dream of presenting the entire story (it's rather poor) but I will include the beginning—partly because they're the very first professional words of mine, and partly because it represents my initial treatment of the satellites of Jupiter:

from "The Callistan Menace" (1940)

"Damn Jupiter!" growled Ambrose Whitefield viciously, and I nodded agreement.

"I've been on the Jovian satellite run," I said, "for fifteen years and I've heard those two words spoken maybe a million times. It's probably the most sincere curse in the Solar System."

Our watch at the controls of the scoutship *Ceres* had just been relieved and we descended the two levels to our room with dragging steps.

"Damn Jupiter—and damn it again," insisted Whitefield morosely. "It's too big for the System. It stays out there behind us and pulls and pulls and *pulls!* We've got to keep the Atomos firing all the way. We've got to check our course—completely—every hour. No relaxation, no coasting, no taking it easy! Nothing but the rottenest kind of work."

There were tiny beads of perspiration on his forehead and he swabbed at them with the back of his hand. He was a young fellow, scarcely thirty, and you could see in his eyes that he was nervous, and even a little frightened.

And it wasn't Jupiter that was bothering him, in spite of his profanity. Jupiter was the least of our worries. It was Callisto! It was that little moon which gleamed a pale blue upon our visiplates that made Whitefield sweat and that had spoiled four nights' sleep for me already. Callisto! Our destination!

Even old Mac Steeden, gray mustachioed veteran who, in his youth, had sailed with the great Peewee Wilson himself, went about his duties with an absent stare. Four days out—and ten days more ahead of us—and panic was reaching out with clammy fingers.

We were all brave enough in the ordinary course of events. The eight of us on the *Ceres* had faced the purple Lectronics and stabbing Disintos of pirates and rebels and the alien environments of half a dozen worlds. But it takes more than run-of-the-mill bravery to face the unknown! to face Callisto, the "mystery world" of the Solar System.

One fact was known about Callisto—one grim, bare fact. Over a period of twenty-five years, seven ships, progressively better equipped, had landed—and never been heard from again. The Sunday supplements peopled the satellite with anything from super-dinosaurs to invisible ghosts of the fourth dimension, but that did not solve the mystery.

We were the eighth. We had a better ship than any of those preceding. We were the first to sport the newly developed beryl-tungsten hull, twice as strong as the old steel shells. We possessed super-heavy armaments and the very latest Atomic Drive engines.

Still—we were only the eighth and every man jack of us knew it.

Don't worry; the mystery was solved. As I recall there was a wormlike creature on Callisto that could project a magnetic field that was intensified by the ordinary steel of ships and space suits. In this case, the spaceship had a nonferrous hull, but the space suits were still steel. The only nonferrous space suit was Peewee Wilson's undersized museum piece.

Fortunately, a boy had stowed away on the ship—

And you can carry on from there.

But did you see what I did with the Jovian system? That's right; I did nothing. I merely mentioned Jupiter's gravitational pull, and I talked about Callisto's "pale blue" appearance. (Why pale blue, I wonder?)

But, then, that was 1938. By the time a dozen years had passed, I had learned a good deal more about astronomy and about writing. I could handle that same system in greater detail and with more authority.

My chance came in one of the six novels which, between 1953 and 1958, I wrote for youngsters. They all dealt with David "Lucky" Starr and his pint-sized pal, John Bigman Jones, who toured the Solar System, fighting criminals, pirates, spies, and the forces of evil in general.

It was Walter I. Bradbury of Doubleday who first suggested the idea that I write them. The intention was that of supplying a serial hero for television, so that both the publishers and I, myself, might make an honest dollar.

But I hesitated. I don't object to money, in principle, but I have a set of hang-ups about what I'm willing to do in exchange. I said, "But the television people may ruin the stories and then I will be ashamed to have my name identified with them."

So Brad said, "Use a pseudonym."

And I did. I chose Paul French and wrote all my Lucky Starr books under that name.

As it turned out, television turned out to be utterly uninterested in the Lucky Starr stories and the precaution was unnecessary. So if you want to know who Paul French is— he is I, Isaac Asimov. There's no reason to keep it secret anymore; nor has there been these dozen years and more.

I have been asked a thousand times, by the way, why I picked that particular pseudonym. Apparently, people expect something subtly disreputable to be at the bottom of it. No such thing. At the time I was selecting a pseudonym, I heard that the suspense writer, Cornell Woolrich, deliberately chose a nationality as his—William Irish. So I chose Paul French. Whether Woolrich was or was not of Irish descent, and whether that weighed with him, either way, I don't know. But to keep the record sparkling clean, I'm not of French descent.

The fifth of my Paul French novels was Lucky Starr and the Moons of Jupiter *(Doubleday, 1957). Its plot centered about an important scientific project which was aiming at the development of an anti-gravity device and the work was based on Jupiter's outermost satellite.*

The project was in trouble, however. Information was leaking out to the Solar System's most inveterate enemies, the human colonies (long since independent and grown despotic and dangerous) in the Sirian system. Actually, the Sirian system is a poor place for human colonies because the star, Sirius, is too large, hot, and bright, and has a white-dwarf companion besides. However, I didn't intend to worry about it till I wrote a Lucky Starr novel set in the Sirian system—and I never got to it.

Lucky Starr and John Bigman Jones are, therefore, coming to the Jovian system to try to locate the source of the leak. Jupiter's outermost satellite is described in the first selection. Later in the book, they travel in toward Jupiter on the first anti-gravity (Agrav) ship, and that flight is described in the second selection:

from LUCKY STARR AND THE MOONS OF JUPITER (*1957*)

Dropping down toward Jupiter Nine reminded Bigman very strongly of similar maneuvers in the asteroid belt. As Lucky had explained on the voyage outward, most astronomers considered Jupiter Nine to have been a true asteroid to begin with; a rather large one that had been captured by Jupiter's tremendous gravity field many millions of years previously.

In fact, Jupiter had captured so many asteroids that here, 15,000,000 miles from the giant planet, there was a kind of miniature asteroid belt belonging to Jupiter alone. The four largest of these asteroid satellites, each from forty to a hundred miles in diameter, were Jupiter Twelve, Eleven, Eight, and Nine. In addition there were at least a hundred additional satellites of less than a mile in diameter, unnumbered and unregarded. Their orbits had been plotted only in the last ten years when Jupiter Nine was first put to use as an anti-gravity research center, and the necessity of traveling to and from it had made the population of surrounding space important.

The approaching satellite swallowed the sky and became a rough world of peaks and rocky channels, unsoftened by any touch of air in the billions of years of its history. Bigman, still thoughtful, said, "Lucky, why in Space do they call this Jupiter Nine, anyway? It isn't the ninth one out from Jupiter according to the Atlas. Jupiter Twelve is a lot closer."

Lucky smiled. "The trouble with you, Bigman, is that you're spoiled. Just because you were born on Mars, you think mankind has been cutting through space ever since creation. Look boy, it's only a matter of a thousand years since mankind invented the first spaceship. . . . Before space travel was invented, men were restricted to Earth and all they knew about Jupiter was what they could see in a telescope. The satellites are numbered in the order they were discovered, see?"

"Oh," said Bigman. "Poor ancestors!" He laughed, as he always did, at the thought of human beings cooped up on one world, peering out longingly.

Lucky went on. "The four big satellites of Jupiter are numbered One, Two, Three, and Four, of course, but the numbers are hardly ever used. The names Io, Europa, Ganymede, and Callisto are familiar names. The nearest satellite of all, a small one, is Jupiter Five, while the farther ones have numbers up to Twelve. The ones past Twelve weren't discovered till after space travel was invented and the men had reached Mars and the asteroid belt . . . Watch out now. We've got to adjust for landing."

It was amazing, thought Lucky, how you could consider tiny a world eighty-nine miles in diameter as long as you were nowhere near it. Of course, such a world is tiny compared to Jupiter or even to Earth. Place it gently on Earth and its diameter is small enough to allow it to fit within the state of Connecticut without lapping over; and its surface area is less than that of Pennsylvania.

And yet, just the same, when you came to enter the small world, when you found your ship enclosed in a large lock and moved by gigantic grapples (working against a gravitational force of almost zero but against full inertia) into a large cavern capable of holding a hundred ships the size of the *Shooting Starr,* it no longer seemed so small.

And then when you came across a map of Jupiter Nine on the wall of an office and studied the network of underground caverns and corridors within which a complicated program was being carried out, it began to seem actually large. Both horizontal and vertical projections of the work volume of Jupiter Nine were shown on the map, and though only a small portion of the satellite was being used, Lucky could see that some of the corridors penetrated as much as two miles beneath the surface and that others spread out just under the surface for nearly a hundred miles.

"A tremendous job," he said softly to the lieutenant at his side.

Lieutenant Augustus Nevsky nodded briefly. His uniform was spotless and gleaming. He had a stiff little blond mustache, and his wide-set blue eyes had a habit of staring straight ahead as though he were at perpetual attention.

He said with pride, "We're still growing."

The days passed. Halfway to Jupiter, they passed the inner and more sparsely populated belt of small moons, of which only Six, Seven, and Ten were numbered. Jupiter Seven was visible as a bright star, but the others were far enough away to melt into the background of the constellations.

Jupiter itself had grown to the size of the Moon as seen from Earth. And because the ship was approaching the planet with the Sun squarely to its rear, Jupiter remained in the "full" phase. Its entire visible surface was ablaze with sunlight. There was no shadow of night advancing across it.

Yet, though the size of the Moon, it was not so bright as the Moon by any means. Its cloud-decked surface reflected eight times as much of the light that reached it, as did the bare powdered rock of the Moon. The trouble was that Jupiter only received one twenty-seventh of the light per square mile that the Moon did. The result was that it was only one-third as bright at that moment as the Moon appeared to be to human beings on Earth.

Yet it was more spectacular than the Moon. Its belts had become quite distinct, brownish streaks with soft

fuzzy edges against a creamy-white background. It was
even easy to make out the flattened straw-colored oval that
was the Great Red Spot as it appeared at one edge, crossed
the face of the planet, then disappeared at the other.

Bigman said, "Hey, Lucky, Jupiter looks as though
it isn't really round. Is that just an optical illusion?"

"Not at all," said Lucky. "Jupiter really isn't round. It's
flattened at the poles. You've heard that Earth is flattened
at the poles, haven't you?"

"Sure. But not enough to notice."

"Of course not. Consider! Earth is twenty-five thousand
miles about its equator and rotates in twenty-four hours,
so that a spot on its equator moves just over a thousand
miles an hour. The resulting centrifugal force bulges the
equator outward so that the diameter of the Earth across
its middle is about twenty-seven miles more than the
diameter from North Pole to South Pole. The difference
in the two diameters is only about a third of one percent,
so that from space Earth looks like a perfect sphere."

"Oh."

"Now take Jupiter. It is two hundred and seventy-six
thousand miles about its equator, eleven times the circum-
ference of Earth, yet it rotates about its axis in only ten
hours; five minutes less than that, to be exact. A point on
its equator is moving at a speed of almost twenty-eight
thousand miles an hour; or twenty-eight times as fast as
any point on Earth. There's a great deal more centrifugal
force and a much larger equatorial bulge, especially since
the material in Jupiter's outer layers is much lighter than
that in the Earth's crust. Jupiter's diameter across its
equator is nearly six thousand miles more than its diameter from North Pole to South Pole. The difference in the
diameters is a full fifteen percent, and that's an easy thing
to see."

Bigman stared at the flattened circle of light that was
Jupiter and muttered, "Sands of Mars!"

The Sun remained behind them and unseen as they
sank toward Jupiter. They crossed the orbit of Callisto,
Jupiter Four, outermost of Jupiter's major satellites, but
did not see it to advantage. It was a world 1,500,000 miles
from Jupiter and as large as Mercury, but it was on the

other side of its orbit, a small pea close to Jupiter and heading into eclipse in its shadow.

Ganymede, which was Jupiter Three, was close enough to show a disc one-third as wide as the Moon seen from Earth. It lay off to one side so that part of its night surface could be seen. It was three-quarters full even so, pale white, and featureless. . . .

Everyone aboard the *Jovian Moon* was watching the day Ganymede eclipsed Jupiter. It wasn't a true eclipse. Ganymede covered only a tiny part of Jupiter. Ganymede was 600,000 miles away, not quite half the size of the Moon as seen from Earth. Jupiter was twice the distance, but it was a swollen globe now, fourteen times as wide as Ganymede, menacing and frightening.

Ganymede met Jupiter a little below the latter's equator, and slowly the two globes seemed to melt together. Where Ganymede cut in, it made a circle of dimmer light, for Ganymede had far less of an atmosphere than Jupiter had and reflected a considerably smaller portion of the light it received. Even if that had not been so, it would have been visible as it cut across Jupiter's belts.

The remarkable part was the crescent of blackness that hugged Ganymede's rear as the satellite moved completely onto Jupiter's disk. As the men explained to one another in breathless whispers, it was Ganymede's shadow falling on Jupiter.

The shadow, only its edge seen, moved with Ganymede, but slowly gained on it. The sliver of black cut finer and finer until in the mid-eclipse region, when Jupiter, Ganymede, and the *Jovian Moon* all made a straight line with the Sun, the shadow was completely gone, covered by the world that cast it.

Thereafter, as Ganymede continued to move on, the shadow began to advance, appearing before it, first a sliver, then a thicker crescent, until both left Jupiter's globe.

The entire eclipse lasted three hours.

The *Jovian Moon* reached and passed the orbit of Ganymede when that satellite was at the other end of its seven-day orbit about Jupiter.

There was a special celebration when that happened. Men with ordinary ships (not often, to be sure) had reached

Ganymede and landed on it, but no one, not one human being, had ever penetrated closer than that to Jupiter. And now the *Jovian Moon* did.

The ship passed within 100,000 miles of Europa, Jupiter Two. It was the smallest of Jupiter's major satellites, only 1900 miles in diameter. It was slightly smaller than the Moon, but its closeness made it appear twice the size of the Moon as seen from Earth. Dark markings could be made out that might have been mountain ranges. Ships' telescopes proved they were exactly that. The mountains resembled those on Mercury, and there was no sign of Moonlike craters. There were brilliant patches, too, resembling ice fields.

And still they sank downward, and left Europa's orbit behind.

Io was the innermost of Jupiter's major satellites, in size almost exactly equal to Earth's moon. Its distance from Jupiter, moreover, was only 285,000 miles, or little more than that of the Moon from Earth.

But there the kinship ended. Whereas Earth's gentle gravitational field moved the Moon about itself in the space of four weeks, Io, caught in Jupiter's gravity, whipped about in its slightly larger orbit in the space of forty-two hours. Where the Moon moved about Earth at a speed of a trifle over 1000 miles an hour, Io moved about Jupiter at a speed of 22,000 miles an hour, and a landing upon it was that much more difficult.

The ship, however, maneuvered perfectly. It cut in ahead of Io and wiped out Agrav at just the proper moment.

With a bound, the hum of the hyperatomics was back, filling the ship with what seemed a cascade of sound after the silence of the past weeks.

The *Jovian Moon* curved out of its path, finally, subject once again to the accelerating effect of a gravitational field, that of Io. It was established in an orbit about the satellite at a distance of less than 10,000 miles, so that Io's globe filled the sky.

They circled about it from dayside to nightside, coming lower and lower. The ship's batlike Agrav fins were retracted in order that they might not be torn off by Io's thin atmosphere.

Then, eventually, there was the keen whistling that came

with the friction of ship against the outermost wisps of that atmosphere.

Velocity dropped and dropped; so did altitude. The ship's sidejets curved it to face stern-downward toward Io, and the hyperatomic jet sprang into life, cushioning the fall. Finally, with one last bit of drop and the softest jar, the *Jovian Moon* came to rest on the surface of Io.

There was wild hysteria on board the *Jovian Moon*. Even Lucky and Bigman had their backs pounded by men who had been avoiding them constantly all voyage long.

One hour later, in the darkness of Io's night, with Commander Donahue in the lead, the men of the *Jovian Moon*, each in his space suit, emerged one by one onto the surface of Jupiter One.

Sixteen men. The first human beings ever to land on Io!

Notice that there is considerable detail about the satellite system in Lucky Starr and the Moons of Jupiter *and, while it isn't completely fair to judge only from a selection out of context, take my word for it that the astronomy didn't unduly slow the story.*

As a matter of fact, one of the special delights of writing science fiction is mastering the art of interweaving science and fiction; in keeping the science accurate and comprehensible without unduly stalling the plot. This is by no means easy to do, and it is as easy to ruin everything by loving science too much as by understanding it too little.

In my case, I loved science too much. I kept getting the urge to explain science without having to worry about plots and characterization.

As I shall explain later, I actually began to write nonfiction in the form of a textbook, which is a very constricted way of doing it. I wanted more freedom, and again I found the answer in the science-fiction magazines.

More and more, as time went on, science-fiction magazines were publishing "science articles"—straightforward pieces on science, usually those branches of science that were felt to be of particular interest to science-fiction readers.

In 1955, I published my first science article of this sort. It was named "Hemoglobin and the Universe" and appeared in the February, 1955, issue of Astounding Science Fiction. *I wrote fifteen more, most of them appearing in* Astounding, *and then came a turning point.*

Robert P. Mills, editor of Venture Science Fiction, *a new magazine, suggested I write a regular science column. It was to be a 1500-word piece and I would write one every two months, for the magazine was a bimonthly. I could have my own choice of topics.*

I was delighted. "Yes, indeed," I said, "yes, yes."

The first of my regular columns appeared in the seventh issue of the magazine (January, 1958) but, alas, the magazine survived only through its tenth issue (July, 1958). I got to write only four articles altogether and worse yet, the dismal thought occurred to me that my articles might have helped kill the magazine.

Fortunately, I had the rudimentary good sense not to mention this gloomy hypothesis of mine to Robert P. Mills. He was editing another magazine, a more firmly established one named The Magazine of Fantasy and Science Fiction, *more commonly known as* F & SF, *and in 1959 he asked me to write a column for that. Apparently, he had not independently thought of the lethal characteristics of my writing and even went so far as to suggest 4000 words instead of 1500. Since* F & SF *was a monthly, this meant I would be writing five times as many words for* F & SF *as for* Venture. *Naturally, I was five times as happy.*

My first science article in F & SF *appeared in the November, 1958, issue. The articles are still appearing now, more than ten years later. I have never missed an issue and I am slowly beginning to relax a little bit, since I am almost convinced now that my monthly column may not be harming the magazine.*

In increasing my wordage five times, Mr. Mills shrewdly increased my total payment four times; and in ten years, that payment hasn't been increased, either. But that's all right. I have no complaints. After all—

I am allowed to write on any subject I choose, and I have chosen them anywhere from pure mathematics to a belligerently controversial view on the social status of women. I am allowed to write in any manner I choose (consistent with good taste and human decency—and I'm glad to say I have never given the editors occasion to call me on either) and I get the proofs for correction before

*the articles appear. What fairer approach to writer's heaven
can be desired, and what is money compared with that?*

*So here is a selection from one of those articles that
deals with the satellites of Jupiter, without the bother of a
fictional frame:*

from "View from Amalthea" (*1968*)

To begin with, Jupiter has twelve known satellites, of
which four are giants with diameters in the thousands of
miles, and the other eight are dwarfs with diameters of
150 miles or less.

Naturally, if we want to see a spectacular display, we
would want to choose an observation post reasonably
close to the four giants. If we do, then seven of the eight
dwarfs are bound to be millions of miles away and would
be seen as starlike points of light at best.

Let's ignore the dwarfs then. There may be some interest
in following a starlike object that shifts its position among
the other stars, but that is not at all comparable to a
satellite that shows a visible disc.

Concentrating on the four giant satellites, we will surely
agree that we don't want to take up an observation post
from which one or more of the satellites will spend much
of its time in the direction of Jupiter. If that happens, we
would be forced to watch it with Jupiter in the sky, and I
defy anyone to pay much attention to any satellite when
there is a close-up view of Jupiter in the field of vision.

For that reason, we would want our observation post in
a position closer to Jupiter than are the orbits of any of
the four giant satellites. Then we can watch all four of
them with our back to Jupiter.

We could build a space station designed to circle
Jupiter at close range and always watch from the side
away from Jupiter, but why bother? There is a perfect
natural station with just the properties we need. It is
Jupiter's innermost satellite, a dwarf that is closer to the
planet than any of the giants.

The four giant satellites of Jupiter were the first satellites
to be discovered anywhere in the Solar System (except
for our own Moon, of course). Three of them were dis-

covered on January 7, 1610, by Galileo, and he spotted the fourth on January 13.

Those remained the only four known satellites of Jupiter for nearly 300 years. And then, on September 9, 1892, the American astronomer, Edward Emerson Barnard, detected a fifth one, much dimmer and therefore smaller, than the giant four, and also considerably closer to Jupiter.

The discovery came as somewhat of a shock, for the astronomical world had grown very accustomed to thinking of Jupiter as having four satellites and no more. The shock was so great, apparently, that astronomers could not bear to give the newcomer a proper name of its own. They called it "Barnard's Satellite" after the discoverer, and also "Jupiter V" because it was the fifth of Jupiter's satellites to be discovered. In recent years, however, it has come to be called Amalthea, after the nymph (or goat) who served as wet nurse for the infant Zeus (Jupiter).

Amalthea's exact diameter is uncertain (as is the diameter of every satellite in the Solar System but the Moon itself). The usual figure given is 100 miles with a question mark after it. I have seen estimates as large as 150 miles. For our purposes, fortunately, the exact size doesn't matter.

There is no direct evidence, but it seems reasonable to suppose that Amalthea revolves about Jupiter with one face turned eternally toward the planet. On half the surface of the satellite, Jupiter's midpoint is always visible. When standing on the very edge of that "sub-Jovian" side, the center of Jupiter is right on the horizon. The planet (as seen from Amalthea) is so huge, however, that one must go a considerable distance into the other hemisphere before *all* of Jupiter sinks below the horizon.

From roughly one-quarter of the surface of Amalthea, all of Jupiter is eternally below the horizon, and the night sky can be contemplated in peace and quiet. For our purposes, since we want to study the satellites of Jupiter, we will take a position (in imagination) at the very center of this "contra-Jovian" side of Amalthea.

One object that will be visible, every so often, in the contra-Jovian sky of Amalthea will be the Sun. Amalthea revolves about Jupiter in 11 hours and 50 minutes. That is its period of rotation, too, with respect to the stars and (with a correction too small to worry about) to the Sun as well. To an observer on Amalthea, the Sun will appear to make a complete circle of the sky in 11 hours and 50 minutes.

Since Amalthea revolves about Jupiter directly (or counterclockwise), the Sun will appear to rise in the east and set in the west, and there will be 5 hours and 55 minutes from sunrise to sunset.

With this statement, which I introduce only to assure you I am not unaware of the existence of the Sun, I will pass on to the matter of satellites exclusively for the remainder of the article.

The four giant satellites, reading outward from Jupiter, are: Io, Europa, Ganymede, and Callisto. Sometimes they are called Jupiter I, Jupiter II, Jupiter III, and Jupiter IV respectively or, in abbreviated form, J-I, J-II, J-III, and J-IV.

Actually, for what we want, the abbreviations are very convenient. The names are irrelevant after all, and it is difficult to keep in mind which is nearer and which is farther if those names are all we go by. With the abbreviations, on the other hand, we can concentrate on the order of distances of the satellites in a very obvious way, and that's what we need to make the data meaningful.

Using the same system, I can and, on occasion, will, call Amalthea J-V. Generally, though, since it is to be our observation point and therefore a very special place, I will use its name.

So let's start with the basic statistics concerning the four giant satellites (see Table 1) with those for Amalthea also included for good measure. On the data in Table 1, the least satisfactory are the values for the diameters. For in-

TABLE 1 — THE FIVE INNER JOVIAN SATELLITES

Satellite	Name	Diameter (miles)	Distance from Jupiter's center (miles)
J-V	Amalthea	100	113,000
J-I	Io	2300	262,000
J-II	Europa	1950	417,000
J-III	Ganymede	3200	666,000
J-IV	Callisto	3200	1,170,000

stance, I have seen figures for Callisto as high as 3220 and as low as 2900. What I have given you is the rough consensus, as far as I can tell from the various sources in my library.

For comparison, the diameter of our own Moon is 2160 miles, so that we can say J-I is a little wider than our Moon, J-II a little thinner, J-III and J-IV are considerably wider.

In terms of volume, the disparity in size between J-III and J-IV, on the one hand, and our Moon, on the other, is larger. Each of the two largest Jovian satellites is 3.3 times as voluminous as the Moon. However, they are apparently less dense than the Moon (perhaps there is more ice mixed with the rocks and less metal) so that they are not proportionately more massive.

Nevertheless, J-III is massive enough. It is not only twice as massive as the Moon; it is the most massive satellite in the Solar System. For the record, here are the figures on mass for the seven giant satellites of the Solar System (see Table 2). The table includes not only the four Jovian giants and our Moon (which we can call E-I), but Triton, which is Neptune's inner satellite and therefore N-I, and Titan, which I will call S-VI for reasons that will be made clear later.

TABLE 2 — MASSES OF SATELLITES

Satellite	Name	Mass (Moon = 1.0)
J-III	Ganymede	2.1
S-VI	Titan	1.9
N-I	Triton	1.9
J-IV	Callisto	1.3
E-I	Moon	1.0
J-I	Io	1.0
J-II	Europa	0.65

If we are going to view the satellites, not from Jupiter's center (the point of reference for the figures on distance given in Table 1) but from the observation post on the contra-Jovian surface of Amalthea, then we have to take some complications into account.

When any of the satellites, say J-I, is directly above Amalthea's contra-Jovian point, it and Amalthea form a straight line with Jupiter. J-I's distance from Amalthea is then equal to its distance from Jupiter's center minus the distance of Amalthea from Jupiter's center. This represents the minimum distance of J-I from Amalthea.

As J-I draws away from this overhead position, its distance from the observation point increases and is considerably higher when it is on the horizon. The distance continues to increase as it sinks below the horizon until it reaches a point exactly on the opposite side of Jupiter from Amalthea. The entire width of Amalthea's orbit would have to be added to the distance between Amalthea and J-I.

Of course, from our vantage point on Amalthea's surface, we would only be able to follow the other satellites to the horizon. We will be faced with a minimum distance at zenith and a maximum distance at either horizon. Without troubling you with the details, I will present those distances in Table 3.

TABLE 3 — DISTANCES OF THE JOVIAN SATELLITES
FROM AMALTHEA

Satellite	Distance from Amalthea (miles)	
	at zenith	at horizon
J-I	149,000	236,000
J-II	304,000	403,000
J-III	553,000	659,000
J-IV	1,057,000	1,168,000

This change in distance from zenith to horizon is not something peculiar to Jupiter's satellites. It is true whenever the point of observation is not at the center of the orbit. The distance of the Moon from a given point on the *surface* of the Earth is greater when the Moon is at the horizon than when it is at the zenith. The average distance of the center of the Moon from a point on Earth's surface is 234,400 miles when the Moon is at zenith and 238,400 when it is at the horizon. This difference is very small because it is only the 4000 mile radius of the Earth that is involved. When the Moon is at the horizon, we must look at it across half the thickness of the Earth, which we need not do when it is at the zenith.

From a point on Amalthea's surface, however, we must look across a considerable part of the 113,000 mile radius of its orbit, which makes more of a difference.

In the case of our Moon, we are dealing with an orbit that is markedly elliptical so that it can be as close as 221,500 miles at one point in its orbit and as far as 252,700 at another point. Fortunately for myself and this article, the orbits of the five Jovian satellites we are discussing, are all almost perfectly circular and ellipticity is a complication we don't have to face here.

Given the distance of each satellite from Amalthea, and the diameter of each satellite, it is possible to calculate the apparent size of each, as seen from our Amalthean viewpoint (see Table 4).

TABLE 4 — APPARENT SIZE OF JOVIAN SATELLITES
AS SEEN FROM AMALTHEA

Satellite	Diameter (minutes of arc)	
	at zenith	at horizon
J-I	53	34
J-II	23	17
J-III	20	17
J-IV	10	9

If you want to compare this with something familiar, consider that the average apparent diameter of the Moon is 31 minutes of arc. This means that J-I, for instance, is just slightly larger than the Moon when it rises, bloats out to a circle half again as wide as the Moon when it reaches zenith and shrinks back to its original size when it sets.

The other three satellites, being farther from Amalthea, do not show such large percentage differences in distance from horizon to zenith and therefore do not show such differences in apparent size either.

Notice that although J-III is considerably farther than J-II, it is also considerably larger. The two effects counterbalance as seen from Amalthea so that J-II and J-III appear indistinguishable in size, at least at the horizon. Of course, J-II, being closer, bloats just a little more at zenith. As for J-IV, it is smallest in appearance, and shows only ⅓ the apparent diameter of our Moon.

The sky of Amalthea puts on quite a display, then. There are four satellites with visible discs, of which one is considerably larger than our Moon.

But never mind size; what about brightness? Here several factors are involved. First there is the apparent surface area of each satellite, then the amount of light received by it from the Sun, and finally the fraction of received Sunlight reflected by it (its albedo). In Table 5, I list each of these bits of data for each of the satellites, using the value for our own Moon as basis for comparison.

If we consider the figures in Table 5, we see that J-I as seen from Amalthea is remarkable. At zenith it will possess an area up to three times that of our Moon. The intensity of Sunlight it receives, however (as do the other Jovian satellites), is only $3/80$ that received by the Moon. This is not surprising. The Moon, after all, is at an average distance of 93,000,000 miles from the Sun as compared to 483,000,000 for the Jovian satellites.

TABLE 5 — THE JOVIAN SATELLITES AND OUR MOON

Satellite	Apparent area (Moon = 1.0)		Sunlight received (Moon = 1.0)	Albedo (Moon = 1.0)
	Maximum	Minimum		
J-I	2.92	1.20	0.037	5
J-II	0.55	0.30	0.037	5.5
J-III	0.42	0.30	0.037	3
J-IV	0.10	0.084	0.037	0.4

The Moon has no atmosphere and therefore no clouds— and it is atmospheric clouds that contribute most to light reflection. The Moon, therefore, showing bare rock, reflects only about $1/14$ of the light it receives from the Sun, absorbing the rest.

The Moon's mark is bettered by J-I, J-II, and J-III. In fact, J-II reflects about $2/5$ of the light it receives, which is every bit as good as the Earth can manage. This doesn't necessarily mean that these three satellites have an atmosphere and clouds like the Earth. It seems more likely that there are drifts of water-ice and ammonia-ice (or both) on the surfaces of the satellites, and that these drifts do the reflecting.

J-IV, for some reason, reflects only $1/30$ of the light it receives and is therefore less than half as reflective as the Moon. Perhaps J-IV is composed of particularly dark rock. Or is it conceivable that astronomers have badly overestimated J-IV's diameter? (If it were smaller than astronomers think it is, it would have to reflect more light to account for its brightness.)

Anyway, we can now calculate the apparent brightness of each satellite (as compared with our Moon) by multiplying the area by the amount of Sunlight received by the albedo. The results are given in Table 6.

TABLE 6 — APPARENT BRIGHTNESS OF THE JOVIAN SATELLITES

| Satellite | Apparent brightness (Moon = 1.0) | |
	Maximum	Minimum
J-I	0.54	0.22
J-II	0.11	0.06
J-III	0.045	0.033
J-IV	0.0015	0.0012

As you see, not one of the Jovian satellites, as seen from Amalthea, can compare in apparent brightness with our Moon as seen from the Earth's surface. Even J-I, the closest to Amalthea and therefore the brightest, is never better than $\frac{1}{2}$ as bright as the Moon; J-II is less than $\frac{1}{7}$ as bright; J-III less than $\frac{1}{20}$; and J-IV less than $\frac{1}{600}$.

And yet who says brightness is everything? Our own Moon is only $\frac{1}{465,000}$ as bright as the Sun, and if we consider beauty alone, it is all the better for that.

Perhaps the Jovian satellites as seen from Amalthea will be still more beautiful than our Moon, for being so softly illuminated. It will result, perhaps, in better contrast, so that craters and maria will be more clearly visible. If the satellites are partly ice-covered, patches of comparative brilliance will stand out against the darkness of bare rock. It will be all the more startling because on Amalthea there will be no air to soften or blur the sharpness of the view.

Callisto may be most beautiful of all, though it may require a fieldglass to see it at its best. It would be a darkling satellite, with its mysteriously low albedo. Perhaps it might look rather like a lump of coal, with its very occasional patches of highly reflecting ice so interspersed by very dark rock that it would seem a cluster of diamonds in the sky, rather than a solid circle of light.

Scientists may go to Amalthea someday for a variety of reasons, but the average tourist may well go for the view alone.

One of the occupational hazards of writing science fiction (or, for that matter, science) is the certainty that you will be quite wrong quite often; that your readers, especially bright thirteen-year-olds, will point that out with great glee; and that you will feel very embarrassed.

Usually, this is because of one's own imperfect understanding of science, but for my own part, I can bear up under that. After all, a science-fiction writer must, on one occasion or another, speak knowingly, or at least with an affectation of knowledge, about every field of science that exists. He is bound to pull a boner every now and then. I am no exception to that general rule.

It is somehow much more irritating, however, to find that though you have gone to a great deal of trouble to be correct and accurate, and are correct and accurate, as far as anyone can tell, at the time of writing—the scientists themselves change their minds. "By the way, old chap," they tell us, "all that stuff we had in all those books— We're going to change all that."

For instance, in the first of my Paul French novels, David Starr: Space Ranger *(Doubleday, 1952), the action was placed on Mars, a Mars that I designed to match meticulously the best opinions of 1952 astronomy. It was a Mars without craters, and in 1965, astronomers discovered that Mars was loaded with craters.*

Then, in Lucky Starr and the Oceans of Venus *(Doubleday, 1954) I pictured a Venus with a planet-wide ocean, and in* Lucky Starr and the Big Sun of Mercury *(Doubleday, 1956) I pictured a Mercury where one side faced the Sun perpetually.*

Both views were in careful accord with the best astronomical knowledge of the middle 1950's.

Unfortunately, by 1956, astronomers began to suspect that Venus was hot, and by 1962 they were certain. The surface temperature of Venus is something like 450° C.

and water can exist on the planet only in gaseous form. Venus can have clouds of water but it cannot have an ocean of water.

And in 1965, astronomers bounced radar waves off Mercury and could tell from the nature of the bouncing that Mercury rotated more quickly than had been thought and did not keep only one side toward the Sun.

This is terribly embarrassing. All the Lucky Starr books are now out of print and they may have to stay out of print. Doubleday has thought of reprinting and, undoubtedly, a new generation of youngsters would be ready to buy them, but what about their scientific outdatedness?

The Mars setting of David Starr: Space Ranger *isn't too bad, since the matter of craters or no craters plays no part in the plot. I could go over the book and, with very little trouble, insert references to craters here and there.*

Not so in the case of the books set on Venus and on Mercury. Almost all the action in Lucky Starr and the Oceans of Venus *takes place under the ocean, including a fight with a two-mile-wide monster something like a giant jellyfish. And everything in* Lucky Starr and the Big Sun of Mercury *turns upon the relative motions of the planet and the Sun, with consequences which I described with meticulous (and, as it turned out, utterly wrong) detail. Those two books simply cannot be patched; they can only be scrapped.*

To reprint the series, then, would mean that I would have to add a special note to the books about Venus and Mercury, explaining that the astronomy was all wrong, and why. And that's rather clumsy and would cast a pall on the series—so maybe it's gone forever.

Just in case it is, I would like to include a passage from my favorite part of the entire series—the aforesaid fight with the giant jellyfish. It had risen out of the deeper portion of the Venusian ocean and had planted its vast cup over a section of the shallower ocean floor which included the ship carrying Lucky and Bigman. Lucky left the ship to find, if he could, a vulnerable spot in the mighty two-hundred-million-ton object:

from LUCKY STARR AND THE OCEANS OF VENUS (*1954*)

Fifty feet or less above, the light ended on a rough, grayish surface, streaked with deep corrugations. Lucky scarcely attempted to brake his rush. The monster's skin was rubbery and his own suit hard. Even as he thought that, he collided, pressing upward and feeling the alien flesh give.

For a long moment, Lucky drew deep gasps of relief. For the first time since leaving the ship, he felt moderately safe. The relaxation did not last, however. At any time the creature could turn its attack on the ship. That must not be allowed to happen.

Lucky played his finger flash about his surroundings with a mixture of wonder and nausea.

Here and there in the undersurface of the monster were holes some six feet across into which, as Lucky could see by the flow of bubbles and solid particles, water was rushing. At greater intervals were slits, which opened occasionally into ten-foot-long fissures that emitted frothing gushes of water.

Apparently this was the way the monster fed. It poured digestive juices into the portion of the ocean trapped beneath its bulk, then sucked in water by the cubic yard to extract the nutriment it contained, and still later expelled water, debris, and its own wastes . . .

Lucky moved jerkily through no action of his own and, in surprise, turned the beam of light on a spot closer to himself. In a moment of stricken horror, he realized the purposes of those deep corrugations he had noticed in the monster's undersurface. One such was forming directly to one side of him and was sucking inward, into the creature's substance. The two sides of the corrugation rubbed against one another, and the whole was obviously a grinding mechanism whereby the monster broke up and shredded particles of food too large to be handled directly by its intake pores.

Lucky did not wait. He could not risk his battered suit against the fantastic strength of the monster's muscles. The wall of his suit might hold, but portions of the delicate working mechanisms might not.

He swung his shoulder so as to turn the suit's jets directly against the flesh of the monster and gave them full energy. He came loose with a sharp smacking sound, then veered around and back.

He did not touch the skin again, but hovered near it and traveled along it, following the direction against gravity, mounting upward, away from the outer edges of the thing, toward its center.

He came suddenly to a point where the creature's under-surface turned down again in a wall of flesh that extended as far as his light would reach on either side. That wall quivered and was obviously composed of thinner tissue.

It was the blowpipe.

Lucky was sure that was what it was—a gigantic cavern a hundred yards across, out of which the fury of rushing water emerged. Cautiously Lucky circled it. Undoubtedly this was the safest place one could be, here at the very base of the blowpipe, and yet he picked his way gingerly.

He knew what he was looking for, however, and he left the blowpipe. He moved away in the direction in which the monster's flesh mounted still higher, until he was at the peak of the inverted bowl, and there it was!

At first, Lucky was aware only of a long-drawn-out rumble, almost too deep to hear. In fact, it was vibration that attracted his attention, rather than any sound. Then he spied the swelling in the monster's flesh. It writhed and beat; a huge mass, hanging thirty feet downward and perhaps as big around as the blowpipe.

That *must* be the center of the organism; its heart, or whatever passed for its heart, must be there. That heart must beat in powerful strokes, and Lucky felt dizzy as he tried to picture it. Those heartbeats must last five minutes at a time, during which thousands of cubic yards of blood (or whatever the creature used) must be forced through blood vessels large enough to hold the *Hilda*. That heartbeat must suffice to drive the blood a mile and back.

What a mechanism it must be, thought Lucky. If one could only capture such a thing alive and study its physiology!

Somewhere in that swelling must also be what brain the monster might have. Brain? Perhaps what passed for its brain was only a small clot of nerve cells without which the monster could live quite well.

Perhaps! But it couldn't live without its heart. The heart had completed one beat. The central swelling had contracted to almost nothing. Now the heart was relaxing for another beat five minutes or more from now, and the swelling was expanding and dilating as blood rushed into it.

Lucky raised his weapon and with his light beam full on that giant heart, he let himself sink down. It might be best not to be too close. On the other hand, he dared not miss.

For a moment a twinge of regret swept him. From a scientific standpoint it was almost a crime to kill this mightiest of nature's creatures.

He dared wait no longer. He squeezed the handgrip of his weapon. The wire shot out. It made contact, and Lucky's eyes were blinded by the flash of light in which the near wall of the monster's heart was burned through.

There is a borderline case of astronomical inaccuracy which bothers me far more than does the matter of the Paul French novels, because it involves an astronomic description of which I am particularly proud.

It is to be found in a story called "The Martian Way" that deals with a colony of Earthmen on Mars. They must import water from Earth and Earth, in a fit of isolationism, refuses to grant further supplies. The Colonists, rather than abandon their Martian homes, decide to trek out to Saturn for their supplies.

But, before going on to the passage, I want to say that the story was written at the height of the McCarthyist period and I included in the story a McCarthy-type politician. My disapproval of Senator Joseph McCarthy was quite manifest in the story and I expected repercussions. I didn't particularly enjoy the thought of repercussions but I felt I had to put myself on record, somehow. Apparently, what I did was done so subtly, however (or so clumsily), that no one either noticed or, possibly, cared. There wasn't a single repercussion and so much for Isaac Asimov, political satirist.

And now to the passage, which begins as the Martian expedition is approaching Saturn:

from "The Martian Way" (*1952*)

Half a million miles above Saturn, Mario Rioz was cradled on nothing and sleep was delicious. He came out of it slowly and for a while, alone in his suit, he counted the stars and traced lines from one to another. . . .

They had aimed high to pass out of the ecliptic while moving through the Asteroid Belt. That had used up water and that had probably been unnecessary. Although tens of thousands of worldlets look as thick as vermin in two-dimensional projection upon a photographic plate, they are nevertheless scattered so thinly through the quadrillions of cubic miles that make up their conglomerate orbit that only the most ridiculous of coincidences would have brought about a collision.

Still, they passed over the Belt and someone calculated the chances of collision with a fragment of matter large enough to do damage. The value was so low, so impossibly low, that it was perhaps inevitable that the notion of the "space float" should occur to someone.

The days were long and many, space was empty, only one man was needed at the controls at any one time. The thought was a natural.

First, it was a particularly daring one who ventured out for fifteen minutes or so. Then another, who tried half an hour. Eventually, before the asteroids were entirely behind, each ship regularly had its off-watch member suspended in space at the end of a cable.

It was easy enough. The cable, one of those intended for operations at the conclusion of their journey, was magnetically attached at both ends, one to the space suit to start with. Then you clambered out the lock onto the ship's hull and attached the other end there. You paused awhile, clinging to the metal skin by the electromagnets in your boots. Then you neutralized those and made the slightest muscular effort.

Slowly, ever so slowly, you lifted from the ship and even more slowly the ship's larger mass moved an equivalently shorter distance downward. You floated incredibly, weightlessly, in solid, speckled black. When the ship had moved far enough away from you, your gauntleted hand, which kept touch upon the cable, tightened its grip slightly. Too tightly, and you would begin moving back toward the ship and it toward you. Just tightly enough, and friction would halt you. Because your motion was equivalent to that of the ship, it seemed as motionless below you as though it had been painted against an impossible background while the cable between you hung in coils that had no reason to straighten out.

It was a half ship to your eye. One half was lit by the light of the feeble Sun, which was still too bright to look at directly without the heavy protection of the polarized spacesuit visor. The other half was black on black, invisible.

Space closed in and it was like sleep. Your suit was warm, it renewed its air automatically, it had food and drink in special containers from which it could be sucked with a minimal motion of the head, it took care of wastes appropriately. Most of all, more than anything else, there was the delightful euphoria of weightlessness.

You never felt so well in your life. The days stopped being too long, they weren't long enough, and there weren't enough of them.

They had passed Jupiter's orbit at a spot some thirty degrees from its then position. For months, it was the brightest object in the sky, always excepting the glowing white pea that was the Sun. At its brightest, some of the Scavangers insisted they could make out Jupiter as a tiny sphere, one side squashed out of true by the night shadow.

Then over a period of additional months it faded, while another dot of light grew until it was brighter than Jupiter. It was Saturn, first as a dot of brilliance, then as an oval, glowing splotch.

("Why oval?" someone asked, and after a while, someone else said, "The rings of course," and it was obvious.)

Everyone spacefloated at all possible times toward the end, watching Saturn incessantly.

("Hey, you jerk, come on back in, damn it. You're on duty." "Who's on duty? I've got fifteen minutes more by my watch." "You set your watch back. Besides, I gave you twenty minutes yesterday." "You wouldn't give two minutes to your grandmother." "Come on in, damn it, or I'm coming out anyway." "All right, I'm coming. Holy howlers, what a racket over a lousy minute." But no quarrel could possibly be serious, not in space. It felt too good.)

Saturn grew until at last it rivaled and then surpassed the Sun. The rings, set at a broad angle to their trajectory of approach, swept grandly about the planet, only a small portion being eclipsed. Then, as they approached, the span of the rings grew still wider, yet narrower as the angle of approach constantly decreased.

The larger moons showed up in the surrounding sky like serene fireflies.

Mario Rioz was glad he was awake so that he could watch again.

Saturn filled half the sky, streaked with orange, the night shadow cutting it fuzzily nearly one-quarter of the way in from the right. Two round little dots in the brightness were shadows of two of the moons. To the left and behind him (he could look over his left shoulder to see, and as he did so, the rest of his body inched slightly to the right to conserve angular momentum) was the white diamond of the Sun.

Most of all he liked to watch the rings. At the left, they emerged from behind Saturn, a tight, bright, triple band of orange light. At the right, their beginnings were hidden in the night shadow, but showed up closer and broader. They widened as they came, like the flare of a horn, growing hazier as they approached, until, while the eye followed them, they seemed to fill the sky and lose themselves.

From the position of the Scavenger fleet just inside the outer rim of the outermost ring, the rings broke up and assumed their true identity as a phenomenal cluster of solid fragments rather than the tight, solid band of light they seemed.

Below him, or rather in the direction his feet pointed, some twenty miles away, was one of the ring fragments. It looked like a large, irregular splotch, marring the symmetry of space, three-quarters in brightness and the night shadow cutting it like a knife. Other fragments were farther off, sparkling like stardust, dimmer and thicker, until, as you followed them down, they became rings once more.

The fragments were motionless, but that was only because the ships had taken up an orbit about Saturn equivalent to that of the outer edge of the rings.

The day before, Rioz reflected, he had been on that nearest fragment, working along with more than a score of others to mold it into the desired shape. Tomorrow he would be at it again.

Today—today he was spacefloating.

Ted Long wandered over the ridged surface of the ring fragment with his spirits as icy as the ground he walked on. It had all seemed perfectly logical back on Mars, but that was Mars. He had worked it out carefully in his mind in perfectly reasonable steps. He could still remember exactly how it went.

It didn't take a ton of water to move a ton of ship. It was not mass equals mass, but mass times velocity equals mass times velocity. It didn't matter, in other words, whether you shot out a ton of water at a mile a second or a hundred pounds of water at twenty miles a second. You got the same final velocity out of the ship.

That meant the jet nozzles had to be made narrower and the steam hotter. But then drawbacks appeared. The narrower the nozzle, the more energy was lost in friction and turbulence. The hotter the steam, the more refractory the nozzle had to be and the shorter its life. The limit in that direction was quickly reached.

Then, since a given weight of water could move considerably more than its own weight under the narrow-nozzle conditions, it paid to be big. The bigger the water-storage space, the larger the size of the actual travel-head, even in proportion. So they started to make liners heavier and bigger. But then the larger the shell, the heavier the bracings, the more difficult the weldings, the more exacting the engineering requirements. At the moment, the limit in that direction had been reached also.

And then he had put his finger on what had seemed to him to be the basic flaw—the original unswervable conception that the fuel had to be placed inside the ship; the metal had to be built to encircle a million tons of water.

Why? Water did not have to be water. It could be ice, and ice could be shaped. Holes could be melted into it. Travel-heads and jets could be fitted into it. Cables could hold travel-heads and jets stiffly together under the influence of magnetic field-force grips.

Long felt the trembling of the ground he walked on. He

was at the head of the fragment. A dozen ships were blasting in and out of sheaths carved in its substance, and the fragment shuddered under the continuing impact.

The ice didn't have to be quarried. It existed in proper chunks in the rings of Saturn. That's all the rings were—pieces of nearly pure ice, circling Saturn. So spectroscopy stated and so it had turned out to be. He was standing on one such piece now, over two miles long, nearly one mile thick. It was almost half a billion tons of water, all in one piece, and he was standing on it.

The colonists manage to overcome their difficulties, bring back the huge fragment of ice from the rings of Saturn and solve the water problems of Mars.

Why am I proud?—In the first place, I consider this the best description of what it's like out there near Saturn that anyone has ever written.

I admit that sounds conceited but how can anyone be a writer and not be conceited? A modest person couldn't possibly suppose that anyone would be willing to pay money for his writings, and he would never get started. A modest writer is a contradiction in terms.

Besides, I have made up my mind that in this book, at least, I lay it right on the line. No stupid facades. If I can't say what I please in My Hundredth Book, there was no use writing the other ninety-nine.

My second reason for pride concerns my description of the "space float," which is these days known under the misleading title of "space walk." When "The Martian Way" was published in 1952, no one had ever stepped out into space at the end of a lifeline. When it finally happened, in the mid-60's, the sensation (judging from the descriptions I read) appears to have been euphoria, exactly as I described it.

I described it accurately, perhaps, because I felt the sensations so thoroughly in writing it. I have a bounding imagination (that, too, like conceit, comes with the territory) and when I picture something, I picture it thoroughly.

I think of that, sometimes, when I am teased about my refusal to get into an airplane. Over and over again, I am told, "You don't know what you're missing."

Hah! I've floated in Saturn's rings. They don't know what they're *missing.*

And now the only trouble rests in the question as to how thick the rings of Saturn are, and how large the particles within them are. Recent estimates of the thicknesses of the rings have dropped enormously. At the time I wrote "The Martian Way," I accepted an estimate that made the rings ten miles thick. In that case, they could easily be composed of particles a mile or two long.

Now, however, estimates tend to be in the yards rather than in the miles, and one suggestion is that the rings are but one foot thick. If so, the particles may be hunks of gravel rather than hunks of mountain, and the story would be ruined.

Everything has its other side, of course. If the changing findings of science ruin a science-fiction story now and then, they certainly make for exciting subject matter in histories of science. At least, this is what I found when I was writing my most ambitious book on astronomy, The Universe (*Walker & Company, 1966*).

That book was not entirely ambitious to begin with, by the way. Edward L. Burlingame, of *Walker & Company*, had an idea that I might write a small book about the recently discovered and fascinatingly mysterious quasars, and I jumped at the chance.

The trouble is, though, that I have an unconquerable aversion against explaining something without first presenting a reasonable background, so I decided to explain a few things before talking about quasars, and then I decided to explain a few other things before that, and then a few other things before that, and so on.

The final result was that, after a short introduction, I began with the statement, "In 600 B.C., the Assyrian Empire had just fallen . . ." So what Ed got was a fairly large history of astronomy in which my discussion of quasars took up the fourth and final section of the nineteenth and final chapter. In a display of excellent good sportsmanship, Ed published the book anyway.

One of the most dramatic episodes in astronomical history occurred in the early 1920's when it first became clear that there was a vast Universe beyond the Milky Way. Step by

step, certain cloudy masses in the heavens turned out to be
enormously large and enormously distant systems of stars—

from THE UNIVERSE (*1966*)

Man's vision of the size of the Universe had increased enormously in 2000 years. Let us recapitulate.

By 150 B.C., the Earth-Moon system had been accurately
defined. The Moon's orbit was seen to be half a million
miles across, and the diameter of the planetary orbits was
suspected to be in the millions of miles.

By 1800 A.D., the scale of the Solar System had been
defined. Its diameter was not merely in the millions of
miles, but in the billions. The distance of the stars was still
unknown but was suspected to be in the trillions of miles
(that is, a couple of light-years) at least.

By 1850 A.D., the distance of the nearer stars had been
defined as not merely trillions of miles, but tens and hundreds of trillions of miles. The diameter of the Galaxy was
still unknown but was suspected to be in the thousands of
light-years.

By 1920 A.D., diameter of the Galaxy had been defined
at not merely thousands of light-years but many tens of
thousands of light-years.

At each new stage, the size of the regions of the Universe
under investigation turned out to exceed the most optimistic
estimates of the past. Furthermore, at each stage, there was
the conservative opinion that the object whose size had
been defined represented all, or almost all the Universe,
and until 1920, that view had always turned out to be
wrong.

The Earth-Moon system had shrunk to insignificance in
the light of the size of the Solar System. The Solar System
had in turn shrunk to insignificance when the distance of
the nearby stars was determined. And the system of the
nearby stars was insignificant in comparison with the
Galaxy as a whole.

Would this process continue or did the Galaxy and its
Magellanic satellites represent an end at last? Had astronomers finally probed to the end of the Universe?

Even as late as 1920, it seemed quite possible that the

conservative view would finally triumph. The Galaxy and the Magellanic Clouds seemed very likely to contain all the matter in the Universe and beyond them, one could maintain, lay nothing . . .

And yet astronomers could not relax completely with their finite Universe 200,000 light-years across. There were grounds for some suspicion that numerous large objects might exist far outside the Galaxy, and it proved extraordinarily difficult to argue that suspicion out of existence.

A particularly troublesome item was a cloudy patch of light in the constellation Andromeda, an object that was called the "Andromeda Nebula" because of its location and appearance.

The Andromeda Nebula is visible to the naked eye as a small object of the fourth magnitude that looks like a faint fuzzy star to the unaided eye. Some Arab astronomers had noted it in their star maps, but the first to describe it in modern times was the German astronomer Simon Marius (1570–1624) in 1612. In the next century, Messier included it in his list of fuzzy objects that were not comets. It was thirty-first on his list, so that the Andromeda Nebula is often known as "M31."

There was no reason, at first, for thinking that the Andromeda Nebula was significantly different from other nebulae such as the Orion Nebula. The Andromeda Nebula seemed a luminous cloud and no more than that.

Some eighteenth-century astronomers even envisaged a place for such clouds in the scheme of things. What if stars developed out of distended rotating masses of gas? Under the effect of their own gravity, such clouds would begin to contract and condense, speeding their rotation as they did so. As they rotated more and more quickly, they would flatten into a lens shape and, eventually, eject a ring of gas from the bulging equator. Later, as rotation continued to speed up, a second ring would separate, then a third ring, and so on. Each ring would coalesce into a small planetary body, and finally what was left of the cloud would have condensed into a large glowing star that would find itself at the center of a whole family of planets.

Such a theory would account for the fact that all the planets of the Solar System were situated nearly in a single plane, that all of them revolved about the Sun in the same direction. Each planet, moreover, tended to have a system of satellites that revolved about it in a single plane and in the same direction, as though the planets, in the process of contracting from gaseous rings, gave off smaller rings of their own.

The first to suggest such an origin of the Solar System was the German philosopher Immanuel Kant (1724–1804) in 1755. A half-century later, the French astronomer Pierre Simon de Laplace (1749–1827) published a similar theory (which he arrived at independently) as an appendix to a popular book on astronomy.

It is interesting that Kant and Laplace had opposing views on the Andromeda Nebula, views that kept astronomers at loggerheads for a century and a half.

Laplace pointed to the Andromeda Nebula as possibly representing a planetary system in the process of formation; indeed its structure is such that it seems to be in the obvious process of rapid rotation. You can almost make out (or convince yourself you are making out) a ring of gas about to be given off. For this reason, Laplace's suggestion as to the method of formation of planetary systems is known as the "nebular hypothesis."

If Laplace were correct and if the Andromeda Nebula were a volume of gas serving as precursor for a single planetary system, it cannot be a very large object and, in view of its apparent size in the telescope, it cannot be a very distant object.

Laplace's nebular hypothesis was popular among astronomers throughout the nineteenth century, and his view of the Andromeda Nebula represented a majority opinion through all that time. In 1907 a parallax determination was reported for the Andromeda Nebula, one that seemed to show it to be at a distance of nineteen light-years. Certainly, that seemed to settle matters.

Yet there was Kant's opposing view. Despite the fact that he, too, had originated a nebular hypothesis, he did not fall prey to the temptation of accepting the Andromeda Nebula as visible support of his theory. He suggested instead that the Andromeda Nebula, and similar bodies, might represent immensely large conglomerations of stars, which appeared as small, fuzzy patches only because they were immensely far away. He felt they might represent "island universes," each one a separate galaxy, so to speak.

However, this suggestion of Kant's was not based on any observational data available to the astronomers of the time. It made very few converts and, if Kant's speculation was thought of at all, it was dismissed as a kind of science fiction.

But Kant's suggestion did not die. Every once in a while some small piece of evidence would arise that would not quite fit the orthodox Laplacian view. Chief among these was the matter of spectroscopic data.

Stars, generally, produce light which, on passing through a prism, broadens into an essentially continuous spectrum, broken by the presence of dark spectral lines. If, however, gases or vapors of relatively simple chemical composition are heated until they glow, the light they emit, when passed through a prism, produces an "emission spectrum" consisting of individual bright lines. (The exact position of the bright lines depends on the chemical composition of the gas or vapor.)

Then, too, a continuous spectrum usually (but not always) implies white light, while an emission spectrum is often the product of colored light, since some of the bright lines of one particular color or another might dominate the entire glow.

Many bright nebulae do indeed show very delicate color effects (that do not show up in ordinary black-and-white photographs) . . .

The light from the Andromeda Nebula was a drab white, however, and in 1899 its spectrum was obtained and shown to be continuous . . .

White light and a continuous spectrum meant that the Andromeda Nebula might consist of a mass of stars and be so far off that those stars could not be made out separately. On the other hand, that conclusion was not inevitable, for gaseous nebulae might, under some circumstances, possess white light and continuous spectra.

This was so because emission spectra were produced by hot gases glowing with their own light. Suppose, though, that a mass of gas was cold and was serving merely as a passive reflector of starlight. In that case, the spectrum of the reflected starlight would be essentially the same as the spectrum of the original starlight itself (just as the spectrum of moonlight is like that of sunlight).

If the Andromeda Nebula were merely reflecting starlight, that would explain everything. Its spectrum would be consistent with the theory that it was a not-very-large patch of gas quite close to the Solar System.

But one catch remained. If the Andromeda Nebula were merely reflecting starlight, where were the stars whose light it was reflecting? . . . None could be found.

At least, no permanent stars could be found. Occasionally, a starlike object was found to be associated temporarily with the Andromeda Nebula. As this turned out to be highly significant, let us pause in order to take up the matter of temporary starlike objects in some detail.

To any casual observer of the heavens, the starry configurations seem permanent and fixed. Indeed, the Greek philosophers had differentiated between the sky and the earth by this fact. On Earth, Aristotle suggested, there was perpetual and continuing change, but the heavens were absolutely changeless.

To be sure, there were occasional "shooting stars" which made it appear, to the uninitiated, that a star had fallen from heaven. However, no matter how many shooting stars appeared, no star was ever observed to be missing from its place as a result. Consequently, such shooting stars were considered to be atmospheric phenomena by the Greeks and therefore, like the shifting of clouds or the falling of rain, to be part of the changing earth and not of the changeless heavens. The very word "meteor" applied to shooting stars is from a Greek term meaning "things in the air."

The Greeks were correct in deciding that the flash of light accompanying a shooting star was an atmospheric phenomenon. The object causing that flash, though, was a speeding body (a "meteoroid") varying in size from less than a pinpoint to a multi-ton object. Before entering the Earth's atmosphere, a meteoroid is an independent body of the Solar System. After entering the atmosphere, it heats through friction to the point where it flashes brilliantly. If small, it is consumed in the process; if large, a remnant may survive to strike the Earth's surface as a "meteorite."

Another class of temporary inhabitants of the sky were the occasional comets, often sporting long, cloudy projections that might be considered as flowing tails or streaming hair. The ancients viewed it as the latter, for "comet" is from the Latin word for "hair." Comets came and went erratically, so the Greek philosophers considered them to be atmospheric phenomena also. Here, they were clearly wrong, for the comets exist far beyond Earth's atmosphere and are actually members of the Solar System, as independent a set of members as the planets themselves.

Nevertheless, suppose we modify the Greek view and say that change is a property of the Solar System, but that the stars far beyond the Solar System are changeless. If we do this, we eliminate not only meteors and comets, but also such changes as the phases of the Moon, the spots on the Sun, and the complicated motions of the planets. Is this restricted view of changelessness tenable?

To the naked eye, it would almost seem to be. To be sure, the intensity of the light produced by some stars varies, but such cases are few and unspectacular, not obvious to the casual eye. Some stars also have significant proper motions, but this is even less noticeable, and it would take many centuries to be sure of the existence of such motions without a telescope.

One type of spectacular change, however, *could* take place in the heavens, and so clearly that the most casual observer could see it. I am referring to the actual appearance of a completely new, and sometimes very bright, star in the sky. Such stars were clearly stars and lacked all trace of the fuzziness of comets. Furthermore, they were not momentary flashes like meteors, but persisted for weeks and months.

Not only were such new stars evidence of change among the stars by the mere fact that they appeared and eventually disappeared, but also they changed brightness radically during the course of their brief stay in the sky as visible objects. Only the fact that such objects were so rarely encountered made it possible for the ancient astronomers to ignore their existence and to continue to accept the assumption of the changelessness of the heavens.

There is evidence, in fact, of only one such new star having appeared during the period of Greek astronomy, and that evidence is none too strong. Hipparchus is supposed to have recorded such a new star in 134 B.C. We do not have his word for this, for virtually none of his works has survived. The Roman encyclopedist Pliny (23–79 A.D.), writing two centuries later, reported it, saying that it was this new star that inspired Hipparchus to prepare the first star map, in order that future new stars might be more easily detected.

Perhaps the most spectacular new star in historic times was not observed in Europe at all, for it appeared in the constellation Taurus in June, 1054, at a time when European astronomy was virtually nonexistent. That we know of it at all is thanks to the observations of Chinese and Japanese astronomers who recorded the appearance of what they called a "guest star" at this time. It persisted for two years and grew so fiercely brilliant at its peak as to outshine Venus and become easily visible by day. For almost a month it was the brightest object in the sky next to the Sun and the Moon.

Then, in November, 1572, another such object, almost as bright, appeared in the constellation Cassiopeia, outshining Venus, at its peak, by five or ten times. By then, however, European astronomy was flourishing again, and an astronomer of the first rank was in his impressionable youth. This was the Danish astronomer Tycho Brahe, who observed the new star carefully and then, in 1573, published a small book about it. A short version of the Latin title of the book is *De Nova Stella* ("Concerning the New Star"). Ever since, a star that suddenly appears where none was observed before has been called a "nova" ("new").

One of the important points made in connection with the nova of 1572 by Brahe was that it lacked a measurable parallax. This meant it had to be many times as distant as the Moon and could not be an atmospheric phenomenon and therefore part of the changeable Earth. (Brahe made the same observation in 1577 for a comet and showed that comets, too, were not atmospheric phenomena.)

Then, in 1604, still another nova appeared, this time in the constellation Ophiuchus. It was observed by Kepler and Galileo. While distinctly less bright than Brahe's nova, that of 1604 was still a remarkable phenomenon and, at its peak, rivaled the planet Jupiter in brilliance.

Oddly enough, no superlatively bright novae have graced the sky in the three and a half centuries since 1604. This is rather a pity, for the telescope was invented a few years after 1604, and astronomy entered a new era in which such spectacular novae could have been studied much more profitably than before.

Nevertheless the telescopic revolution in astronomy at once affected the views concerning these novae. In the first place, it was quickly seen that the stars visible to the naked eye were not all the stars there were by any means. A nova, therefore, need not be a truly new star, despite its name. It might merely be a dim star—too dim to be seen by the naked eye, ordinarily—which, for some reason, brightened sufficiently to become visible. As astronomers began to discover more and more variable stars, such changes in brightness came to seem neither phenomenal nor even unusual in themselves. What was unusual about novae was not the fact that their brightness changed, but the *extent* to which it changed. Novae could be classified as a type of variable star, but a particular type called "cataclysmic variables." Their changes in brightness seemed not merely the result of some more or less quiet periodic process, but rather the consequence of some vast cataclysm —somewhat like the difference between a periodic geyser spout and an erratic and unpredictable volcanic eruption.

Then, too, whereas in pretelescopic days, only those sudden brightenings which reached unusual peaks could readily be observed, the telescope made it possible to observe much less drastic events.

Since novae were associated with such brightness, dim ones were not searched for, and for two and a half centuries no novae were reported. Then, in 1848, the English astronomer John Russell Hind (1823–1895) happened to observe a star in Ophiuchus that suddenly brightened. At it's brightest, it only reached the fifth magnitude so that it was never anything more than a dim star to the naked eye, and in pretelescope days it might easily have gone unnoticed. Nevertheless, it was a nova.

Thereafter, novae of all brightness were searched for and discovered in surprising numbers. One of them, appearing in the constellation of Aquila in 1918 ("Nova Aquilae"), shone, briefly, as brightly as Sirius. None, however, approached the planetary brightness of the novae of 1054, 1572, and 1604.

It is now estimated that some two dozen novae appear each year, here and there in the Galaxy, although relatively few of them are so situated as to be visible from the Earth.

The matter of the novae entered the problem of the Andromeda Nebula when, in 1885, one appeared in the central portions of the nebula. For the first time, a prominent star was seen in connection with the Andromeda Nebula.

There were two possibilities here. The star might exist between the Andromeda Nebula and ourselves and be seen in the nebula only because that object was in the line of sight. In that case the star and the nebula would have no true connection. The second possibility was that the Andromeda Nebula was made up of stars too dim to be seen and that one of them had flared up into a nova and had become visible in a telescope.

If the latter were the case, it might be possible to determine the distance of the Andromeda Nebula if one assumed that novae always reached about the same peak of luminosity. In that case, variations in apparent brightness would be caused entirely by a difference in distance. If the distance of any nova could be determined, the distance of all the rest could then be calculated. The opportunity came with a nova that appeared in the constellation Perseus ("Nova Persei") in 1901. It was an unusually close nova and its distance was estimated by parallax to be about 100 light-years.

The nova that had appeared in the Andromeda Nebula, referred to now as "S Andromedae," reached only the seventh magnitude at its peak (so that it would never have been visible without a telescope) as compared with a magnitude of 0.2 reached by Nova Persei. If the two novae had indeed attained the same luminosity, S Andromedae would have to be some sixteen times as distant as Nova Persei to account for the difference in brightness. It was argued in 1911, then, that the distance of S Andromedae was 1600 light-years.

If S Andromedae were indeed part of the Andromeda Nebula, that meant the nebula, too, was 1600 light-years distant. If S Andromedae were merely in the line of sight of the nebula, the latter would have to be beyond the nova and even more than 1600 light-years from us. In either case, the nebula was at least 800 times as far from us as had been calculated from the apparent parallactic data obtained in 1907. If the nebula were 1600 light-years distant, it had to be quite large to seem as large in our telescopes as it does. It could scarcely represent a single planetary system in the process of formation as Laplace had supposed. Still, one could not yet accept the Kantian view either. Even at 1600 light-years, the Andromeda Nebula had to be merely a feature of the Galaxy.

This line of argument assumed, however, that S Andromedae and Nova Persei actually reached the same luminosity. What if this assumption were not valid? What if S Andromedae were actually much more luminous than Nova Persei ever was? Or much less luminous? How could one tell?

The American astronomer Heber Doust Curtis (1872–1942) believed that the one way of deciding this matter was to search for more novae in the Andromeda Nebula. What could not be judged in the case of one specimen might become clear in the comparative study of many. He therefore tracked down and studied a number of novae in the Andromeda Nebula, and found himself able to make two points.

First, the number of novae located in the nebula was so high that there was no possibility that they were not associated with the nebula. To suppose that all those novae just happened to spring up among stars located in the line of sight between ourselves and the nebula was ridiculous. Such a fortuitous concentration of novae was completely unlikely. This further implied that the Andromeda Nebula was not merely a cloud of dust and gas passively reflecting sunlight. It had to consist of numerous stars—a very large number indeed to have so many novae (a very rare type of star) appear among them. That such stars could not be made out even by large telescopes argued that the nebula was at a great distance. Secondly, all the novae observed in the Andromeda Nebula after 1885 were far dimmer than S Andromedae had been. Curtis suggested in 1918 that these other novae should be compared with Nova Persei, and that S Andromedae was an exceptional, extraordinarily bright nova.

If the ordinary novae in the Andromeda Nebula were set equal in luminosity to Nova Persei, then the distance that would account for the unusual dimness of the former would have to be in hundreds of thousands of light-years, at the very least. Such a distance would also account for the fact that the nebula could not be resolved into stars.

At such a distance, individual stars were simply too faint to be made out—unless they brightened enormously, nova-fashion.

But if the Andromeda Nebula were indeed at such a distance, it must be far outside the limits of the Galaxy and, to appear as large as it does, it must be a huge conglomeration of a vast number of stars. It was indeed an island universe of the type Kant had once described.

Curtis' conclusion was by no means accepted by other astronomers, and even Shapley was opposed to him.

Entering the lists, however, was the American astronomer Edwin Powell Hubble (1889–1953). It seemed clear to him that the argument involving novae would always seem inconclusive since not enough was known about them. If, however, the Andromeda Nebula were actually an island universe, then perhaps a new telescope—more powerful than any available to nineteenth-century astronomers—might settle the issue by revealing the individual stars in the nebula. From the ordinary stars, far less mysterious than the novae, it might be possible to draw firmer conclusions concerning the nebula.

In 1917, a new telescope had been installed on Mt. Wilson, just northeast of Pasadena. It had a mirror that was an unprecedented 100 inches in diameter, making it by far the most powerful telescope in the world (and it was to remain the most powerful for a generation).

Hubble turned the Mt. Wilson telescope on the Andromeda Nebula and succeeded in making out individual stars on the outskirts. That was the final settlement of one problem: the nebula consisted of stars and not of gas and dust . . .

By the mid-1920's, then, the matter was settled, and it has not been questioned since. The Andromeda Nebula is not a member of the Galaxy but is located far beyond its bounds. It is a vast and independent conglomeration of stars, an island universe indeed. Kant was right; Laplace was wrong.

There is more than one dimension to writing, of course. Not only can you write on different subjects, you can also aim at different audiences. And since I am the greediest writer alive and want to write on every subject for every audience, I fall easy prey to certain propositions.

Mrs. Julian May Dikty, of the Follett Publishing Company, wrote to me in 1965, reminding me that we had met at a recent science-fiction convention in Chicago, and suggesting I write a series of books on astronomy for eight-year-olds.

I am easily reached by an appeal to sentiment, as it happens. I told myself that Mrs. Dikty was a fellow conventioneer and that requests from fellow conventioneers deserved special consideration, so I agreed.

But I was cheating, you know, just to give myself a good argument for doing what I wanted to do. I knew very well that I had never been to that particular science-fiction convention (it's a long story but, through no fault of my own, I was maneuvered into being in Chicago a week after the convention) and that Mrs. Dikty only thought she had met me.

Oh, well, I have by now written four of those little books, and a fifth is in press.

One of the little books is Galaxies (Follett, 1968) and I treat the Andromeda Galaxy, for eight-year-olds, as follows:

from GALAXIES *(1968)*

Our Sun is part of a great gathering of many billions of stars. This is shaped like a pinwheel and it turns around and around in space. There is a thick cluster of stars at the center of the pinwheel, and streams of stars called spiral arms come from the center. Our Sun is out in one of the spiral arms, far from the center.

When we look through the pinwheel of stars longways, we can see a band of many faint stars that make a dim, milky glow in the sky. This is called the Milky Way.

The great group of stars we belong to is called a Galaxy . . .

Elsewhere in space there are Galaxies just as huge as our own. In the constellation of Andromeda, we can see a small hazy spot of light. A large telescope shows that this spot is another great Galaxy, more than two million light-years away from our Milky Way Galaxy.

Our own Galaxy is shaped much like the Andromeda Galaxy.

Beyond the Andromeda Galaxy in every direction are still other Galaxies. Many of them have pinwheel shapes and are called spiral Galaxies. Other Galaxies without spiral arms look like great balls of stars or have no special shape.

All the Galaxies put together and the space between them make up the Universe.

That may sound like pretty hard going for eight-year-olds, but I'm only quoting the words, of course. There are useful and accurate pictures on every page of these little books, which help the young readers over the hurdles, and for them I can claim no credit, of course. The illustrators of Galaxies *are Alex Ebel and Denny McMains.*

PART 2
ROBOTS

MY NAME in science fiction is most often associated with robots. I had occasion recently to explain why in an article written for a British popular-science magazine, Science Journal, *at the request of its editor, Robin Clarke.*

You may wonder why so specialized a subject as my relationship to robots appeared in so estimable a periodical, and I can only say that it happens now and then. I get a request to speak or write on a vastly complicated and specialized subject and I answer, as I must, that I am not really an authority on that particular subject. (I am not really an authority on any subject, but I hate to say so too openly.)

Invariably, the answer comes back: "Oh, we know that, but we want you to speak or write on this vastly complicated and specialized subject in its relation to the future."

Well, Science Journal *was preparing a special issue labled "Machines Like Men," for October, 1968, and after panning a progression of serious articles on progressively more complex robots, they decided on a final article on the ultimate robots of the future and so they asked me to do an article, entitled "The Perfect Machine."*

Part of its beginning went as follows:

from "The Perfect Machine" (1968)

The science-fiction writers . . . could not rid themselves of the notion that the manufacture of robots involved forbidden knowledge, a wicked aspiration on the part of man to abilities reserved for God. The attempt to create artificial life was an example of hubris and demanded punishment. In story after story, with grim inevitability, the robot destroyed its creator before being itself destroyed. There were exceptions, to be sure, and occasional tales were written in which robots were sympathetic or even virtuous. But it was not until 1939 that, for the first time as far as I know, a science-fiction writer approached the robots from a systematic engineering standpoint.

Without further coyness, I will state that that science-fiction writer was myself. Since then I have written some two dozen short stories and two novels in which robots were treated as machines, created by human beings to fulfill human purposes. There was no hint of "forbidden knowledge," only rational engineering. Those robot stories killed the Frankenstein motif in respectable science fiction as dead as ever "Don Quixote" killed knight errantry.

To me, the applied science of manufacturing robots, of designing them, of studying them, was "robotics." I used this word because it seemed the obvious analogue of physics, mechanics, hydraulics, and a hundred other terms. In fact, I was sure it was an existing word. Recently, however, it was pointed out to me that "robotics" does not appear in any edition of Webster's unabridged dictionary so I suppose I invented the word.

My engineering attitude toward robots did not spring to life, full blown. I can trace the development neatly through the stories themselves.

I wrote my first robot story in 1939 and had trouble selling it at first. (As a matter of fact, it was not until 1941 that rejection slips and I became almost total—never quite total, of course—strangers.)

It was about a robot nursemaid, named "Robbie." It was loved by the little girl it cared for and distrusted by the little girl's mother. The mother finally got rid of the robot, the little girl was inconsolable, and, eventually, events twisted themselves in such a fashion that the little girl found the robot, had her life saved by it, and all were reunited in a perfect happy ending.

I called the story "Robbie" but the editor, Frederik Pohl, who finally accepted and published it, changed the title to "Strange Playfellow." Fred, an amiable fellow, exceedingly intelligent, and a friend of mine of thirty years' standing (since before I was a writer and he an editor) does have a tendency in that direction. Some editors are more inveterate title changers than others, and Fred is a title-change addict.

On rare occasions, he improves a title by changing it; but this, in my opinion, was not one of those occasions.

Anyway, the important thing about the story was the existence of one paragraph. The girl's mother is expressing her doubts about Robbie, and the girl's father says:

from "Strange Playfellow" (*1940*)

"Dear! A robot is infinitely more to be trusted than a human nursemaid. Robbie was constructed for only one purpose—to be the companion of a little child. His entire 'mentality' has been created for the purpose. He just can't help being faithful and loving and kind. He's a machine —*made so.*"

It is the reverse of the Frankenstein attitude, you see, but I don't go any farther than to say "made so."

The question of being "made so" grew sharper in my mind with time. My third robot story was "Liar!" It was about a robot who could read minds, and who thus knew what people wanted to hear. It had to tell them what they wanted to hear even when that was a lie, for otherwise it would make them feel bad. The robot, reading minds, would sense their unhappiness so that truth-telling was, in those cases, inadmissible.

The robot caused considerable trouble before this was understood.

Susan Calvin, the robopsychologist (who appears in a number of my robot stories), is the first to understand. Here's a passage as she begins to explain:

from "Liar!" (*1941*)

Lanning's voice was hostile. "What is all this, Dr. Calvin?"

She faced them and spoke wearily. "You know the fundamental law impressed upon the positronic brain of all robots, of course."

The other two nodded together. "Certainly," said Bogert. "On no condition is a human being to be injured in any way, even when such injury is directly ordered by another human."

What had been a simple "made so" in "Strange Playfellow" had now become a "fundamental law" of robotics.

There was more than that, though. In the course of a discussion with John W. Campbell, Jr., editor of Astounding Science Fiction, sometime in 1941, two more laws were added, and thus were evolved the "Three Laws of Robotics." These, in some form or another will, I honestly think, eventually form the basis of robotics when the science is truly developed and it is for them, if anything, that I may be remembered by posterity.

They were first mentioned specifically in my fifth robot story, "Runaround," which was set on Mercury (with only one side facing the Sun, of course). A robot had gone out of order and it was necessary that it be repaired quickly, or else disaster would follow. The two heroes of the story, Gregory Powell and Mike Donovan, their lives in balance, try to figure out what to do and decide to go back to fundamentals:

from "Runaround" (*1942*)

Powell's radio voice was tense in Donovan's ear: "Now, look, let's start with the three fundamental Rules of Robotics—the three rules that are built most deeply into a robot's positronic brain." In the darkness, his gloved fingers ticked off each point.

"We have: One, a robot may not injure a human being under any conditions—and, as a corollary, must not permit a human being to be injured because of inaction on his part."

"Right!"

"Two," continued Powell, "a robot must follow all orders given by qualified human beings as long as they do not conflict with Rule One."

"Right!"

"Three: a robot must protect his own existence, as long as that does not conflict with Rules One and Two."

"Right! Now where are we?"

By 1950, nine of my robot stories were collected into a book—I, Robot. This was my second book and after all these years it is still in print and is still selling briskly, to my infinite satisfaction. Its first few years were rocky, however.

You see, although Doubleday and Houghton Mifflin publish the lion's share of my books (sixty of the Hundred between the two of them) the rest have been distributed for a variety of reasons among thirteen other publishers. My relations with all of these but one have always been entirely satisfactory. The exception was Gnome Press which, in the early 1950's, published I, Robot and three other books. All four books have since been taken over, to my delight, by Doubleday.

In the collection, I adjusted the stories in minor ways to remove internal inconsistencies and to place the Three Laws firmly in those stories which preceded "Runaround." I also changed the title of the first story from "Strange Playfellow" back to "Robbie." (A snap of the finger to you, Fred Pohl, old friend.)

Just before the contents page of I, Robot was a special listing of the Three Laws, and these give the "official version" which differed only inconsequentially from the wording in "Runaround" but which I ought to present here:

from I, ROBOT (1950)

THE THREE LAWS OF ROBOTICS

1. A robot may not injure a human being or, through inaction, allow a human being to come to harm.

2. A robot must obey the orders given it by human beings except where such orders would conflict with the First Law.

3. A robot must protect its own existence as long as such protection does not conflict with the First or Second Law.

—HANDBOOK OF ROBOTICS
56th Edition, 2058 A.D.

The concept of robots continued to develop in my mind and I could see no limits to their perfection. Computers, it seems to me (and a robot's brain is, after all, merely a compact computer), can grow complex and versatile without foreseeable limit. Why not a computer (or robot), then, as intelligent as man. For that matter, why not a computer (or robot) more intelligent than man.

I took up this matter as the final and climactic paragraphs of a book entitled The Intelligent Man's Guide to Science *which had its ups and downs.*

Its history began in May, 1959, when an editor from Basic Books asked me to do a book on twentieth-century science. I agreed, but then, exactly as in the case of the later Universe, *I found it necessary to go back to ancient times in every branch of science which I discussed. The book turned out to be more than twice as long as the editor had anticipated—nearly 400,000 words long.*

The editor agreed to do it anyway, but when I received the galley proof, I hit the ceiling and bounced. It seems that the editor, wielding his blue pencil with an energy and intensity I had never encountered before (or since), had greatly condensed my book. When the book was published in 1960, I refused to read it or, indeed, even to open it.

I must interrupt here to say that I generally read my own books after they are published. In part, this is to catch any still-surviving errors so that they may be corrected in the next printing (if any). Mostly, though, I am forced to admit it is because I love to read my own books for their own sake.

This sounds ridiculous, perhaps, but why not? I like the way I write. How else could I write as much as I do, if I didn't enjoy my own writing? Think of it! I've got to read the stuff as it comes out of the typewriter, and then again when I correct the first draft, and then again when I retype it, and then again when I read the final copy, and then again in copyedited version, and then again in galley proof and in page proof. If I didn't like my writing, how could I stand it all?

Of course, I could hire a secretary to do most of this, but since I like reading my writing I don't have to. I can thus remain a one-man operation, running at my own speed without interference, and without the frictional delay of having to deal with typists, secretaries, agents, or any other middlemen at all.

But to get back to The Intelligent Man's Guide to Science—

It was a critical and financial success, so I cannot and do not say that the editorial modifications in any way damaged the book. What's more, my relationship with Basic Books did not suffer. However, what made me unhappy was that the book was not *mine. A book with my name on it doesn't have to be a critical or a financial success; but it does have to be* mine.

Anyway, in 1964, Basic Books asked me to bring the book up to date, and this time I was not to be caught again. I set my conditions. I was to see all changes before *the galley-proof stage, and I implied that the fewer I saw the happier I would be. I was assured that this would be so (and this agreement was honored rigorously by them).*

I got to work with great vigor, therefore, made a thoroughgoing revision of the book and produced The New Intelligent Man's Guide to Science *which is* my *book, and which I love, and open and read frequently. And it is a critical and financial success also.*

Let me quote the last two paragraphs then, which deal with the ultimate end of the computer and which are the same, as it happens, in both editions:

from THE INTELLIGENT MAN'S GUIDE TO SCIENCE (*1960*)

All these attempts to mimic the mind of man are in their earliest infancy. Not in the foreseeable future can we envision any possibility of a machine matching the human brain. The road, however, is open, and it conjures up thoughts which are exciting but also, in some ways, frightening. What if man eventually were to produce a mechanical creature equal or superior to himself in all respects, including intelligence and creativity? Would it replace man, as the superior organisms of the earth have replaced or subordinated the less well adapted in the long history of evolution?

It is a queasy thought: that we represent, for the first time in the history of life on the Earth, a species capable of bringing about its own possible replacement. Of course, we have it in our power to prevent such a regrettable denouement by refusing to build machines that are too intelligent. But it is tempting to build them nevertheless. What achievement could be grander than the creation of an object that surpasses the creator? How could we consummate the victory of intelligence over nature more gloriously than by passing on our heritage, in triumph, to a greater intelligence—of our own making.

And here we come to an advantage science fiction holds over straightforward science exposition. When it comes to really far-out ideas, much more can be done in a fictional frame. Several years before I wrote the above passage, I had written a story called "The Last Question."

This story has a rather curious aftermath. More people have written me to ask if I were the author of this particular story than of any other story I have ever written. They not only can't remember for sure that I am the author; they also can't remember where they read it; and, invariably, they can't remember the title.

Perhaps this is because it is a bad title, but I don't think so. I think that the content of the story attracts them, yet frightens them, too. Unconsciously, they try to forget and don't quite succeed.

It is also the only story of mine that (as far as I know) was the subject of a sermon. It was read from the pulpit in a Unitarian church at Bedford, Massachusetts, while I sat quietly in the back row (I didn't tell them I was coming) and listened.

Anyway, it is one of the three or four stories I am most pleased with having written. It represents my ultimate thinking on the matter of computers/robots and so I am presenting it here, in full:

"The Last Question" (1956)

The last question was asked for the first time, half in jest, on May 21, 2061, at a time when humanity first stepped into the light. The question came about as a result of a five-dollar bet over highballs, and it happened this way:

Alexander Adell and Bertram Lupov were two of the

faithful attendants of Multivac. As well as any human beings could, they knew what lay behind the cold, clicking, flashing face—miles and miles of face—of that giant computer. They had at least a vague notion of the general plan of relays and circuits that had long since grown past the point where any single human could possibly have a firm grasp of the whole.

Multivac was self-adjusting and self-correcting. It had to be, for nothing human could adjust and correct it quickly enough or even adequately enough. So Adell and Lupov attended the monstrous giant only lightly and superficially, yet as well as any men could. They fed it data, adjusted questions to its needs, and translated the answers that were issued. Certainly they, and all others like them, were fully entitled to share in the glory that was Multivac's.

For decades, Multivac had helped design the ships and plot the trajectories that enabled man to reach the Moon, Mars, and Venus, but past that, Earth's poor resources could not support the ships. Too much energy was needed for the long trips. Earth exploited its coal and uranium with increasing efficiency, but there was only so much of both.

But slowly Multivac learned enough to answer deeper questions more fundamentally, and on May 14, 2061, what had been theory, became fact.

The energy of the Sun was stored, converted, and utilized directly on a planet-wide scale. All Earth turned off its burning coal, its fissioning uranium, and flipped the switch that connected all of it to a small station, one mile in diameter, circling the Earth at half the distance of the Moon. All Earth ran by invisible beams of sunpower.

Seven days had not sufficed to dim the glory of it, and Adell and Lupov finally managed to escape from the public function and to meet in quiet where no one would think of looking for them, in the deserted underground chambers, where portions of the mighty buried body of Multivac showed. Unattended, idling, sorting data with contented lazy clickings, Multivac, too, had earned its vacation and the boys appreciated that. They had no intention, originally, of disturbing it.

They had brought a bottle with them, and their only concern at the moment was to relax in the company of each other and the bottle.

"It's amazing when you think of it," said Adell. His broad face had lines of weariness in it, and he stirred his drink slowly with a glass rod, watching the cubes of ice slur clumsily about. "All the energy we can possibly ever use for free. Enough energy, if we wanted to draw on it, to melt all Earth into a big drop of impure liquid iron, and still never miss the energy so used. All the energy we could ever use, forever and forever and forever."

Lupov cocked his head sideways. He had a trick of doing that when he wanted to be contrary, and he wanted to be contrary now, partly because he had had to carry the ice and glassware. "Not forever," he said.

"Oh, hell, just about forever. Till the Sun runs down, Bert."

"That's not forever."

"All right, then. Billions and billions of years. Twenty billion, maybe. Are you satisfied?"

Lupov put his fingers through his thinning hair as though to reassure himself that some was still left and sipped gently at his own drink. "Twenty billion years isn't forever."

"Well, it will last our time, won't it?"

"So would the coal and uranium."

"All right, but now we can hook up each individual spaceship to the Solar Station, and it can go to Pluto and back a million times without every worrying about fuel. You can't do *that* on coal and uranium. Ask Multivac, if you don't believe me."

"I don't have to ask Multivac. I know that."

"Then stop running down what Multivac's done for us," said Adell, blazing up. "It did all right."

"Who says it didn't? What I say is that the Sun won't last forever. That's all I'm saying. We're safe for twenty billion years, but then what?" Lupov pointed a slightly shaky finger at the other. "And don't say we'll switch to another star."

There was silence for a while. Adell put his glass to his lips only occasionally, and Lupov's eyes slowly closed. They rested.

Then Lupov's eyes snapped open. "You're thinking we'll switch to another star when our Sun is done, aren't you?"

"I'm not thinking."

"Sure you are. You're weak on logic, that's the trouble

with you. You're like the guy in the story who was caught in a sudden shower and who ran to a grove of trees and got under one. He wasn't worried, you see, because he figured when one tree got wet through, he would just get under another one."

"I get it," said Adell. "Don't shout. When the Sun is done, the other stars will be gone, too."

"Darn right they will," muttered Lupov. "It all had a beginning in the original cosmic explosion, whatever that was, and it'll all have an end when all the stars run down. Some run down faster than others. Hell, the giants won't last a hundred million years. The Sun will last twenty billion years and maybe the dwarfs will last a hundred billion for all the good they are. But just give us a trillion years and everything will be dark. Entropy has to increase to maximum, that's all."

"I know all about entropy," said Adell, standing on his dignity.

"The hell you do."

"I know as much as you do."

"Then you know everything's got to run down someday."

"All right. Who says they won't?"

"You did, you poor sap. You said we had all the energy we needed, forever. You said 'forever.' "

It was Adell's turn to be contrary. "Maybe we can build things up again someday," he said.

"Never."

"Why not? Someday."

"Never."

"Ask Multivac."

"You ask Multivac. I dare you. Five dollars says it can't be done."

Adell was just drunk enough to try, just sober enough to be able to phrase the necessary symbols and operations into a question which, in words, might have corresponded to this: Will mankind one day without the net expenditure of energy be able to restore the Sun to its full youthfulness even after it had died of old age?

Or maybe it could be put more simply like this: How can the net amount of entropy of the universe be massively decreased?

Multivac fell dead and silent. The slow flashing of lights

ceased, the distant sounds of clicking relays ended.

Then, just as the frightened technicians felt they could hold their breath no longer, there was a sudden springing to life of the teletype attached to that portion of Multivac. Five words were printed: INSUFFICIENT DATA FOR MEANINGFUL ANSWER.

"No bet," whispered Lupov. They left hurriedly.

By next morning, the two, plagued with throbbing head and cottony mouth, had forgotten the incident.

Jerrodd, Jerrodine, and Jerrodette I and II watched the starry picture in the visiplate change as the passage through hyperspace was completed in its non-time lapse. At once, the even powdering of stars gave way to the predominance of a single bright marble-disc, centered.

"That's X–23," said Jerrodd confidently. His thin hands clamped tightly behind his back and the knuckles whitened.

The little Jerrodettes, both girls, had experienced the hyperspace passage for the first time in their lives and were self-conscious over the momentary sensation of inside-outness. They buried their giggles and chased one another wildly about their mother, screaming, "We've reached X–23—we've reached X–23—we've—"

"Quiet children," said Jerrodine sharply. "Are you sure, Jerrodd?"

"What is there to be but sure?" asked Jerrodd, glancing up at the bulge of featureless metal just under the ceiling. It ran the length of the room, disappearing through the wall at either end. It was as long as the ship.

Jerrodd scarcely knew a thing about the thick rod of metal except that it was called a Microvac, that one asked it questions if one wished; that if one did not it still had its task of guiding the ship to a preordered destination; of feeding on energies from the various Sub-galactic Power Stations; of computing the equations for the hyperspatial jumps.

Jerrodd and his family had only to wait and live in the comfortable residence quarters of the ship.

Someone had once told Jerrodd that the ac at the end of "Microvac" stood for "analogue computer" in ancient English, but he was on the edge of forgetting even that.

Jerrodine's eyes were moist as she watched the visiplate. "I can't help it. I feel funny about leaving Earth."

"Why, for Pete's sake?" demanded Jerrodd. "We had nothing there. We'll have everything on X–23. You won't be alone. You won't be a pioneer. There are over a million people on the planet already. Good Lord, our great-grand-children will be looking for new worlds because X–23 will be overcrowded." Then, after a reflective pause, "I tell you, it's a lucky thing the computers worked out interstellar travel the way the race is growing."

"I know, I know," said Jerrodine miserably.

Jerrodette I said promptly, "Our Microvac is the best Microvac in the world."

"I think so, too," said Jerrodd, tousling her hair.

It *was* a nice feeling to have a Microvac of your own and Jerrodd was glad he was part of his generation and no other. In his father's youth, the only computers had been tremendous machines taking up a hundred square miles of land. There was only one to a planet. Planetary AC's they were called. They had been growing in size steadily for a thousand years and then, all at once, came refinement. In place of transistors had come molecular valves so that even the largest Planetary AC could be put into a space only half the volume of a spaceship.

Jerrodd felt uplifted, as he always did when he thought that his own personal Microvac was many times more complicated than the ancient and primitive Multivac that had first tamed the Sun, and almost as complicated as Earth's Planetary AC (the largest) that had first solved the problem of hyperspatial travel and had made trips to the stars possible.

"So many stars, so many planets," sighed Jerrodine, busy with her own thoughts. "I suppose families will be going out to new planets forever, the way we are now."

"Not forever," said Jerodd, with a smile. "It will all stop someday, but not for billions of years. Many billions. Even the stars run down, you know. Entropy must increase."

"What's entropy, Daddy?" shrilled Jerrodette II.

"Entropy, little sweet, is just a word which means the amount of running-down of the universe. Everything runs down, you know, like your little walkie-talkie robot, remember?"

"Can't you just put in a new power unit, like with my robot?"

"The stars *are* the power units, dear. Once they're gone, there are no more power units."

Jerrodette I at once set up a howl. "Don't let them, Daddy. Don't let the stars run down."

"Now look what you've done," whispered Jerrodine, exasperated.

"How was I to know it would frighten them?" Jerrodd whispered back.

"Ask the Microvac," wailed Jerrodette I. "Ask him how to turn the stars on again."

"Go ahead," said Jerrodine. "It will quiet them down." (Jerrodette II was beginning to cry, also.)

Jerrodd shrugged. "Now, now, honeys. I'll ask Microvac. Don't worry, he'll tell us."

He asked the Microvac, adding quickly, "Print the answer."

Jerrodd cupped the strip of thin cellufilm and said cheerfully, "See now, the Microvac says it will take care of everything when the time comes so don't worry."

Jerrodine said, "And now, children, it's time for bed. We'll be in our new home soon."

Jerrodd read the words on the cellufilm again before destroying it: INSUFFICIENT DATA FOR MEANINGFUL ANSWER.

He shrugged and looked at the visiplate. X–23 was just ahead.

VJ–23X of Lameth stared into the black depths of the three-dimensional, small-scale map of the Galaxy and said, "Are we ridiculous, I wonder, in being so concerned about the matter?"

MQ–17J of Nicron shook his head. "I think not. You know the Galaxy will be filled in five years at the present rate of expansion."

Both seemed in their early twenties, both were tall and perfectly formed.

"Still," said VJ–23X, "I hesitate to submit a pessimistic report to the Galactic Council."

"I wouldn't consider any other kind of report. Stir them up a bit. We've got to stir them up."

VJ–23X sighed. "Space is infinite. A hundred billion Galaxies are there for the taking. More."

"A hundred billion is *not* infinite and it's getting less infinite all the time. Consider! Twenty thousand years ago, mankind first solved the problem of utilizing stellar energy, and a few centuries later, interstellar travel became possible. It took mankind a million years to fill one small world and then only fifteen thousand years to fill the rest of the Galaxy. Now the population doubles every ten years—"

VJ–23X interrupted. "We can thank immortality for that."

"Very well. Immortality exists and we have to take it into account. I admit it has its seamy side, this immortality. The Galactic AC has solved many problems for us, but in solving the problem of preventing old age and death, it has undone all its other solutions."

"Yet you wouldn't want to abandon life, I suppose."

"Not at all," snapped MQ–17J, softening it at once to, "Not yet. I'm by no means old enough. How old are you?"

"Two hundred twenty-three. And you?"

"I'm still under two hundred. —But to get back to my point. Population doubles every ten years. Once this Galaxy is filled, we'll have filled another in ten years. Another ten years and we'll have filled two more. Another decade, four more. In a hundred years, we'll have filled a thousand Galaxies. In a thousand years, a million Galaxies. In ten thousand years, the entire known Universe. Then what?"

VJ–23X said, "As a side issue, there's a problem of transportation. I wonder how many sunpower units it will take to move Galaxies of individuals from one Galaxy to the next."

"A very good point. Already, mankind consumes two sunpower units per year."

"Most of it's wasted. After all, our own Galaxy alone pours out a thousand sunpower units a year and we only use two of those."

"Granted, but even with a hundred percent efficiency, we only stave off the end. Our energy requirements are going up in a geometric progression even faster than our population. We'll run out of energy even sooner than we run out of Galaxies. A good point. A very good point."

"We'll just have to build new stars out of interstellar gas."

"Or out of dissipated heat?" asked MQ–17J, sarcastically.

"There may be some way to reverse entropy. We ought to ask the Galactic AC."

VJ–23X was not really serious, but MQ–17J pulled out his AC-contact from his pocket and placed it on the table before him.

"I've half a mind to," he said. "It's something the human race will have to face someday."

He stared somberly at his small AC-contact. It was only two inches cubed and nothing in itself, but it was connected through hyperspace with the great Galactic AC that served all mankind. Hyperspace considered, it was an integral part of the Galactic AC.

MQ–17J paused to wonder if someday in his immortal life he would get to see the Galactic AC. It was on a little world of its own, a spider webbing of force-beams holding the matter within which surges of sub-mesons took the place of the old clumsy molecular valves. Yet despite its sub-etheric workings, the Galactic AC was known to be a full thousand feet across.

MQ–17J asked suddenly of his AC-contact, "Can entropy ever be reversed?"

VJ–23X looked startled and said at once, "Oh, say, I didn't really mean to have you ask that."

"Why not?"

"We both know entropy can't be reversed. You can't turn smoke and ash back into a tree."

"Do you have trees on your world?" asked MQ–17J.

The sound of the Galactic AC startled them into silence. Its voice came thin and beautiful out of the small AC-contact on the desk. It said: THERE IS INSUFFICIENT DATA FOR A MEANINGFUL ANSWER.

VJ–23X said, "See!"

The two men thereupon returned to the question of the report they were to make to the Galactic Council.

Zee Prime's mind spanned the new Galaxy with a faint interest in the countless twists of stars that powered it. He had never seen this one before. Would he ever see them all? So many of them, each with its load of humanity —but a load that was almost a dead weight. More and more, the real essence of men was to be found out here, in space.

Minds, not bodies! The immortal bodies remained back

on the planets, in suspension over the eons. Sometimes they roused for material activity but that was growing rarer. Few new individuals were coming into existence to join the incredibly mighty throng, but what matter? There was little room in the Universe for new individuals.

Zee Prime was roused out of his reverie upon coming across the wispy tendrils of another mind.

"I am Zee Prime," said Zee Prime. "And you?"

"I am Dee Sub Wun. Your Galaxy?"

"We call it only the Galaxy. And you?"

"We call ours the same. All men call their Galaxy their Galaxy and nothing more. Why not?"

"True. Since all Galaxies are the same."

"Not all Galaxies. On one particular Galaxy the race of man must have originated. That makes it different."

Zee Prime said, "On which one?"

"I cannot say. The Universal AC would know."

"Shall we ask him? I am suddenly curious."

Zee Prime's perceptions broadened until the Galaxies themselves shrank and became a new, more diffuse powdering on a much larger background. So many hundreds of billions of them, all with their immortal beings, all carrying their load of intelligences with minds that drifted freely through space. And yet one of them was unique among them all in being the original Galaxy. One of them had, in its vague and distant past, a period when it was the only Galaxy populated by man.

Zee Prime was consumed with curiosity to see this Galaxy and he called out: "Universal AC! On which Galaxy did mankind originate?"

The Universal AC heard, for on every world and throughout space, it had its receptors ready, and each receptor led through hyperspace to some unknown point where the Universal AC kept itself aloof.

Zee Prime knew of only one man whose thoughts had penetrated within sensing distance of Universal AC, and he reported only a shining globe, two feet across, difficult to see. "But how can that be all of Universal AC?" Zee Prime had asked.

"Most of it," had been the answer, "is in hyperspace. In what form it is there I cannot imagine."

Nor could anyone, for the day had long since passed, Zee Prime knew, when any man had any part of the

making of a Universal AC. Each Universal AC designed
and constructed its successor. Each, during its existence
of a million years or more, accumulated the necessary
data to build a better and more intricate, more capable
successor in which its own store of data and individuality
would be submerged.

The Universal AC interrupted Zee Prime's wandering
thoughts, not with words, but with guidance. Zee Prime's
mentality was guided into the dim sea of Galaxies and
one in particular enlarged into stars.

A thought came, infinitely distant, but infinitely clear.
THIS IS THE ORIGINAL GALAXY OF MAN.

But it was the same after all, the same as any other,
and Zee Prime stifled his disappointment.

Dee Sub Wun, whose mind had accompanied the other,
said suddenly, "And is one of these stars the original star
of Man?"

The Universal AC said, MAN'S ORIGINAL STAR HAS GONE
NOVA. IT IS A WHITE DWARF.

"Did the men of its system die?" asked Zee Prime,
startled and without thinking.

The Universal AC said, A NEW WORLD, AS IN SUCH
CASES WAS CONSTRUCTED FOR THEIR PHYSICAL BODIES IN
TIME.

"Yes, of course," said Zee Prime, but a sense of loss
overwhelmed him even so. His mind released its hold on
the original Galaxy of Man, let it spring back and lose
itself among the blurred pinpoints. He never wanted to
see it again.

Dee Sub Wun said, "What is wrong?"

"The stars are dying. The original star is dead."

"They must all die. Why not?"

"But when all energy is gone, our bodies will finally die,
and you and I with them."

"It will take billions of years."

"I do not wish it to happen even after billions of years.
Universal AC! How may stars be kept from dying?"

Dee Sub Wun said in amusement, "You're asking how
entropy might be reversed in direction."

And the Universal AC answered: THERE IS AS YET IN-
SUFFICIENT DATA FOR A MEANINGFUL ANSWER.

Zee Prime's thoughts fled back to his own Galaxy. He
gave no further thought to Dee Sub Wun, whose body

might be waiting on a Galaxy a trillion light-years away, or on the star next to Zee Prime's own. It didn't matter.

Unhappily, Zee Prime began collecting interstellar hydrogen out of which to build a small star of his own. If the stars must someday die, at least some could yet be built.

Man considered with himself, for in a way, Man, mentally, was one. He consisted of a trillion, trillion, trillion ageless bodies, each in its place, each resting quiet and incorruptible, each cared for by perfect automatons, equally incorruptible, while the minds of all the bodies freely melted one into the other, indistinguishable.

Man said, "The Universe is dying."

Man looked about at the dimming Galaxies. The giant stars, spendthrifts, were gone long ago, back in the dimmest of the dim far past. Almost all stars were white dwarfs, fading to the end.

New stars had been built of the dust between the stars, some by natural processes, some by Man himself, and those were going, too. White dwarfs might yet be crushed together and of the mighty forces so released, new stars built, but only one star for every thousand white dwarfs destroyed, and those would come to an end, too.

Man said, "Carefully husbanded, as directed by the Cosmic AC, the energy that is even yet left in all the Universe will last for billions of years."

"But even so," said Man, "eventually it will all come to an end. However it may be husbanded, however stretched out, the energy once expended is gone and cannot be restored. Entropy must increase forever to the maximum."

Man said, "Can entropy not be reversed? Let us ask the Cosmic AC."

The Cosmic AC surrounded them but not in space. Not a fragment of it was in space. It was in hyperspace and made of something that was neither matter nor energy. The question of its size and nature no longer had meaning in any terms that Man could comprehend.

"Cosmic AC," said Man, "how may entropy be reversed?"

The Cosmic AC said, THERE IS AS YET INSUFFICIENT DATA FOR A MEANINGFUL ANSWER.

Man said, "Collect additional data."

The Cosmic AC said, I WILL DO SO. I HAVE BEEN DOING

SO FOR A HUNDRED BILLION YEARS. MY PREDECESSORS AND I HAVE BEEN ASKED THIS QUESTION MANY TIMES. ALL THE DATA I HAVE REMAINS INSUFFICIENT.

"Will there come a time," said Man, "when data will be sufficient or is the problem insoluble in all conceivable circumstances?"

The Cosmic AC said, NO PROBLEM IS INSOLUBLE IN ALL CONCEIVABLE CIRCUMSTANCES.

Man said, "When will you have enough data to answer the question?"

The Cosmic AC said, THERE IS AS YET INSUFFICIENT DATA FOR A MEANINGFUL ANSWER.

"Will you keep working on it?" asked Man.

The Cosmic AC said, I WILL.

Man said, "We shall wait."

The stars and Galaxies died and snuffed out, and space grew black after ten trillion years of running down.

One by one, Man fused with AC, each physical body losing its mental identity in a manner that was somehow not a loss but a gain.

Man's last mind paused before fusion, looking over a space that included nothing but the dregs of one last dark star and nothing besides but incredibly thin matter, agitated randomly by the tag ends of heat wearing out, asymptotically, to an equilibrium level near absolute zero.

Man said, "AC, is this the end? Can this chaos not be reversed into the Universe once more? Can that not be done?"

AC said, THERE IS AS YET INSUFFICIENT DATA FOR A MEANINGFUL ANSWER.

Man's last mind fused and only AC existed—and that in hyperspace.

Matter and energy had ended and with it space and time. Even AC existed only for the sake of the one last question that it had never answered from the time a half-drunken computer attendant ten trillion years before had asked the question of a computer that was to AC far less than was a man to Man.

All other questions had been answered, and until this last question was answered also, AC might not release his consciousness.

All collected data had come to a final end. Nothing was left to be collected.

But all collected data had yet to be completely correlated and put together in all possible relationships.

A timeless interval was spent in doing that.

And it came to pass that AC learned how to reverse the direction of entropy.

But there was now no man to whom AC might give the answer of the last question. No matter. The answer—by demonstration—would take care of that, too.

For another timeless interval, AC thought how best to do this. Carefully, AC organized the program.

The consciousness of AC encompassed all of what had once been a Universe and brooded over what was now Chaos. Step by step, it must be done.

And AC said, LET THERE BE LIGHT!

And there was light—

PART 3
MATHEMATICS

WHEN I WAS IN GRADE SCHOOL, I had an occasional feeling that I might be a mathematician when I grew up. I loved the math classes because they seemed so easy. As soon as I got my math book at the beginning of a new school term, I raced through it from beginning to end, found it all beautifully clear and simple, and then breezed through the course without trouble.

It is, in fact, the beauty of mathematics, as opposed to almost any other branch of knowledge, that it contains so little unrelated and miscellaneous factual material one must memorize. Oh, there are a few definitions and axioms, some terminology—but everything else is deduction. And, if you have a feel for it, the deduction is all obvious, or becomes obvious as soon as it is once pointed out.

As long as this holds true, mathematics is not only a breeze, it is an exciting intellectual adventure that has few peers. But then, sooner or later (except for a few transcendent geniuses), there comes a point when the breeze turns into a cold and needle-spray storm blast. For some it comes quite early in the game: long division, fractions, proportions, something shows up which turns out to be no longer obvious no matter how carefully it is explained. You may get to understand it but only by constant concentration; it never becomes obvious.

And at that point mathematics ceases to be fun.

When there is a prolonged delay in meeting that barrier, you feel lucky, but are you? The longer the delay, the greater the trauma when you do meet the barrier and smash into it.

I went right through high school, for instance, without finding the barrier. Math was always easy, always fun, always an "A-subject" that required no studying.

To be sure, I might have had a hint there was something

wrong. My high school was Boys High School of Brooklyn and in the days when I attended (1932 to 1935) it was renowned throughout the city for the skill and valor of its math team. Yet I was not a member of the math team.

I had a dim idea that the boys on the math team could do mathematics I had never heard of, and that the problems they faced and solved were far beyond me. I took care of that little bit of unpleasantness, however, by studiously refraining from giving it any thought, on the theory (very widespread among people generally) that a difficulty ignored is a difficulty resolved.

At Columbia I took up analytical geometry and differential calculus and, while I recognized a certain unaccustomed intellectual friction heating up my mind somewhat, I still managed to get my A's.

It was when I went on to integral calculus that the dam broke. To my horror, I found that I had to study; that I had to go over a point several times and that even then it remained unclear; that I had to sweat away over the homework problems and sometimes either had to leave them unsolved or, worse still, worked them out incorrectly. And in the end, in the second semester of the year course, I got (oh shame!) a B.

I had, in short, reached my own particular impassable barrier, and I met that situation with a most vigorous and effective course of procedure—I never took another math course.

Oh, I've picked up some additional facets of mathematics on my own since then, but the old glow was gone. It was never the shining gold of "Of course" anymore, only the dubiously polished pewter of "I think I see it."

Fortunately, a barrier at integral calculus is quite a high one. There is plenty of room beneath it within which to run and jump, and I have therefore been able to write books on mathematics. I merely had to remember to keep this side of integral calculus.

In June, 1958, Austin Olney of Houghton Mifflin (whose acquaintance I had first made the year before and whose suggestion is responsible for this book you are holding) asked me to write a book on mathematics for youngsters. I presume he thought I was an accomplished mathematician and I, for my part, did not see my way clear to disabusing him. (I suppose he is disabused now, though.)

*I agreed readily (with one reservation which I shall come
to in due course) and proceeded to write a book called
Realm of Numbers which was as far to the safe side of integral calculus as possible.*

*In fact, it was about elementary arithmetic, to begin with,
and it was not until the second chapter that I as much as
got to Arabic numerals, and not until the fourth chapter
that I got to fractions.*

*However, by the end of the book I was talking about
imaginary numbers, hyperimaginary numbers, and trans-
finite numbers—and that was the real purpose of the book.
In going from counting to transfiinites, I followed such a
careful and gradual plan that it never stopped seeming easy.*

*Anyway, here's part of a chapter from the book, rather
early on, while I am still reveling in the simplest matters,
but trying to get across the rather subtle point of the importance of zero.*

from REALM OF NUMBERS *(1959)*

The Hindus began with nine different symbols, one for
each of the numbers from one through nine. These have
changed through history but reached their present form in
Europe in the sixteenth century and are now written: 1, 2,
3, 4, 5, 6, 7, 8, and 9.

This in itself was not unique. The Greeks and Hebrews,
for instance, used nine different symbols for these numbers.
In each case, the symbols were the first nine letters of their
alphabets. The Greeks and Hebrews went on, though, to
use the next nine letters of their alphabets for ten, twenty,
thirty, and so on; and the nine letters after that for one
hundred, two hundred, three hundred, and so on. If the
alphabet wasn't long enough for the purpose (twenty-eight
letters are required to reach a thousand by this system)
archaic letters or special forms of letters were added.

The use of letters for numbers gave rise to confusion
with words. For instance, the Hebrew number "fifteen"
made use of the two letters that began the name of God (in
the Hebrew language) and so some other letter combination
had to be used.

On the other hand, ordinary words could be converted
into numbers by adding up the numerical value of the

letters composing it. This was done especially for words
and names in the Bible (a process called "gematria") and
all sorts of mystical and occult meanings were read into it.
The most familiar example is the passage in the Revelation
of St. John where the number of the "beast" is given as six
hundred and sixty-six. This undoubtedly meant that some
contemporary figure, whom it was unsafe to name openly
(probably the Roman Emperor Nero) had a name which,
in Hebrew or Greek letters, added up to that figure. Ever
since then, however, people have been trying to fit the
names of their enemies into that sum.

Where the Hindus improved on the Greek and Hebrew
system, however, was in using the same nine figures for
tens, hundreds, and indeed for any rung of the abacus. Out
of those nine figures, they built up all numbers. All that
was necessary was to give the figures positional values.

For instance, the number twenty-three, on the abacus,
consisted of three counters moved to the right on the "ones"
rung and two on the "tens" rung. The number can therefore be written 23, the numeral on the right representing
the bottom rung on the abacus and the one on the left the
next higher one.

Obviously, thirty-two would then be written 32 and the
positional values become plain since 23 and 32 are not the
same number. One is two tens plus three ones and the
other three tens plus two ones.

It is very unlikely that the clever Greeks did not think
of this; they thought of many much more subtle points.
What must have stopped them (and everyone else until
the day of the unknown Hindu genius) was the dilemma of
the untouched rung on the abacus.

Suppose you wanted, instead of twenty-three, to write
two hundred and three. On the abacus, you would move
two counters on the "hundreds" rung and three on the
"ones" rung. The "tens" rung would remain untouched.
Using the Hindu system, it might seem you would still have
to write 23, only this time the 2 means "two hundreds,"
not "two tens."

For that matter, how would you write two thousand and
three, or two thousand and thirty, or two thousand three
hundred? In each case, you would have to move two
counters on one rung and three on another. They would all
seem to be 23.

One solution might be to use different symbols for each rung, but that was what the Greeks did and that was unsatisfactory. Or you might use some sort of symbol above each figure to indicate the rung. You might write twenty-

three as $\overset{\cdot\cdot}{23}$ and two hundred and three as $\overset{\cdot\cdot}{23}$, indicating that in the second case, the 2 was in the third or "hundreds" rung, rather than in the second or "tens" rung. This would make the numbers rather difficult to read in a hurry, though the system would work in theory.

No, the great Hindu innovation was the *invention of a special symbol for an untouched abacus row*. This symbol the Arabs called "sifr," meaning "empty," since the space at the right end of an untouched abacus rung was empty. This word has come down to us as "cipher" or, in more corrupt form, as "zero."

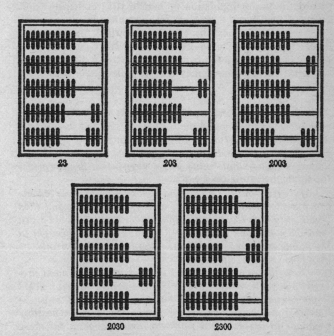

NUMBERS WITH ZERO ON ABACUS

Our symbol for zero is 0, and so we write twenty-three as 23, two hundred and three as 203, two thousand and three as 2003, two hundred and thirty as 230, two thousand and thirty as 2030, two thousand three hundred as 2300, and so on. In each case, we show the untouched rungs on the abacus by using zeros.

(Twenty-three could be written as 0023 or 0000000023, depending on the size of the abacus, but this is never done. It is always assumed that all rungs of the abacus above the first one mentioned and all numerals to the left of the first one mentioned are zero.)

It was the zero that made our so-called Arabic numerals practical and revolutionized the use of numbers. (Strange that the discovery of "nothing" could be so world-shakingly important; and stranger still that so many great mathematicians never saw that "nothing.")

Such is the importance of zero that, to this day, one word for the manipulation of numbers is "ciphering" and when we work out a problem (even one not involving numbers), we "decipher" it. The awe in which the numerals were held by people who didn't understand their working is recalled to us by the fact that any secret writing, usually called a "cryptogram," may also be called a "cipher."

The best part of Realm of Numbers *was that it restored my long-lost feeling about math that I had had before the integral-calculus disaster. More than any other book I've ever written it poured out the typewriter in a series of "Of courses." The whole thing was written—first draft, correction, final copy, everything—in thirteen days.*

My wife, who is shrewd and practical-minded, urged me to put the manuscript aside for, say, six months, and then walk into the Houghton Mifflin offices with a work-worn and haggard look on my face. She said that if I brought in a manuscript two weeks after starting it, they would be convinced it was no good.

I saw the reasoning behind her argument but found myself incapable of putting it into practice. A completed manuscript simply burns a hole in my desk. It must be brought to the publishers. What's more, I can't possibly manage to make myself work-worn and haggard, for there

*is something about a completed manuscript that gives me
an expression of eager delight.*

*So I brought it in promptly and capered about in my
usual fashion and thank goodness no one seemed to think
any the less of the manuscript as a result.*

*In fact, it was followed up by similar books on measuring units and on algebra. It was my intention (and still is)
to sneak up on calculus by very small steps and, eventually,
live dangerously indeed by maneuvering myself immediately
under my impassable barrier.*

*The trouble is I get easily sidetracked. A new book appeared which gave a method for quickly manipulating numbers in one's head through the use of shortcut rules. The
only trouble was that memorizing the rules and keeping
them straight seemed to me to be infinitely harder than
going about it by pencil and paper.*

*I felt that what was needed was only the very simplest
rules for handling only the very simplest problems. It was
my theory, you see, that most people are faced with those
very simplest problems ninety percent of the time. The
difficult problems that involve complicated rules and feats
of memory come up only infrequently and they can be handled by pen and paper.*

So I wrote Quick and Easy Math, *of which part of a
chapter is included here:*

from QUICK AND EASY MATH (*1964*)

I think it would be generally agreed that addition and subtraction are the simplest of the arithmetical operations. Even
without timesaving devices, most people would accept them
without much trouble. Multiplication, however, is considerably harder and more tedious; mistakes are easier to
make; and most people hesitate more over working out particular problems.

Yet multiplication is only a form of addition, and is itself a kind of shortcut.

Thus, let's consider the multiplication problem 9 times 8,
or to use the "multiplication sign" ($\times$), 9×8. The number 9 is the "multiplicand" in this case (from a Latin word
meaning "that which is to be multiplied") while the num-

ber 8 is the "multiplier." As you all surely know, $9 \times 8 = 72$, and 72 is the "product."

But what is there in $9 \times 8 = 72$ that makes the problem a kind of addition? Remember that you can read 9×8 as "nine times eight." You are asked to take 8 "nine times." Well, if you take nine 8's and add them together: $8 + 8 + 8 + 8 + 8 + 8 + 8 + 8 + 8$, you do indeed get 72.

Because multiplication is a form of addition, it shares some of the properties of addition. Just as $a + b = b + a$, so $a \times b = b \times a$. (In algebra, the multiplication sign is generally omitted, so we can express the last statement as $ab = ba$.) Consequently if $9 \times 8 = 72$, then $8 \times 9 = 72$. Sure enough, if you add eight 9's together: $9 + 9 + 9 + 9 + 9 + 9 + 9 + 9$, the sum there too comes to 72.

The fact that multiplication is a shortcut for at least some problems in addition is at once plain. It is easier to memorize that $8 \times 9 = 72$ than to have to add all those 9's and 8's.

In the third grade or so we are usually set to memorizing the "multiplication table," a table which gives the products of all possible combinations of single digits. As a result, it soon becomes second nature for us to say $3 \times 2 = 6$, $7 \times 7 = 49$, $5 \times 9 = 45$, and so forth. We ought to be able to rattle off any combination from $0 \times 0 = 0$ to $9 \times 9 = 81$.

The multiplication table I learned as a child ran all the way up through 12, so that I also learned that $8 \times 11 = 88$, $11 \times 12 = 132$, and $12 \times 12 = 144$. It might not be a bad idea for people who want to make multiplication easier for themselves to memorize all the combinations up to 20 so that they can say, at the drop of a hat, $6 \times 15 = 90$, $17 \times 12 = 204$, $18 \times 19 = 342$, and $20 \times 20 = 400$. However, these extra memorizations, involving two-digit numbers, though handy, are not absolutely necessary. You can make out perfectly well if you memorize a multiplication table that takes you only to 9×9.

The simplest part of multiplication involves zero. Any number at all, no matter how large, when multiplied by zero gives zero as the product. We can say that $2 \times 0 = 0$; $75 \times 0 = 0$; $6,354,876 \times 0 = 0$. And, of course, $0 \times 0 = 0$.

This behavior of zero simplifies certain types of multiplication problems. Suppose, for instance, you want to multiply 10 by 10 and that you decide to do it by the step-by-step method you were taught in school. First, you multiply 10 by 0, writing down the answer; then you multiply 10 by 1, indenting the second answer; finally you add the two answers. I am sure that you all know how to do this and, in fact, that you do this sort of thing every time you multiply. The problem 10×10 would then be worked out as follows:

$$
\begin{array}{r}
10 \\
\times\ 10 \\
\hline
00 \\
10\ \ \\
\hline
100
\end{array}
$$

The numbers that lie between the two horizontal lines are called "partial products." Notice that the first partial product comes out 00, because that partial product is the result of multiplying 10 by 0, and all multiplications by 0 yield 0. We might write 00 or 000 or even 000000000000, but all numbers made up only of zeros are equal to 0.

We get these zeros as partial products whenever there is a zero as one of the digits in the multiplier. Let's take some more cases of multiplications involving numbers made up of a 1 followed by several zeros.

$$
\begin{array}{r}
100 \\
\times\ \ \ 100 \\
\hline
000 \\
0\ 00\ \ \\
10\ 0\ \ \ \ \\
\hline
10,000
\end{array}
\qquad
\begin{array}{r}
1,000 \\
\times\ \ \ \ 10 \\
\hline
0\ 000 \\
10\ 00\ \ \\
\hline
10,000
\end{array}
$$

In short, $100 \times 100 = 10,000$ and $1000 \times 10 = 10,000$. If we stick to numbers of this type and study the answers, we find that the product contains as many zeros as do the multiplicand and multiplier put together.

In multiplying 10×10, multiplicand and multiplier end in one zero apiece and the product 100 ends in two zeros. In multiplying 100×100, multiplicand and multiplier end in two zeros apiece and the product, 10,000, ends in four zeros. Again, in multiplying 1000×10, the total number of zeros in multiplicand and multiplier is four and the product is also 10,000.

Without bothering to multiply out in full, you can tell that 10,000 × 1000, with a total of seven zeros, must have a product of 10,000,000.

If the numbers being multiplied contain but a single digit before the various zeros and one or both of these digits is not 1, things are hardly any more complicated. Suppose that we wish to multiply 300 by 500. We can write 300 as 3 × 100 and 500 as 5 × 100. This means that 300 × 500 = 3 × 100 × 5 × 100. But we know from the multiplication table that 3 × 5 = 15 and we know from adding zeros that 100 × 100 = 10,000. Therefore 3 × 100 × 5 × 100 = 15 × 10,000, or 150,000.

If you consider this preceding paragraph carefully, you see that what we are doing is to add the zeros of multiplicand and multiplier and put the product of the non-zero digits in front of the sum of those zeros.

In multiplying 300 × 500 we could, without ado, count zeros and see that the answer must end in four zeros, 0000. We then multiply 3 × 5 and place the product, 15, in front of the four zeros. That gives us our complete answer, 150,000.

Using this system, you can see quickly that 700 × 4000 has an answer in which 28 (that is, 7 × 4) is followed by five zeros. Therefore 700 × 4000 = 2,800,000. In the same way 5 × 50 has as its product 25 followed by a single zero, or 250; 100 × 80 = 8000; 20 × 60 = 1200, and so on.

Sometimes it is possible to have more zeros in the product than you might expect from merely counting the zeros in multiplicand and multiplier. Suppose you were multiplying 40 × 50. You know the answer will end in two zeros, 00, and that these will be preceded by the product of 4 × 5, which is 20. Therefore, 40 × 50 = 2000, which, as it turns out, ends in three zeros, not in two. The third zero, however, was added by way of the product of 4 × 5, and not by adding the zeros in multiplicand and multiplier.

This is not a matter of concern, of course. The method of counting zeros and putting the product of the single digits before those zeros will give the correct answer in any case. If an additional zero is needed, it will be added automatically.

What we see, then, is that we have learned more from

the multiplication table than we perhaps supposed. In memorizing the product of 8 × 9 as 72, we also made it possible for ourselves to tell, at a glance, the product of 80 × 9, of 8 × 90, of 80 × 90, of 8000 × 900, and so on.

But if we think that's all there is to multiplication, we are living in a fool's paradise. What if one of the numbers contains more than one digit that is not zero? What if it is not the product of 8 × 9 that we want but the product of 83 × 9?

This is something we haven't memorized in any multiplication table. Instead, we usually work it out digit by digit in the manner taught us in school. First, we multiply the 3 by the 9, which gives us 27. We put down 7 and carry 2. Then we multiply 8 × 9, which gives us 72. Adding the 2 we have carried, gives us the sum of 74. Writing this down before the 7 we had previously written down, the answer is 747. This system of multiplying without actually writing down the partial products is "short multiplication." If we multiply 83 × 9 by short multiplication, it would look like this:

$$
\begin{array}{r}
83 \\
\times\ \ 9 \\
\small 2 \\
\hline
747
\end{array}
$$

If we wrote out the partial products in full, we would have "long multiplication," thus:

$$
\begin{array}{r}
83 \\
\times\ \ 9 \\
\hline
27 \\
72\ \ \\
\hline
747
\end{array}
$$

Is there any way of simplifying this? Yes, there is, if we follow our basic principle of changing a difficult problem into an easy one. We have already decided that once the multiplication table is memorized it is easy to multiply numbers that consist of only single digits, plus zeros. How, then, can we convert 83 into such numbers? The logical way is to write 83 as 80 + 3. The number 3 is a single digit, and the number 80 is a single digit plus a zero.

But how can one multiply $80 + 3$ by 9?

Using algebraic symbolism we are multiplying a sum $a + b$ by a number c and this is written $(a + b)c$. If we clear parentheses, we find that $(a + b)c = ac + bc$. In other words, to multiply $80 + 3$ by 9, we first multiply 80×9, then 3×9, then add the two products.

This may strike you as a step backward. How can we make a multiplication simpler by changing it into two multiplications? Are we not just making it harder? Not at all. We are converting one difficult multiplication into two easy ones, and this is a step forward, not backward. We know at a glance that $80 \times 9 = 720$, and that $3 \times 9 = 27$. Since $720 + 27 = 747$, there is our answer.

You can do this in your head without trouble, in all likelihood, but if you want to do it on paper it would look like this:

$$
\begin{array}{r}
80 + 3 \\
\times\ 9 \\
\hline
720 + 27 = 747
\end{array}
$$

Naturally you can use this method on numbers involving final zeros. If you are faced with the multiplication 83×90, work out 83×9 and add the zero. Since you know that $83 \times 9 = 747$, then $83 \times 90 = 7470$. Furthermore, $830 \times 9 = 7470$ also; $8300 \times 900 = 7,470,000$ and so on.

Now let's look back a bit to the point where I multiplied 83×9 by the usual method of long multiplication. The partial products were:

$$
\begin{array}{r}
27 \\
72 \\
\hline
\end{array}
$$

The indented 72 might just as well have a zero after it, for that would not change things. In that case we would have:

$$
\begin{array}{r}
83 \\
\times\ \ 9 \\
\hline
27 \\
720 \\
\hline
747
\end{array}
$$

This means that in ordinary long multiplication we are adding 27 and 720 to get 747, while in the method I recommend, we are adding 720 and 27. Since we are doing the same thing either way, why should one method be preferable to the other?

The answer is this: the school method works from right to left. This is to simplify the written work. Any number you write down will not have to be changed as a result of any number that you will later carry (just as in addition). The trouble is that we think of numbers from left to right, no matter how much we may work with them from right to left, and that makes for confusion.

If we try to multiply 83×9 mentally, in the usual manner, we begin by saying $3 \times 9 = 27$, put down 7 and carry 2, but since we think of 27 as "two-seven" we might carelessly put down 2 and carry 7. We then end with a completely wrong answer.

In the left-to-right method, however, we are thinking of numbers in the customary left-to-right way. We say $(80 + 3) \times 9 = 720 + 27 = 747$. It may not be any easier arithmetically, but it is certainly easier psychologically.

In the same way you can say $44 \times 6 = (40 + 4) \times 6 = 240 + 24 = 264$; and $46 \times 7 = (40 + 6) \times 7 = 280 + 42 = 322$; and so on.

Furthermore, the left-to-right method is more versatile in that it allows subtractions as well as additions. The school method of right-to-left does not allow this.

Suppose that we must multiply 89×7. We can write this $(80 + 9) \times 7 = 560 + 63 = 623$. However, adding 560 and 63 mentally might produce a bit of hesitation. Why not, then, consider 89 to be $90 - 1$, rather than $80 + 9$? Now we can say that $89 \times 7 = (90 - 1) \times 7 = 630 - 7 = 623$.

Most people would find it easier to deal with $630 - 7$ than with $560 + 63$, and the left-to-right method allows such people to make the necessary shift from addition to subtraction.

In the same way, $49 \times 8 = (50 - 1) \times 8 = 400 - 8 = 392$. And $38 \times 3 = (40 - 2 \times 3 = 120 - 6 = 114$.

Of course, you can pass this system on to numbers with more than two digits. The problem 546×6 can be expressed as $(500 + 40 + 6) \times 6 = 3000 + 240 + 36 =$

3276. Or, $329 \times 5 = (300 + 30 - 1) \times 5 = 1500 + 150 - 5 = 1645$.

If you try this technique on larger numbers, you may well find it difficult to keep all the partial products in your head while trying to sum them. Enough practice will make it easier to do so but if you would rather not devote the necessary time to such practice, all is not yet lost. You can use pencil and paper after all.

In multiplying 7625×7, you can mentally break up 7625 into $7000 + 600 + 20 + 5$, and multiply each of these portions by 7. You then write down the partial products only:

$$
\begin{array}{r}
49,000 \\
4,200 \\
140 \\
35 \\
\hline
53,375
\end{array}
$$

You may still find this faster than the usual method taught in school.

When the British edition of this book came out, it seemed to me I found an egregious error on the book jacket. This sometimes happens but, fortunately, very rarely. Still, it remains the nightmare of all right-thinking authors and editors.

In the case of Realm of Numbers, *for instance, the worst of all book-jacket mistakes took place—my name was misspelled. Houghton Mifflin had to paint in a black strip on every book jacket and place my name, correctly spelled, on that strip. If you have a copy of that book, you will see the black strip.—And now you will know why, unless Houghton Mifflin censors out this paragraph in order to hide their shame.*

For that matter, in the first printing of my story collection The Martian Way and Other Stories *published in 1955 by Doubleday, my name was misspelled on the spine of the book itself. Usually I never think to remove the book jacket and look at the book itself, but some obscure inner feeling drove me to do it that time and waves of horror broke wildly over me.*

My second name received an unwanted z. *Actually the name is pronounced as though that letter were a* z, *and it should be a* z. *It was my father that misspelled it, through ignorance of the Latin alphabet (though he had the Hebrew and Cyrillic alphabets down cold). Still, it is an* s *now and it must stay an* s. *It is* A-S-I-M-O-V. *I've reached the ridiculous point now where I snap at strangers who write me letters in which the* z *is present in my name and insist they write again before I answer properly.*

I tell myself that I do this because name recognition is my greatest asset and that I owe it to my writing career to keep my name purely and wholesomely spelled—but that's just rationalization. Actually, I'm a nut.

The mistake I found on the British edition of Quick and Easy Math (*to get back from the digression—and I suspect this book will turn out to be little more than a collection of digressions) was in the title, so I could afford to smile tolerantly. The innocent Englishman had written it* Quick and Easy Maths. *I pointed out this mistake to Houghton Mifflin, laughing heartily, and they told me that "maths" was the standard British abbreviation for "mathematics."*

Well, it's their language, I suppose.

Of course, having indicated how to do simple problems in one's head, I had to write another book on how to do complicated problems on a slide rule.

Here I had a momentary hesitation. After all, there are a number of books telling people how to use a slide rule. In fact, any decent slide rule comes equipped with a little booklet explaining how to use it. Did I have to add another?

But that kind of argument must *be squelched. There are also books written on every other subject I discuss in my own volumes and if I begin worrying about one item, I will have to worry about every other item I add to the set of infinitely-retold tales.*

So I reasoned it out once and for all. I write on a subject, however often it has previously been treated, because it is my pleasure to do so and because it is an honest living. Then, too, I have managed to convince myself I do it better than anyone else, and I'll thank you not to disillusion me in this respect.

Mathematics has an oddly uncomfortable relationship to science fiction. It is easy to write a science-fiction story centered about an astronomic idea, or a chemical one, or a physical, or biological one. Every time some startling new discovery is made in the natural sciences, there are bound to be a rash of science-fiction stories exploiting it. Heavens, when the atom bomb dropped, atomic-doom science-fiction stories grew to be so numerous that editors began refusing them on sight.

But what do you do with mathematics? Generally, it doesn't lend itself to exciting science fiction, and new and startling mathematical discoveries are generally so rarefied that expounding them in fictional guise is almost impossible.

To be sure, something can be done. I've tried my own hand at mathematical science fiction, remaining as carefully below the integral calculus ceiling in fiction as in fact. Indeed, I got down to the simplest of arithmetic in a tale that was a fictional precursor of Realm of Numbers. *And just to show you what can be done with the most elementary of arithmetic, here's the story (not a very long one) in full:*

"The Feeling of Power" (*1958*)

Jehan Shuman was used to dealing with the men in authority on long-embattled Earth. He was only a civilian but he originated programming patterns that resulted in self-directing war computers of the highest sort. Generals consequently listened to him. Heads of congressional committees, too.

There was one of each in the special lounge of New Pentagon. General Weider was space-burned and had a small mouth puckered almost into a cipher. Congressman Brant was smooth-cheeked and clear-eyed. He smoked Denebian tobacco with the air of one whose patriotism was so notorious, he could be allowed such liberties.

Shuman, tall, distinguished, and Programmer-first-class, faced them fearlessly.

He said, "This, gentlemen, is Myron Aub."

"The one with the unusual gift that you discovered quite by accident," said Congressman Brant placidly. "Ah." He inspected the little man with the egg-bald head with amiable curiosity.

The little man, in return, twisted the fingers of his hands

anxiously. He had never been near such great men before. He was only an aging low-grade Technician who had long ago failed all tests designed to smoke out the gifted ones among mankind and had settled into the rut of unskilled labor. There was just this hobby of his that the great Programmer had found out about and was now making such a frightening fuss over.

General Weider said, "I find this atmosphere of mystery childish."

"You won't in a moment," said Shuman. "This is not something we can leak to the firstcomer. —Aub!" There was something imperative about his manner of biting off that one-syllable name, but then he was a great Programmer speaking to a mere Technician. "Aub! How much is nine times seven?"

Aub hesitated a moment. His pale eyes glimmered with a feeble anxiety. "Sixty-three," he said.

Congressman Brant lifted his eyebrows. "Is that right?"

"Check it for yourself, Congressman."

The congressman took out his pocket computer, nudged the milled edges twice, looked at its face as it lay there in the palm of his hand, and put it back. He said, "Is this the gift you brought us here to demonstrate. An illusionist?"

"More than that, sir. Aub has memorized a few operations and with them he computes on paper."

"A paper computer?" said the general. He looked pained.

"No, sir," said Shuman patiently. "Not a paper computer. Simply a sheet of paper. General, would you be so kind as to suggest a number?"

"Seventeen," said the general.

"And you, Congressman?"

"Twenty-three."

"Good! Aub, multiply those numbers and please show the gentlemen your manner of doing it."

"Yes, Programmer," said Aub, ducking his head. He fished a small pad out of one shirt pocket and an artist's hairline stylus out of the other. His forehead corrugated as he made painstaking marks on the paper.

General Weider interrupted him sharply. "Let's see that."

Aub passed him the paper, and Weider said, "Well, it looks like the figure seventeen."

Congressman Brant nodded and said, "So it does, but

I suppose anyone can copy figures off a computer. I think I could make a passable seventeen myself, even without practice."

"If you will let Aub continue, gentlemen," said Shuman without heat.

Aub continued, his hand trembling a little. Finally he said in a low voice, "The answer is three hundred and ninety-one."

Congressman Brant took out his computer a second time and flicked it, "By Godfrey, so it is. How did he guess?"

"No guess, Congressman," said Shuman. "He computed that result. He did it on this sheet of paper."

"Humbug," said the general impatiently. "A computer is one thing and marks on paper are another."

"Explain, Aub," said Shuman.

"Yes, Programmer. —Well, gentlemen, I write down seventeen and just underneath it, I write twenty-three. Next, I say to myself: seven times three—"

The congressman interrupted smoothly, "Now, Aub, the problem is seventeen times twenty-three."

"Yes, I know," said the little Technician earnestly, "but I *start* by saying seven times three because that's the way it works. Now seven times three is twenty-one."

"And how do you know that?" asked the congressman.

"I just remember it. It's always twenty-one on the computer. I've checked it any number of times."

"That doesn't mean it always will be, though, does it?" said the congressman.

"Maybe not," stammered Aub. "I'm not a mathematician. But I always get the right answers, you see."

"Go on."

"Seven times three is twenty-one, so I write down twenty-one. Then one times three is three, so I write down a three under the two of twenty-one."

"Why under the two?" asked Congressman Brant at once.

"Because—" Aub looked helplessly at his superior for support. "It's difficult to explain."

Shuman said, "If you will accept his work for the moment, we can leave the details for the mathematicians."

Brant subsided.

Aub said, "Three plus two makes five, you see, so the twenty-one becomes a fifty-one. Now you let that go for a while and start fresh. You multiply seven and two, that's fourteen, and one and two, that's two. Put them down like this and it adds up to thirty-four. Now if you put the thirty-four under the fifty-one this way and add them, you get three hundred and ninety-one and that's the answer."

There was an instant's silence and then General Weider said, "I don't believe it. He goes through this rigmarole and makes up numbers and multiplies and adds them this way and that, but I don't believe it. It's too complicated to be anything but horn-swoggling."

"Oh no, sir," said Aub in a sweat. "It only *seems* complicated because you're not used to it. Actually, the rules are quite simple and will work for any numbers."

"Any numbers, eh?" said the general. "Come then." He took out his own computer (a severely styled GI model) and struck it at random. "Make a five seven three eight on the paper. That's five thousand seven hundred and thirty-eight."

"Yes, sir," said Aub, taking a new sheet of paper.

"Now" (more punching of his computer), "seven two three nine. Seven thousand two hundred and thirty-nine."

"Yes, sir."

"And now multiply those two."

"It will take some time," quavered Aub.

"Take the time," said the general.

"Go ahead, Aub," said Shuman crisply.

Aub set to work, bending low. He took another sheet of paper and another. The general took out his watch finally and stared at it. "Are you through with your magic-making, Technician?"

"I'm almost done, sir. —Here it is, sir. Forty-one million, five hundred and thirty-seven thousand, three hundred and eighty-two." He showed the scrawled figures of the result.

General Weider smiled bitterly. He pushed the multiplication contact on his computer and let the numbers whirl to a halt. And then he stared and said in a surprised squeak, "Great Galaxy, the fella's right."

The President of the Terrestrial Federation had grown haggard in office and, in private, he allowed a look of settled melancholy to appear on his sensitive features. The Denebian war, after its early start of vast movement and great popularity, had trickled down into a sordid matter of maneuver and countermaneuver, the discontent rising steadily on Earth. Possibly, it was rising on Deneb, too.

And now Congressman Brant, head of the important Committee on Military Appropriations, was cheerfully and smoothly spending his half-hour appointment spouting nonsense.

"Computing without a computer," said the President impatiently, "is a contradiction in terms."

"Computing," said the congressman, "is only a system for handling data. A machine might do it, or a human brain might. Let me give you an example." And, using the new skills he had learned, he worked out sums and products until the President, despite himself, grew interested.

"Does this always work?"

"Every time, Mr. President. It is foolproof."

"Is it hard to learn?"

"It took me a week to get the real hang of it. I think you would do better."

"Well," said the President, considering, "it's an interesting parlor game, but what is the use of it?"

"What is the use of a newborn baby, Mr. President? At the moment there is no use, but don't you see that this points the way toward liberation from the machine. Consider, Mr. President," the congressman rose and his deep voice automatically took on some of the cadences he used in public debate, "that the Denebian war is a war of computer against computer. Their computers can forge an impenetrable shield of counter-missiles against our missiles, and ours forge one against theirs. If we advance the efficiency of our computers, so do they theirs, and for five years a precarious and profitless balance has existed.

"Now, we have in our hands a method of going beyond the computer, leapfrogging it, passing through it. We will combine the mechanics of computation with human thought; we will have the equivalent of intelligent computers; billions of them. I can't predict what the consequences will be in detail but they will be incalculable. And if Deneb beats us to the punch, they may be unimaginably catastrophic."

The President said, troubled, "What would you have me do?"

"Put the power of the administration behind the establishment of a secret project on human computation. Call it Project Number, if you like. I can vouch for my committee, but I will need the administration behind me."

"But how far can human computation go?"

"There is no limit. According to Programmer Shuman, who first introduced me to this discovery—"

"I've heard of Shuman, of course."

"Yes. Well, Dr. Shuman tells me that in theory there is nothing the computer can do that the human mind can not do. The computer merely takes a finite amount of data and performs a finite number of operations upon them. The human mind can duplicate the process."

The President considered that. He said, "If Shuman says this, I am inclined to believe him—in theory. But, in practice, how can anyone know how a computer works?"

Brant laughed genially. "Well, Mr. President, I asked the same question. It seems that at one time computers were designed directly by human beings. Those were simple computers, of course, this being before the time of the rational use of computers to design more advanced computers had been established."

"Yes, yes. Go on."

"Technician Aub apparently had, as his hobby, the reconstruction of some of these ancient devices and in so doing he studied the details of their workings and found he could imitate them. The multiplication I just performed for you is an imitation of the workings of a computer."

"Amazing!"

The congressman coughed gently. "If I may make another point, Mr. President—the further we can develop this thing, the more we can divert our Federal effort from computer production and computer maintenance. As the human brain takes over, more of our energy can be directed into peacetime pursuits and the impingement of war on the ordinary man will be less. This will be most advantageous for the party in power, of course."

"Ah," said the President, "I see your point. Well, sit down, Congressman, sit down. I want some time to think about this. —But meanwhile, show me that multiplication trick again. Let's see if I can't catch the point of it."

Programmer Shuman did not try to hurry matters. Loesser was conservative, very conservative, and liked to deal with computers as his father and grandfather had. Still, he controlled the West European computer combine, and if he could be persuaded to join Project Number in full enthusiasm, a great deal would be accomplished.

But Loesser was holding back. He said, "I'm not sure I like the idea of relaxing our hold on computers. The human mind is a capricious thing. The computer will give the same answer to the same problem each time. What guarantee have we that the human mind will do the same?"

"The human mind, Computer Loesser, only manipulates facts. It doesn't matter whether the human mind or a machine does it. They are just tools."

"Yes, yes. I've gone over your ingenious demonstration that the mind can duplicate the computer but it seems to me a little in the air. I'll grant the theory but what reason have we for thinking that theory can be converted to practice?"

"I think we have reason, sir. After all, computers have not always existed. The cave men with their triremes, stone axes, and railroads had no computers."

"And possibly they did not compute."

"You know better than that. Even the building of a railroad or a ziggurat called for some computing, and that must have been without computers as we know them."

"Do you suggest they computed in the fashion you demonstrate?"

"Probably not. After all, this method—we call it 'graphitics,' by the way, from the old European word 'grapho' meaning 'to write'—is developed from the computers themselves so it cannot have antedated them. Still, the cave men must have had *some* method, eh?"

"Lost arts! If you're going to talk about lost arts—"

"No, no. I'm not a lost-art enthusiast, though I don't say there may not be some. After all, man was eating grain before hydroponics, and if the primitives ate grain, they must have grown it in soil. What else could they have done?"

"I don't know, but I'll believe in soil-growing when I see someone grow grain in soil. And I'll believe in making fire by rubbing two pieces of flint together when I see that, too."

Shuman grew placative. "Well, let's stick to graphitics. It's just part of the process of etherealization. Transportation by means of bulky contrivances is giving way to direct mass-transference. Communications devices become less massive and more efficient constantly. For that matter, compare your pocket computer with the massive jobs of a thousand years ago. Why not, then, the last step of doing away with computers altogether? Come, sir, Project Number is a going concern; progress is already headlong. But we want your help. If patriotism doesn't move you, consider the intellectual adventure involved."

Loesser said skeptically, "What progress? What can you do beyond multiplication? Can you integrate a transcendental function?"

"In time, sir. In time. In the last month I have learned to handle division. I can determine, and correctly, integral quotients and decimal quotients."

"Decimal quotients? To how many places?"

Programmer Shuman tried to keep his tone casual. "Any number!"

Loesser's jaw dropped. "Without a computer?"

"Set me a problem."

"Divide twenty-seven by thirteen. Take it to six places."

Five minutes later, Shuman said, "Two point zero seven nine six two three."

Loesser checked it. "Well, now, that's amazing. Multiplication didn't impress me too much because it involved integers after all, and I thought trick manipulation might do it. But decimals—"

"And that is not all. There is a new development that is, so far, top secret and which, strictly speaking, I ought not to mention. Still— We may have made a breakthrough on the square-root front."

"Square roots?"

"It involves some tricky points and we haven't licked the bugs yet, but Technician Aub, the man who invented the science and who has an amazing intuition in connection with it, maintains he has the problem almost solved. And he is only a Technician. A man like yourself, a trained and talented mathematician ought to have no difficulty."

"Square roots," muttered Loesser, attracted.

"Cube roots, too. Are you with us?"

Loesser's hand thrust out suddenly, "Count me in."

General Weider stumped his way back and forth at the head of the room and addressed his listeners after the fashion of a savage teacher facing a group of recalcitrant students. It made no difference to the general that they were the civilian scientists heading Project Number. The general was the overall head, and he so considered himself at every waking moment.

He said, "Now square roots are all fine. I can't do them myself and I don't understand the methods, but they're fine. Still, the Project will not be sidetracked into what some of you call the fundamentals. You can play with graphitics any way you want to after the war is over, but right now we have specific and very practical problems to solve."

In a far corner, Technician Aub listened with painful attention. He was no longer a Technician, of course, having been relieved of his duties and assigned to the Project, with a fine-sounding title and good pay. But, of course, the social distinction remained and the highly placed scientific leaders could never bring themselves to admit him to their ranks on a footing of equality. Nor, to do Aub justice, did he, himself, wish it. He was as uncomfortable with them as they were with him.

The general was saying, "Our goal is a simple one, gentlemen; the replacement of the computer. A ship that can navigate space without a computer on board can be constructed in one-fifth the time and at one-tenth the expense of a computer-laden ship. We could build fleets five times, ten times as great as Deneb could if we could but eliminate the computer.

"And I see something even beyond this. It may be fantastic now; a mere dream; but in the future I see the manned missile!"

There was an instant murmur from the audience.

The general drove on. "At the present time, our chief bottleneck is the fact that missiles are limited in intelligence. The computer controlling them can only be so large, and for that reason they can meet the changing nature of anti-missile defenses in an unsatisfactory way. Few missiles, if any, accomplish their goal, and missile warfare is coming to a dead end; for the enemy, fortunately, as well as for ourselves.

"On the other hand, a missile with a man or two within, controlling flight by graphitics, would be lighter, more mobile, more intelligent. It would give us a lead that might well mean the margin of victory. Besides which, gentlemen, the exigencies of war compel us to remember one thing. A man is much more dispensable than a computer. Manned missiles could be launched in numbers and under circumstances that no good general would care to undertake as far as computer-directed missiles are concerned—"

He said much more but Technician Aub did not wait.

Technician Aub, in the privacy of his quarters, labored long over the note he was leaving behind. It read finally as follows:

"When I began the study of what is now called graphitics, it was no more than a hobby. I saw no more in it than an interesting amusement, an exercise of mind.

"When Project Number began, I thought that others were wiser than I; that graphitics might be put to practical use as a benefit to mankind, to aid in the production of really practical mass-transference devices perhaps. But now I see it is to be used only for death and destruction.

"I cannot face the responsibility involved in having invented graphitics."

He then deliberately turned the focus of a protein-depolarizer on himself and fell instantly and painlessly dead.

They stood over the grave of the little Technician while tribute was paid to the greatness of his discovery.

Programmer Shuman bowed his head along with the rest of them but remained unmoved. The Technician had done his share and was no longer needed, after all. He might have started graphitics, but now that it had started, it would carry on by itself overwhelmingly, triumphantly, until manned missiles were possible with who knew what else.

Nine times seven, thought Shuman with deep satisfaction, is sixty-three, and I don't need a computer to tell me so. The computer is in my own head.

And it was amazing the feeling of power that gave him.

Two things come to mind in connection with "The Feeling of Power." One involves the matter of anthologization. Almost every one of my science fiction short stories and novelettes has been anthologized in one place or another (one of them in fifteen different collections so far, with three more in press at the moment of writing). Usually, though, these collections are devoted to science fiction exclusively.

Some of my stories, however, are anthologized in collections that are intended for general reading in the classroom, and here "The Feeling of Power" is particularly prominent. Perhaps that is because the story deals with arithmetic as a method of making a rather subtle (I think) point. And the "satire" in the story usually receives particular attention in the questions placed at the end of the story in such collections.

I always read those questions with profound interest. When I was in school myself I was forever being asked questions about literary works and I used to wonder whether the writers themselves could have answered the questions satisfactorily. Since I try not to let even the most fugitive of thoughts go to waste, I wrote a short-short based on that notion in 1953, long after I was out of school. In the tale, Shakespeare is brought into the present and is enrolled in a college course on his own plays. You guessed it! He flunked!

Anyway, I now had a chance to see for myself. For instance, here are some of the questions asked about the story in these collections:

"Any good science fiction story is based upon certain assumptions as to what is going to happen during the next few centuries. What are the assumptions in this story?"

"What general failings of the human race are satirized in this story?"

"What is the main interest for the reader in this story? Is it in the action, the character, or the theme? Support your answer."

"What details which are casually introduced into the story establish that it takes place in the far-distant future?"

I think I can answer all those questions, but what would happen if I did and sneaked them into a class which had been reading my story. Would they be the best set of answers in the class? Would the teacher write "Very good" on them, or would she write, "I think you missed the point"? Would I pass?

Well, I'm not going to try.

As a matter of fact, I don't even feel guilty about it. I just write my stories, clickety-click, as they come pouring out of me. I don't sit around and analyze them, either be-fore I write them or after I write them. That's for the reader to do, if he wishes. If he happens to see something there that was more or less vaguely in my mind as I wrote, I'm happy for both of us—but if he sees something that wasn't anywhere in my mind (as far as I know) who's to say he's wrong?

I once listened to a German philosopher (he was really German and he was a professor of philosophy) discuss one of my stories in detail, when he didn't know I was in the audience. After his lecture, I came up to dispute the points he had made in his interpretation and presented him with what I felt was a blockbuster when I said, "After all, I happen to be the author of the story."

"Oh," said he, "are you Isaac Asimov? I'm pleased to meet you and I admire your work but tell me— What makes you think, just because you wrote the story that you know anything at all about it?"

I've tried never to forget that little lesson.

The second item that comes to mind in connection with "The Feeling of Power" concerns the disconcerting effect a literal mind can have.

I know a very fine man, the soul of kindness and gener-osity, who publishes a magazine devoted to computers. He asked if he might reprint one of my stories dealing with computers so I sent him a copy of "The Feeling of Power."

He sent it right back with the simple comment, "I don't believe it is possible for human beings to forget how to do arithmetic."

It isn't easy to strike me speechless (as you may guess from this book alone) but he managed it with that com-ment.

PART 4
PHYSICS

I ONCE TOOK a course in high school physics which, for some reason forever buried in the murky mind of the teacher, began with a long and detailed study of the incandescent lamp. I never recovered.

I did poorly in the course, naturally, and I did not do remarkably well in my one college course in the science, either. Press the button marked "physics" in my brain and the first free-association response is "Electric lights. Fooey."

My chance for recovery came in 1962, when Mr. Truman M. Talley (Mac, for short) of New American Library set about talking me into doing a whole series of small introductory paperback books on science. For the purpose, I remember, he came up to Boston, had me out to dinner, and spun such a web of charm about me that, at the crucial moment, when he whipped out the contract all set for my signing—I signed it.

Mac calmly placed his copy of the contract in his inner jacket pocket and said, "Which science do you want to handle first?"

At once I said, "If you don't mind, I'd like to tackle physics."

You see, here was my chance. At last I would sit down and undo the electric-light damage that had been done me in high school. I would introduce physics the way it ought to be introduced; or, at the very least, the way I thought it ought to be introduced.

Mac and the New American Library were only going to handle the paperback version of the books, of course, and the hard-cover editions were signed over to Walker & Company. (Part of the reason for this was that Ed Burlingame, whom I mentioned before in connection with The Universe, *was Mac's associate at the time I was working on the book. When he resigned to become editor in chief of Walker &*

Company, he had inside knowledge of the book's existence and grabbed it. Editors sometimes carry me around like a virus when they change jobs, and that's one of the reasons I have so many publishers.)

The book came out under the title Understanding Physics but it was in three volumes. That was by no means intentional to begin with.

The agreement was that I was to do books, not more than 90,000 words long, on each of the sciences. But who counts? When I'm writing and having fun, the last thing in the world I want to do is to cut myself short. I hadn't gone very far in my lovingly slow explanation of physics before I realized that there wasn't the slightest possibility of covering the necessary ground in 90,000 words. A quick estimate showed me that I would, by then, have dealt with only one-third of the subject matter.

So I devoted the first book to "Motion, Sound, and Heat," the second book to "Light, Magnetism, and Electricity," and the third book to "The Electron, Proton, and Neutron." In other words I had three introductions: one to Mechanics, one to Electromagnetics, and one to Subatomics.

I handed them in to New American Library as three separate books, but Mac decided to run them as three volumes of a single book. This publishing decision was accepted by Walker & Company, and out it came as a single book in three volumes.

This presented me with a serious problem. Do I count the book as one book or as three books in my list?

And don't ask what difference it makes.

It makes a lot of difference. When the book came out in 1966, I was three-quarters of the way toward My Hundredth Book and three books would give me three times the push ahead that one book would. I wanted it to be three books—yet I also wanted to be honest.

I told myself that I had written it as three separate books; I had submitted it as three separate books; that it had been entirely a publisher's decision to count it as a single book—and yet I couldn't quite convince myself that I wasn't just stretching matters for the sake of that Hundredth.

So I asked Ed Burlingame. I said, "Ed, when you publish

Understanding Physics, *do you think of it as one book or as three books?"*

And Ed said with a phenomenally straight face, "Why, three books of course, Isaac."

I went off in a state of high satisfaction to enter them on my list in that fashion, refusing to let myself consider for one moment that Ed, as a good editor, knew what was bugging me and felt it his first duty to give me the answer I wanted.

The three volumes of Understanding Physics approached the science from a historical viewpoint. I believe in the historical approach for a number of reasons and make use of it whenever I can.

The most elaborate historical account of science I have yet attempted arose out of a suggestion made to me in 1961 by T. O'Conor Sloane of Doubleday. His letter aroused the liveliest interest in me because when I was a nine-year-old and picked up the August, 1929, issue of Amazing Stories, the very first science-fiction magazine I ever read, its editor had been T. O'Conor Sloane. That editor had been an aged man at the time and had since died, but surely there must be some connection.

There was! T. O'Conor Sloane III was the grandson of the onetime editor.

Could I refuse under those circumstances?

Tom Sloane asked me to do 250 short biographies of the most important scientists in history, arranged chronologically. In principle, that was easy, but it was clearly going to be a difficult task to pick out the 250 most important scientists, so I avoided the necessity of too many decisions by writing 1000 short biographies.

By the time I was finished I was extremely nervous about the length of the book, and it seemed to me there was a distinct possibility that Tom might kill me when I brought it in. So I used strategy.

I plunked six boxes full of manuscript in front of him and said, "I have finished the original plus carbon of the book."

He looked at it in astonishment and said, "It looks a little on the long side."

I let that sink in, hoping he would estimate three boxes

*original and three boxes carbon. When I thought he had
adjusted himself sufficiently, I brought in the other six
boxes which I had hidden outside his door and said, "And
this is the carbon I spoke of."*

Fortunately, he had a sense of humor and started laughing.

*Then came the problem of naming the book. I had called
it on my manuscript:* A Biographical History of Science
and Technology, *which was a perfect description. However,
publishers are concerned about the selling aspects of titles
even more than about their descriptive aspects. Tom said
"history" was a bad title word and "encyclopedia" was a
good one from the sales point of view, so it became* A Biographical Encyclopedia of Science and Technology.

*And then Tom said he thought my name had become
sufficiently well known to add luster to the title and, to my
horror, suggested it become* Asimov's Biographical Encyclopedia of Science and Technology. *That, indeed, proved to
be the final title.*

*I'm not kidding about my horror. I really did object.
Partly it was because, although I am terribly fond of myself, I am not as conceited as all* that. *Besides, if the book
did badly I might not be able to persuade myself it wasn't
my name in the title that had turned the trick and then I
would feel rotten. But neither Tom nor anyone else at
Doubleday would listen, and it came out with my name in
the title, bold as brass.*

*And it did well, at that. Doubleday has since put my
name at the head of the title of two more books, and may
even continue doing so, too.*

*Among the scientific biographies contained in the book
were some that were as short at 100 words and others that
were as long as 10,000 words, and I must admit that the
choice of whom to include and how thoroughly to deal with
him was entirely a matter of my own prejudices. If he
were someone I liked, he got in at considerable length and
that's all there was to it.*

*One of the scientists I particularly like is Galileo, so he
got a pretty full treatment and here he is:*

from ASIMOV'S BIOGRAPHICAL ENCYCLOPEDIA
OF SCIENCE AND TECHNOLOGY (*1964*)

GALILEO (gahl-ih-lay'oh)
    Italian astronomer and physicist
    Born: Pisa, February 15, 1564
    Died: Arcetri (near Florence), January 8, 1642

Universally known by his first name only, Galileo's full
name is Galileo Galilei. He was born three days before
Michelangelo died; a kind of symbolic passing of the palm
of learning from the fine arts to science.

Galileo was destined by his father, a mathematician, to
the study of medicine and was deliberately kept away from
mathematics. In those days (and perhaps in these) a physician earned thirty times a mathematician's salary. Galileo
would undoubtedly have made a good physician, as he
might also have made a good artist or musician, for he was
a true Renaissance man, with many talents.

However, fate took its own turning and the elder Galilei
might as well have saved himself the trouble. The young
student, through accident, happened to hear a lecture on
geometry. He promptly talked his reluctant father into
letting him study mathematics and science.

This was fortunate for the world, for Galileo's career
was a major turning point in science. He was not content merely to observe; he began to measure, to reduce
things to quantity, to see if he could not derive some mathematical relationship that would describe a phenomenon
with simplicity and generality. He was not the first to do
this, for it had been done even by Archimedes eighteen
centuries before, but Galileo did it more extensively than
his predecessors and, what is more, he had the literary
ability (another talent) to describe his work so clearly and
beautifully that he made his quantitative method famous
and fashionable.

The first of his startling discoveries took place in 1581,
when he was a teen-ager studying medicine at the University of Pisa. Attending services at the Cathedral of Pisa,
he found himself watching a swinging chandelier, which

air currents shifted now in wide arcs, now in small ones. To Galileo's quantitative mind, it seemed that the time of swing was the same, regardless of the amplitude. He tested this by his pulsebeat. Then, upon returning home, he set up two pendulums of equal length and swung one in larger, one in smaller sweeps. They kept together and he found he was correct.

(In later experiments, Galileo was to find that the difficulty of accurately measuring small intervals of time was his greatest problem. He had to continue using his pulse, or to use the rate at which water trickled through a small orifice and accumulated in a receiver. It is ironic then, that after Galileo's death Huygens was to use the principle of the pendulum, discovered by Galileo, as the means by which to regulate a clock, thus solving the problem Galileo himself could not. Galileo also attempted to measure temperature, devising a thermoscope for the purpose in 1593. This was a gas thermometer which measured temperature by the expansion and contraction of gas. It was grossly inaccurate, and not until the time of Amontons, a century later, was a reasonable beginning made in thermometry. It should never be forgotten that the rate of advance of science depends a great deal on advances in techniques of measurement.)

In 1586 Galileo published a small booklet on the design of a hydrostatic balance he had invented and this first brought him to the attention of the scholarly world.

Galileo began to study the behavior of falling bodies. Virtually all scholars still followed the belief of Aristotle that the rate of fall was proportional to the weight of the body. This, Galileo showed, was a conclusion erroneously drawn from the fact that air resistance slowed the fall of light objects that offered comparatively large areas to the air. (Leaves, feathers, and snowflakes are examples.) Objects that were heavy enough and compact enough to reduce the effect of air resistance to a quantity small enough to be neglected, fell at the same rate. Galileo conjectured that in a vacuum *all* objects would fall at the same rate. (A good vacuum could not be produced in his day, but when it finally was, Galileo was proved to be right.)

Legend has it that Galileo demonstrated his views by simultaneously dropping two cannonballs, one ten times heavier than the other, from the Leaning Tower of Pisa.

Both were seen and heard to strike the ground simultaneously. This seems to be nothing more than a legend, but a similar experiment was actually performed, or at least described, some years earlier by Stevinus.

Nevertheless, the experiments that Galileo did indeed perform were quite sufficient to upset Aristotelian physics.

Since his methods for measuring time weren't accurate enough to follow the rate of motion of a body in free fall, he "diluted" gravity by allowing a body to roll down an inclined plane. By making the slope of the inclined plane a gentle one, he could slow the motion as much as he wished. It was then quite easy to show that the rate of fall of a body was quite independent of its weight.

He was also able to show that a body moved along an inclined plane at a constantly accelerated velocity; that is, it moved more and more quickly. Da Vinci had noted this a century earlier but had kept it to himself.

This settled an important philosophic point. Aristotle had held that in order to keep a body moving, a force had to be continually applied. From this it followed, according to some medieval philosophers, that the heavenly bodies, which were continually moving, had to be pushed along by the eternal labors of angels. A few even used such arguments to deduce the existence of God. On the other hand, some philosophers of the late Middle Ages, such as Buridan, held that constant motion required no force after the initial impulse. By that view, God in creating the world could have given it a start and then let it run by itself forever after. If a continuous force *were* applied, said these philosophers, the resulting motion would become ever more rapid.

Galileo's experiments decided in favor of this second view and against Aristotle. Not only did the velocity of a falling ball increase steadily with time under the continuous pull of the earth, but the total distance it covered increased as the square of the time.

He also showed that a body could move under the influence of two forces at one time. One force, applying an initial force horizontally (as the explosion of a gun), could keep a body moving horizontally at a constant velocity. Another force, applied constantly in a vertical direction, could make the same body drop downward at an accelerated velocity. The two motions superimposed would cause the body to follow a parabolic curve. In this way Galileo was able to make a science out of gunnery.

This concept of one body influenced by more than one force also explained how it was that everything on the surface of the earth, including the atmosphere, birds in flight, and falling stones, could share in the earth's rotation and yet maintain their superimposed motions. This disposed of one of the most effective arguments against the theories of Copernicus and showed that one need not fear that the turning and revolving earth would leave behind those objects not firmly attached to it.

(Galileo's proofs were all reached by the geometric methods of the Greeks. The application of algebra to geometry and the discovery of infinitely more powerful methods of mathematical analysis than those at Galileo's disposal had to await Descartes and Newton. Yet Galileo made do with what he had and his discoveries marked the beginning of the science of mechanics and served as the basis a century later for the three laws of motion propounded by Newton.)

In his book on mechanics Galileo also dealt with the strength of materials, founding that branch of science as well. He was the first to show that if a structure increased in all dimensions equally it would grow weaker—at least he was the first to explain the theoretical basis for this. This is what is now known as the square cube law. The volume increases as the cube of linear dimensions, but the strength only as the square. For that reason larger animals require proportionately sturdier supports than small ones. A deer expanded to the size of an elephant and kept in exact proportion would collapse. Its legs would have to be thickened out of proportion for proper support.

The success of Galileo and his successors, particularly Newton, in accounting for motion by pushes and pulls ("forces") gave rise to the thought that everything in the universe capable of measurement could be explained on the basis of pushes and pulls no more complicated in essence than the pushes and pulls of levers and gears within a machine. This mechanistic view of the universe was to gain favor until a new revolution in science three centuries after Galileo showed matters to be rather more complicated than the mechanists had assumed.

Galileo's work made him unpopular at Pisa and he

moved to a better position at Padua. Galileo was always making himself unpopular with influential people, for he had a brilliant and caustic wit and he could not resist using that wit to make jackasses—and therefore bitter enemies—of those who disagreed with him. Even as a college student, he had been nicknamed "the wrangler" because of his argumentativeness. Besides, he was so brilliant a lecturer that students flocked to hear him while his colleagues mumbled away in empty halls, and nothing will infuriate a colleague more than that.

In Padua, Galileo was corresponding with the great astronomer Kepler and came to believe in the truth of the theories of Copernicus, though he prudently refrained for a while from saying so publicly. However, in 1609, he heard that a magnifying tube, making use of lenses, had been invented in Holland. Before six months had passed, Galileo had devised his own version of the instrument, one that had a magnifying power of thirty-two and had turned it on the heavens. Thus began the age of telescopic astronomy.

Using his telescope, Galileo found that the Moon had mountains and the Sun had spots, which showed once again that Aristotle was wrong in his thesis that the heavens were perfect and that only on Earth was there irregularity and disorder. Tycho Brahe had already refuted Aristotle in his studies on his nova and his comet, and Fabricus had done it in his studies of a variable star, but Galileo's findings attacked the Sun itself. (Other astronomers discovered the sunspots at almost the same time as Galileo and there was wrangling over priority, which made Galileo additional enemies. Galileo, however, whether he had priority in the discovery or not, did more than merely see the spots. He used them to show that the Sun rotated about its axis in twenty-seven days, by following individual spots around the Sun. He even determined the orientation of the Sun's axis in that fashion.)

The stars, even the brighter ones, remained mere dots of light in the telescope, while the planets showed as little globes. Galileo deduced from this that the stars must be much farther away than the planets and that the universe might be indefinitely large.

Galileo also found that there were many stars in existence that could be seen by telescope but not by naked eye. The Milky Way itself owed its luminosity to the fact that it was composed of myriads of such stars.

More dramatically, he found that Jupiter was attended by four subsidiary bodies, visible only by telescope, that circled it regularly. Within a few weeks of observation he was able to work out the periods of each. Kepler gave these latter bodies the name of satellites and they are still known as the Galilean satellites. They are known singly by the mythological names of Io, Europa, Ganymede, and Callisto. Jupiter with its satellites was a model of a Copernican system—small bodies circling a large one. It was definite proof that not all astronomical bodies circled the Earth.

Galileo observed that Venus showed phases entirely like those of the Moon, from full to crescent, which it must do if the Copernican theory was correct. According to the Ptolemaic theory, Venus would have to be a perpetual crescent. The discovery of the phases of Venus definitely demonstrated, by the way, the fact that planets shine by reflected sunlight. Galileo discovered that the dark side of the Moon had a dim glow that could only arise from light shining upon it from the Earth ("Earthshine"). This showed that Earth, like the planets, gleamed in the Sun, and removed one more point of difference between the Earth and the heavenly bodies.

All these telescopic discoveries meant the final establishment of Copernicanism more than half a century after Copernicus had published his book.

Galileo announced his discoveries in special numbers of a periodical he called *Sidereus Nuncius* ("Starry Messenger"), and these aroused both great enthusiasm and profound anger. He built a number of telescopes and sent them all over Europe, including one to Kepler, so that others might confirm his findings. Galileo visited Rome in 1611, where he was greeted with honor and delight, though not everyone was happy. The thought of imperfect heavens, of invisible objects shining there, and worst of all of the Copernican system enthroned and the Earth demoted from its position as center of the universe was most unsettling. Galileo's conservative opponents persuaded Pope Pius V to declare Copernicanism a heresy, and Galileo was forced into silence in 1616.

Intrigue continued. Now Galileo's friends, now his enemies, seemed to have gained predominance. In 1632 Galileo was somehow persuaded that the Pope then reigning (Urban VIII) was friendly and would let him speak out. He therefore published his masterpiece, *Dialogue on the Two Chief World Systems,* in which he had two people, one representing the view of Ptolemy and the other the view of Copernicus, present their arguments before an intelligent layman. (Amazingly enough, despite his long friendship with Kepler, Galileo did not mention Kepler's modification of Copernicus' theory, a modification that improved it beyond measure.)

Galileo of course gave the Copernican the brilliant best of the battle. The Pope was persuaded that Simplicio, the character who upheld the views of Ptolemy in the book, was a deliberate and insulting caricature of himself. Galileo was brought before the Inquisition on charges of heresy (his indiscreet public statements made it easy to substantiate the charge) and was forced to renounce any views that were at variance with the Ptolemaic system. Romance might have required a heroic refusal to capitulate, but Galileo was nearly seventy and he had the example of Bruno to urge him to caution.

Legend has it that when he rose from his knees, having completed his renunciation, he muttered, *"Eppur si muove!"* ("And yet it moves"—referring to the Earth). This was indeed the verdict given by the world of scholarship, and the silencing af Galileo for the remaining few years of his old age (during which—in 1637—he made his last astronomical discovery, that of the slow swaying or "libration" of the Moon as it revolves) was an empty victory for the conservatives. When he died they won an even shallower victory by refusing him burial in consecrated ground.

The Scientific Revolution begun with Copernicus had been opposed for nearly a century at the time of Galileo's trial, but by then the fight was lost. The Revolution not only existed, but also had prevailed, although, to be sure, there remained pockets of resistance. Harvard, in the year of its founding (1636), remained firmly committed to the Ptolemaic theory.

My bad habit of exceeding all planned bounds, either because I have too much to say, or because I want to "begin

*at the beginning" makes itself felt in one way or another
in almost all my books. In one of my smaller books on
physics,* The Neutrino—

But let me begin at the beginning. (You see?)

*My first book editor was, as I mentioned earlier, Walter
I. Bradbury of Doubleday. After I had done a baker's
dozen of science-fiction books with him, he left Doubleday
and took a position with Henry Holt. This was profoundly
disturbing to me, for all my editors quickly become father
figures to me (even when, as is increasingly true lately,
they are younger than I am).*

*After all, editors let me make long-distance collect calls
to them whenever my attic becomes lonely; they treat me
to lunches at the slightest excuse, or none at all; and, most
of all, they are indefatigable in reassuring me that everyone
of the publishing house, from the president to the elevator
operator, loves me. (I can't help it. Writing is a lonely
occupation.)*

*Naturally, losing a father figure rattles one, and the in-
terval that passes before one gets an appropriate fixation
on the next editor is cold and dismal. What's more, the
longer and closer an editor has been with you, the greater
the trauma of separation when it comes. At my two major
publishing houses, particularly (Houghton Mifflin and
Doubleday) the various editors with whom I am involved
now have strict instructions never to resign, whatever purely
material advantages may be held out to them elsewhere.
(They will assure me in the most soothing way that they
never will and, to give them credit, they say it with the
most serious expressions you can imagine.)*

*But Brad did leave and I was lost for a while until it
occurred to me that perhaps I might write a book for him
at his new place. I eventually visited him at Holt and we
talked about a book, and then, a few days later, I got a
letter from him telling me that for reasons entirely uncon-
nected with my visit, he had resigned his position.*

*Eventually, he was at Harper's, and eventually, I tried
again. One effort came to naught under circumstances I will
describe later. A second time, though, we again discussed
a book and this time we actually got as far as signing
a contract—and then Brad left Harper's and returned to
Doubleday!*

Quite aware that I would be terrified of being left with

strangers, he arranged to carry the contract with him and, when the book was finally completed, it was Doubleday that published it. It turned out to be The Neutrino.

This was the first time Brad was involved with a manuscript of mine that was nonfiction, and he wasn't used to my meandering. When I said that I was going to write a book about the neutrino, I suppose he thought I would start more or less: "Once upon a time there was a neutrino."

I didn't. I had to pave the way in my own fashion. I began by laying a solid foundation and discussing the development of the conservation laws in physics. At precisely the midpoint of the book, I began a section which bore the subheading, "Enter the Neutrino," *and Brad penciled lightly in the margin,* "At last!"

I have my reasons for meandering, of course. One of my problems, for instance, is that I have a fixation on counting. No matter what the subject may be on which I am writing, if I reach a place where it is possible to compare numbers (especially large numbers), I detour. I made a point of this in the introduction to Only a Trillion, *which I'll come back to later but which I'll now content myself with describing as the very first collection of my science articles to be published:*

from ONLY A TRILLION (*1957*)

One of the stories my mother likes to tell about me as a child is that once, when I was nearly five, she found me standing rapt in thought at the curbing in front of the house in which we lived. She said, "What are you doing, Isaac?" and I answered, "Counting the cars as they pass."

I have no personal memory of this incident but it must have happened, for I have been counting things ever since. At the age of nearly five I couldn't have known many numbers and, even allowing for the relatively few cars roaming the streets thirty years ago, I must have quickly reached my limit. Perhaps it was the sense of frustration I then experienced that has made me seek ever since for countable things that would demand higher and higher numbers.

With time I grew old enough to calculate the number of snowflakes it would take to bury Greater New York under ten feet of snow and the number of raindrops it would take to fill the Pacific Ocean. There is even a chance that I was subconsciously driven to make chemistry my lifework out of a sense of gratitude to that science for having made it possible for me to penetrate beyond such things and take—at last—to counting atoms.

There is a fascination in large numbers which catches at most people, I think, even those who are easily made dizzy.

For instance, take the number one million; a 1 followed by six zeros; 1,000,000; or, as expressed by physical scientists, 10^6, which means $10 \times 10 \times 10 \times 10 \times 10 \times 10$.

Now consider what "one million" means.

How much time must pass in order that a million seconds may elapse?—Answer: just over 11½ days.

What about a million minutes?—Answer: just under 2 years.

How long a distance is a million inches?—Answer: just under 16 miles.

Assuming that every time you take a step your body moves forward about a foot and a half, how far have you gone when you take a million steps?—Answer: 284 miles.

In other words:

The secretary who goes off for a week to the mountains has less than a million seconds to enjoy herself.

The professor who takes a year's Sabbatical leave to write a book has just about half a million minutes to do it in.

Manhattan Island from end to end is less than a million inches long.

And, finally, you can walk from New York to Boston in less than a million steps.

Even so, you may not be impressed. After all, a jet plane can cover a million inches in less than a minute. At the height of World War II, the United States was spending a million dollars every six minutes.

So—let's consider a trillion. A trillion is a million million; a 1 followed by 12 zeros: 1,000,000,000,000; 10^{12}.

A trillion seconds is equal to 31,700 years.

A trillion inches is equal to 15,800,000 miles.

In other words, a trillion seconds ago, Stone Age man lived in caves, and mastodons roamed Europe and North America.

Or, a trillion-inch journey will carry you 600 times

around the Earth, and leave more than enough distance to carry you to the Moon and back.

And yet . . . even a trillion can become a laughably small figure in the proper circumstances.

After considerable computation one day recently I said to my long-suffering wife: "Do you know how rare astatine-215 is? If you inspected all of North and South America to a depth of ten miles, atom by atom, do you know how many atoms of astatine-215 you would find?"

My wife said, "No. How many?"

To which I replied, "Practically none. Only a trillion."

This fetish of mine was one thing that slowed up The Neutrino. *At the point where I got a chance to talk about solar energy, I went into it in far greater detail than I had to because I could not resist playing with numbers—*

from THE NEUTRINO (1966)

Consider the Sun. The most obvious characteristic of that body is the quantity of light and heat it delivers despite the fact that it is 93,000,000 miles from us. It lights and warms all the Earth and has done so constantly through all of history.

The energy in the form of light and heat pouring down from the noonday Sun upon a single square centimeter of the Earth's surface in a single minute is 1.97 calories. This quantity, 1.97 cal/cm^2/min, is called the *solar constant*.

A cross section of the Earth in a plane perpendicular to the radiation reaching it from the Sun is about 1,280,000,-000,000,000,000 or 1.28×10^{18} square centimeters in area. Therefore the total radiation striking the Earth each minute is about 2,510,000,000,000,000,000 or 2.51×10^{18} calories.

Even this by no means expresses all the radiation of the Sun. The Sun radiates energy in all directions and only very little of it strikes the tiny Earth.

Imagine a huge, hollow sphere with the Sun enclosed at its center, with every part of the sphere 93,000,000 miles from the Sun. The Sun would light and heat every part of that sphere just as it does the Earth, and the area of this huge sphere would be over two billion times the cross-sectional area of the Earth. That means that the Sun radiates more than two billion times as much energy as the Earth manages to intercept.

The total energy radiated by the Sun is 5,600,000,000,-000,000,000,000,000,000 or 5.6×10^{27} cal/min. What's more the Sun has been radiating 5.6×10^{27} cal/min through all of recorded history and for an indefinitely long period before that, with only slight variations.

Here, then, is the crucial question: Where is all that energy coming from? If the law of conservation of energy applies to the Sun as well as to the Earth, then the incredibly vast supply of energy being poured into space by the Sun cannot be created out of nothing. Energy can only be changed from one form to another, and therefore the Sun's radiation must be at the expense of another form of energy. But what other form?

A person pondering the problem might think first of chemical energy, as the form of the disappearing energy. A coal fire, for example, delivers light and heat as the Sun does, when the carbon of the coal and the oxygen of the air combine to form carbon dioxide.

Can it be, then, that the Sun is nothing more than a vast coal fire and that its radiant energy is obtained at the expense of chemical energy?

This possibility can be eliminated without trouble. Chemists know quite well exactly how much energy is given off by the burning of a given quantity of coal. Suppose the Sun's enormous mass (which is 333,500 times that of the Earth) were nothing but coal and oxygen and that the two were combining at such a rate as to produce 5.6×10^{27} cal/min. The Sun would then, indeed, be a coal fire lighting and heating the solar system as it is observed to do. But how long could such a coal fire continue to burn at such a rate before nothing is left but carbon dioxide? The answer is easily determined and works out to be a trifle over 1500 years.

This is a small stretch of time. It covers only a fraction of the civilized history of mankind (to say nothing of the long eons before that). Since the Sun was shining in its present fashion at the time of the height of the Roman Empire then we know without further investigation that it cannot be a coal fire, for it would be extinguished by now.

Indeed, there is no known chemical reaction which would supply the Sun with the necessary energy for even a fraction of mankind's civilized existence.

Some alternatives to chemical energy must be examined, and one of them involves kinetic energy. We on Earth have a good display of the meaning of such energy every time a meteor strikes the upper atmosphere. Its kinetic energy is converted into heat by the effect of air resistance. Even a tiny meteor, the size of a pinhead, is heated to a temperature that causes it to blaze out for miles. A meteorite weighing a gram and moving at an ordinary velocity for meteorites (say, twenty miles per second) would have a kinetic energy of more than 5,000,000,000,000 or 5×10^{12} ergs—or about 120,000 calories.

A similar meteorite striking the Sun rather than the Earth would be whipped by the Sun's far stronger gravitational force to a far greater velocity. It would therefore deliver considerably more energy to the Sun. It is estimated, in fact, that a gram of matter falling into the Sun from a great distance would supply the Sun with some 44,000,000 calories of radiation. To take care of all the Sun's radiation, therefore, about 120,000,000,000,000,000,000 or 1.2×10^{20} grams of meteoric matter would have to strike the Sun every minute. This is equivalent to over a hundred trillion tons of matter.

This works well on paper but astronomers would view such a situation with the deepest suspicion. In the first place, there is no evidence that the solar system is rich enough in meteoric material to supply the Sun with a hundred trillion tons of matter every minute over long eons of history.

Besides, this would affect the mass of the Sun. If meteoric material were collecting on the Sun at this rate then its mass would be increasing at the rate of about one percent in 30,000 years. This may not seem much, but it would seriously affect the Sun's gravitational pull, which depends upon its mass. If the Sun were increasing its mass even at this apparently slow rate, the Earth would be moving steadily closer to the Sun and our year would be growing steadily shorter. Each year would, in fact, be two seconds shorter than the one before, and astronomers would detect that fact at once, if it were indeed a fact. Since no such variation in the length of the year is observed, the possibility of meteorites serving as the source of the Sun's radiation must be abandoned.

Helmholtz, one of the architects of the law of conservation of energy, came up with a more reasonable alternative in 1853. Why consider meteorites falling into the Sun, when the Sun's own material might be falling? The Sun's surface is fully 432,000 miles from the Sun's center. Suppose that surface were slowly falling. The kinetic energy of that fall could be converted into radiation. Naturally, if a small piece of the Sun's surface fell a short way toward the Sun's center, very little energy would be made available. However, if all the Sun's vast surface fell, that is, if the Sun were contracting, a great deal of energy might be made available.

Helmholtz showed that if the Sun were contracting at a rate of 0.014 centimeters per minute, that would account for its radiation. This was a very exciting suggestion, for it involved no change in the Sun's mass and therefore no change in its gravitational effects. Furthermore, the change in its diameter as a result of its contraction would be small. In all the six thousand years of man's civilized history, the Sun's diameter would have contracted by only 560 miles which, in a total diameter of 864,000 miles, can certainly be considered insignificant. The shrinkage in diameter over the two hundred fifty years from the invention of the telescope to Helmholtz's time would be only twenty-three miles, a quantity that would pass unnoticed by astronomers.

The problem of the Sun's radiation seemed solved, and yet a flaw—a most serious one—remained. It was not only during man's civilized history that the Sun had been radiating, but for extended stretches of time before mankind had appeared upon the Earth.

How long those extended stretches had been no one really knew in Helmholtz's time. Helmholtz, however, felt this could be reasoned out. If the material of the Sun had fallen inward from a great distance, say from the distance of the Earth's orbit, enough energy could have been supplied to allow the Sun to radiate at its present rate for 18,000,000 years. This would mean that the Earth could not be more than 18,000,000 years old, however, for it could scarcely be in existence in anything like its present form when the matter of the Sun extended out to the regions through which the Earth is now passing.

It might have seemed that a lifetime of 18,000,000 years for the Earth was enough for even the most demanding theorist, but it was not. Geologists, who studied slow changes in the Earth's crust, estimated by what seemed irrefutable arguments that to achieve the present situation, the Earth must have been in existence not for merely tens of millions of years, but for hundreds of millions of years, possibly for billions of years; and that through all that time, the Sun must have been shining in much its present fashion.

Then, too, in 1859, the theory of evolution by natural selection had been advanced by the English naturalist Charles Robert Darwin. If evolution was to have proceeded as biologists were then beginning to think it must have, then, again, the Earth had to be in existence for hundreds of millions of years at least, with the Sun shining throughout that time much as it is today.

During the second half of the nineteenth century, therefore, the law of conservation of energy was shored up, with respect to the Sun, in a most controversial fashion. A plausible theory had been proposed which astronomers were willing to accept, but which geologists and biologists objected to vigorously.

Apparently there were three alternatives:

1) The law of conservation of energy did not hold everywhere in the universe and, in particular, did not hold on the Sun—in which case "all bets were off."

2) The law of conservation did hold on the Sun, and the geologists and biologists were somehow wrong in their interpretation of the evidence they had mustered, so that the Earth was only a brief few million years old.

3) The law of conservation did hold on the Sun, but there was some source of energy as yet unknown to science which, when discovered, would allow for the Sun's radiating in its present fashion for billions of years, thus reconciling physical theory with the views of geologists and biologists.

In the end, it was alternative 3 which won out.

The Neutrino *was by no means the first book I had devoted to subatomics. The very first book I had written on physics was, in fact,* Inside the Atom, *where, for the first time, I wrote up a serious description, for youngsters, of the development of the atomic bomb.*

I have always been ambivalent about the atomic bomb. Of all the recent discoveries of science, the atomic bomb was the first that was clearly "science fictional."

For one thing, work on it had been held utterly secret, so that it burst upon the world as a horrid surprise. For another, science-fiction writers had been dealing with such bombs in their stories all through the early 1940's. It is my understanding that the FBI, at one time, tried to stop the stories, but they were, very properly, informed that to stop atomic-bomb stories would give away the whole deal to 50,000 science-fiction fans at once. For a wonder, the FBI saw the point, and the stories were allowed to continue.

So, with no one but science-fiction writers saying anything, it ended up seeming science-fictional indeed.

My own personal science-fiction output, however, never included any reference to atomic bombs. This was not because I was unaware of the possibility, but precisely because I was aware and detested the possibility. I preferred instead to foresee the peaceful uses of atomic power. Thus, I had a passage in a story called "Superneutron" (a very poor story for which I have never permitted anthologization) in which atomic power plants were described, in essence, with reasonable accuracy. The passage was written in late 1940, nearly fourteen years before such plants were actually established.

I claim no great foresight for making the prediction; everyone in science fiction was doing the same. Anyway, in the story a group of men are talking and here are two paragraphs of that conversation:

from "Superneutron" (*1941*)

"Good," agreed Hayes, "but we'll pass on to another point for a moment. Do any of you remember the first atomic power plants of a hundred and seventy years ago and how they operated?"

"I believe," muttered Levin, "that they used the classic uranium fission method for power. They bombarded uranium with slow neutrons and split it up into masurium, barium, gamma rays and more neutrons, thus establishing a cyclic process."

Exactly right!

Except that three years before the story was written, the element I call "masurium" was formed by atomic bombardment. The earlier "discovery" of that element had proved erroneous and the new formation was the first real isolation of the element. The element was therefore given the new and permanent name of "technetium."

I had been able to foresee fourteen years into the future with crystal clarity, but, alas, I had not been able to look three years into the past.

Well, the atomic bomb came, and it finally made science fiction "respectable." For the first time, science-fiction writers appeared to the world in general to be something more than a bunch of nuts; we were suddenly Cassandras whom the world ought to have believed.

But I tell you, I would far rather have lived and died a nut in the eyes of all the world than to have been salvaged into respectability at the price of nuclear war hanging like a sword of Damocles over the world forever.

PART 5
CHEMISTRY

ALTHOUGH I have written on every branch of science and at every level, chemistry is the field in which I have received formal training. At least I majored in chemistry in college and then took a whole mess of additional chemistry courses in graduate school. As a result the three degrees I obtained from Columbia (B.S. 1939; M.A. 1941; and Ph.D. 1948) were all in chemistry.

But then, when Boston University School of Medicine offered me a faculty position in 1949, it was in the department of biochemistry.

You may ask: So what?

So a lot. There's a difference. Biochemistry is the study of the chemical processes that go on within living tissue and it has strong physiological and medical components. (That's why it is taught in a medical school.) It is a highly specialized branch of chemistry and it is one that is growing with enormous celerity. No one who has received his education only in "straight" chemistry is entirely fit to teach biochemistry.

As it happened, I had had no courses in biochemistry at all and was therefore not entirely fit to teach biochemistry. But I wasn't going to toss away what (at that time) seemed like a good position. I reasoned that in a medical school no one faculty member teaches the entire course; we were each assigned specific lectures. I felt that I might be lucky and be assigned lectures that were among the more heavily "straight" and the less heavily "bio."—And if not, I could teach myself biochemistry when no one was looking and stay a lecture ahead of the students. Besides, I was still under the impression, in 1949, that I preferred research to teaching and it was in research (I thought) that I would make my mark.

So I kept a cheerful smile on my face, did my best to

exude self-confidence and accepted the position.

I managed. Fortunately my science-fiction writing had inured me to self-education, and I got away with it. In fact, so sure of myself did I grow that I had not been at the job much more than a year when I let myself be talked into co-authoring a medical school text on biochemisty.

I told the story of the birth of the textbook and some of what it meant to write (and in collaboration, yet) in an article of mine called "The Sound of Panting" in which I discussed the difficulties of keeping up with the subject in general. Here is the way the article begins:

from "The Sound of Panting" (*1955*)

Back in September of 1950, Dr. William C. Boyd, Professor of Immunochemistry at Boston University School of Medicine—where I work—having just come back from several months in Egypt, and feeling full of spirit, lured me to one side and suggested that we write a textbook on biochemistry for medical students. This struck me as a terrific idea. Dr. Boyd had already written textbooks on blood-grouping, on immunology, and on anthropology, so there was no doubt in my mind that he could supply the experience. As for myself, although a science-fiction writer, I am not too proud to write textbooks, so I felt I could supply enthusiasm. We then rung in Dr. Burnham S. Walker, who is the head of our Department of Biochemistry and who has an encyclopedic knowledge of the subject. He went along not only with the notion but also with alacrity.

There followed a hectic interval in which we laid our plans, corralled a publisher, and had a lot of fun. But there came a time when all the preliminaries were over and we came face to face with a typewriter and a clean sheet of paper.

It took us a year and a half before the first edition was done and I learned a lot about textbooks.

A textbook, after all, is an orderly presentation of what is known in a given branch of science and is intended to be used for the instruction of students. Note the word "orderly." It implies that a textbook must begin at the beginning, proceed through the various stages of the middle, and end at the end. Unfortunately, unless the science concerned is a deductive one such as mathematics or logic, this neat procedure is hampered by the fact that there is no beginning, no middle, and no end.

An inductive science such as biochemistry consists, essentially, of a vast conglomeration of data out of which a number of thinkers have abstracted certain tentative conclusions. It resembles a three-dimensional lacework all knotted together. To expound any portion of biochemistry properly, a certain knowledge of other areas of the science must be assumed. It is, therefore, the task of the writer to decide what one-dimensional order of presentation is least confusing. What subjects can he discuss in the earlier chapters with the best chance of being understood despite the absence of information contained in the later chapters? How often must an author stop to explain at a given point and how often can he get away with a simple reference to a page halfway up the book, or even with a curt "See Appendix"? (I, by the way, was a devotee of the "stop and explain" philosophy and I was consequently periodically crushed by the democratic procedure of being outvoted two to one.)

. . . Three collaborators have three different styles. True! Fortunately, by dint of revising each other's work and then beating out the results in triple conference, a reasonably uniform style was achieved with elimination of extremes. Dr. Walker, for instance, whose natural style is extremely condensed, was forced to include occasional conjunctions and to allow the existence of a few subordinate clauses. I, on the other hand, found that my more passionate outbursts of lyricism were ruthlessly pruned. Many was the gallant rearguard fight by one or another of us in favor of inserting a comma or of deleting it; many the anguished search through the Unabridged in defense of a maligned word.

Though I treat the situation lightly in the above passage, I did not really enjoy collaboration. I was outvoted far too many times and the final product, though quite a decent and respectable textbook, never really felt, to me, as though it were mine.

To be sure, my two collaborators, Drs. Walker and Boyd, were and are wonderful human beings with whom it was a pleasure to be associated, but I am simply not made for collaboration, that's all, where that collaboration extends to my writing.

I was trapped, far more reluctantly, into writing a second text (for student nurses this time) in collaboration, though there the machinery of collaboration was looser. That was it, though. I never did it again and I don't think I ever will. Besides the two texts, four books in my Hundred are collaborations if we go by the title page, but in those four the collaboration was for reasons that did not involve the actual writing. I did all the actual writing.

As it happened, Biochemistry and Human Metabolism was rather a flop. Oh, the publisher (Williams & Wilkins) didn't lose money on it, but it didn't make much either. And our royalties, considering the time we spent on it were, while not actually beneath contempt, not very far above it.

The reasons for that are by no means mysterious, either, for shortly after our text appeared, two other texts were published, each of which was longer, more detailed, more thorough and (oh, well) better than ours. So, after the third edition, when Dr. Walker left the Medical School for greener pastures and Dr. Boyd was too busy with other projects, we just let the book lapse. The publishers were very polite and hid their relief masterfully, but made no perceptible effort to induce us to reconsider.

Still, the first edition of the text has a certain personal importance to me since it was the first nonfiction book I ever wrote. In fact, it was the first professional nonfiction of any kind that I ever published. Considering that I am now far more a non-fiction writer than a fiction writer, that makes it a milestone for me.

The first chapter of the text was not mine in any of the editions. It was written almost entirely by Dr. Boyd. The second chapter, on the other hand, was virtually entirely mine, in all three editions. Consequently, here is the first page of Chapter 2—the first bit of my nonfiction writing, which now stretches itself over seventy-three of my Hundred Books:

from BIOCHEMISTRY AND HUMAN METABOLISM (*1952*)

In a very real sense, life may be looked upon as a struggle on the part of the body to maintain the internal structure of the enormously complex protein molecules of which it is composed. The difficult nature of such a task may be judged from the fact that a distinctive property of most protein molecules is their extreme instability as compared with other chemical structures. Environmental factors as mild as the warmth of a human hand or the gentle bubbling of air would suffice, in many cases, to so alter the properties of a protein solution as to render it biologically useless.

That life should be built on such fragile, almost evanescent, molecules is not at all surprising. It would seem, upon reflection, to be inevitable. Life implies change—quick adjustments to altered conditions. There must be something then in a living organism which can vary with the absorption of a few quanta of light, with trifling changes in air pressure, oxygen concentration, temperature, or any of the other hundreds of variables that beset us every moment of time. That something is the protein molecule.

It might be tempting for beginning students to equate complexity of structure with mere size of molecules. Thus, the beta-lactoglobulin of milk has an empirical formula which is thought to be $C_{1864}H_{3012}N_{468}S_{21}O_{576}$. Here we have a molecule in which we can count almost six thousand individual atoms of five different kinds. The molecular weight is over forty thousand, which means that the molecule is some twenty-three hundred times as heavy as a water molecule and more than two hundred times as heavy as a molecule of the amino acid, tryptophane. And yet beta-lactoglobulin is a protein of comparatively simple structure. Certainly, its molecular weight is well below the average for proteins. Molecular weights in the hundreds of thousands are common and those in the millions are not unknown. There are protein molecules, in other words, which compare with beta-lactoglobulin as that protein compares with tryptophane.

Yet, knowing size, we know comparatively little. There are other types of molecules produced by living organisms which compare with proteins in molecular weight. There is cellulose, for instance, impressive in size, and yet used for nothing more in the living plant than to enclose the cell in a sturdy box. It is a huge molecule, yet so stable that we build houses out of it. Size alone is therefore no guarantee that a molecule will possess the flexibility and instability needed to have within it the potentiality of life.

Through the year and a half that our collaboration on the first edition of the text continued, I grew steadily more chafed and more anxious to try my hand at a book on biochemistry in which I would not be interfered with.

While the book was being written and I was chafing, I attended a lecture by George Wald on the biochemistry of vision, a lecture given at an American Chemical Society meeting at M.I.T.

Wald is the best lecturer on chemistry that I have ever heard, and this particular talk I heard in 1951 was the best and most entertaining one I ever listened to until I heard another talk on the biochemistry of vision given in Washington, D.C., on December 28, 1966, during the American Association for the Advancement of Science meetings. This 1966 lecture was also given by Wald. (And he won a share of the 1967 Nobel Prize in Physiology and Medicine for his work in this field.)

Wald speaks without notes and with no perceptible hesitation. Without seeming to simplify, he arranges matters so that even those who do not have specialized knowledge of the field can follow. What's more, he makes it seem interesting. And the acid test is this: even if, for some reason, you don't follow the line of argument, it still sounds interesting.

I came out of the lecture in 1951 with an absolutely unbearable desire to write biochemistry for the general public; something that would read as well as Wald's talks sounded. With great enthusiasm I turned out some sample chapters of biochemistry that would serve as a kind of text for the general public.

I tried the result on Doubleday, to whom up to that time I had sold four books. Brad read the manuscript and handed it back with one of the gentlest verbal rejection slips I have ever received. "Isaac," he said, very mildly, "stick to fiction."

I didn't give in without a struggle. I tried several other publishers. One and all agreed with Brad. Chagrined, I retired the manuscript sample (fortunately, I had never got around to writing the complete book) and returned to fiction.

I might have continued doing so to this day but for a rather unlooked-for accident. My erstwhile collaborator, William C. Boyd, had written an excellent book on genetics (his specialty) for the general public. Mr. Henry Schuman, who at that time owned a small publishing firm in New York, had come to visit Bill, hoping he could get him to write a simplified version of the book for teen-agers.

Bill, however, was drowned in work and could not undertake the task. Since he is a gentle soul who hated to have Mr. Schuman come 200 miles to see him and then have to leave empty-handed, he introduced him to me, as someone who was longing to write on scientific subjects for the general public.

I had almost forgotten that, but Bill's reminder had my eyes glistening at once and poor Mr. Schuman found himself avalanched in instant response.

It was all different this time. In my previous attempt, I had been trying to rewrite the text in more general terms, but now I threw all that away. I started from scratch and wrote a book for teen-agers without any thought of the textbook at all, and that worked. Here, for instance, is how I handled the same subject matter I had discussed in the quoted section of the textbook:

from THE CHEMICALS OF LIFE (1954)

What makes proteins so unusual? Well, for one thing, the protein molecule is very large. To show what we mean by that, let's consider the weight of different kinds of atoms and molecules.

Naturally, all atoms are exceedingly light. It takes billions upon billions of them to make up the weight of even the tiniest particle of dust. It is one of the miracles of science that man has been able to weigh atoms despite their minuteness.

Now it turns out that the hydrogen atom is the lightest one that can exist and it is customary to call its weight 1 for convenience. Or, to put it just a little more scientifically, 1 is called the ATOMIC WEIGHT of hydrogen. The carbon atom is 12 times as heavy as the hydrogen atom and carbon's atomic weight is therefore 12. In the same way, we can say that the atomic weight of nitrogen is 14, of oxygen is 16, and of sulfur is 32.

In order to find out how much a molecule weighs, it is only necessary to add up the atomic weights of the various atoms it contains. For instance, the hydrogen molecule consists of two hydrogen atoms, each with an atomic weight of 1. The MOLECULAR WEIGHT of hydrogen is therefore 2. Similarly, the nitrogen molecule is made up of two nitrogen atoms which weigh 14 each. The oxygen molecule is made up of two oxygen atoms which weigh 16 each. The molecular weight of nitrogen is therefore 28 and that of oxygen is 32.

The same rule holds where the atoms in a molecule are of different types. The water molecule, with one oxygen and two hydrogen atoms, has a molecular weight of $16 + 1 + 1$, or 18.

As we said in the previous section, the water molecule is a rather small one. A molecule of table sugar, by contrast, has 12 carbon atoms, 22 hydrogen atoms, and 11 oxygen atoms. The 12 carbons weigh 144 all together, the 22 hydrogens weigh 22, and the 11 oxygens weigh 176. Add them all together and the molecular weight of sugar turns out to be 342. This is a more sizable figure than that for water, but it is by no means tops. A molecule of a typical fat contains as many as 170 atoms and has a molecular weight of nearly 900.

Now we are ready to consider the protein molecule. How does it compare with fat and sugar in this respect? Of course, there are innumerable different kinds of protein molecules, but we can pick a protein that occurs in milk and has been studied quite a bit. *In its molecule are no less than 5,941 atoms.* Of these, 1,864 are carbon, 3,012 are hydrogen, 576 are oxygen, 468 are nitrogen, and 21 are sulfur. The molecular weight, as you can see for yourself, is quite large. It comes to 42,020. The molecule of this protein is thus 45 times as large as a molecule of fat and 120 times as large as a molecule of sugar.

But is this protein a fair example? Actually, it is not, because it is a rather *small* protein. The average protein has a molecular weight of 60,000. Many go much higher. Some of the proteins in clam-blood, for instance, have a molecular weight of 4,000,000. And some of the viruses consist of protein molecules with molecular weights in the tens of millions and even the hundreds of millions.

Now size in itself can be very useful. The body can do things with a protein molecule that it could not do with smaller molecules. It is as though you were given the choice of having a birthday party in the large ballroom of an expensive hotel or in a little one-room tenement flat. Obviously the ballroom would have many more possibilities (provided money were no object).

But is size alone enough? One could imagine a large ballroom with no furniture and no ventilation. It might then be preferable to give the birthday party in the small flat after all.

Actually, there are molecules that are just as large as proteins but that are nevertheless much more limited in their usefulness than proteins. For instance, the chief compound of ordinary wood is CELLULOSE. Its molecule is very large but its only use to the plant is as stiffening substance in the "walls" around the living plant cells. Again, the starchlike substance called GLYCOGEN, that occurs in animal livers, has a large molecule and yet is used only as a body fuel. Proteins, on the other hand, have millions and billions of different functions in the body.

Why is this so? Well, the key to the mystery can be found if cellulose or glycogen are treated with certain acids. These acids cause the cellulose or glycogen molecule to break up into smaller pieces. The smaller pieces turn out to be the same in both cases. They are molecules of GLUCOSE, a kind of sugar which is found in blood and which is somewhat simpler than ordinary table sugar.

The cellulose molecule, in other words, seems to resemble a necklace made up of thousands of individual glucose molecules strung together like so many beads. The glycogen molecule is made up of these same glucose molecules strung together in a somewhat different pattern.

Apparently, the fact that cellulose and glycogen are made up of only one type of smaller molecule limits their versatility. This also holds true for other such giant molecules (*with the exception of proteins*) which almost always consist of only one (or sometimes two) sub-units. It is as though you were given the job of making up a language but were only allowed to use a single letter. You could have words like *aa* and *aaaa*, and *aaaaaaaaaaaaaa*. In fact you could have any number of words, depending on how many *a*'s you wished to string together, but it wouldn't be a satisfactory language. Things would be a little better if you were allowed to use two letters; still better if allowed to use three; and very much better if allowed to use twenty.

The last is exactly the case in proteins. When proteins are exposed to acid, their molecules also break apart into a number of smaller molecules. These smaller molecules are known as AMINO ACIDS, and they are *not all the same*. There are about twenty different amino acids, varying in size from a molecular weight of 90 to one of about 250. They can be strung together to form proteins in every which way. And each time they are strung together in a slightly different way, they make a slightly different protein.

How many different combinations are there possible in a protein molecule? Well, an average protein molecule would contain about 500 amino acids, altogether, but we can start with a much smaller number. Suppose we start with only two different amino acids and call them *a* and *b*. They can be arranged in two different ways: *ab* and *ba*. If we had three different amino acids, *a*, *b*, and *c*, we could make six combinations: *abc, acb, bac, bca, cab*, and *cba*. With four different amino acids, we could make 24 different combinations. They are easy to figure out and the reader may wish to amuse himself by listing them.

However, the number of possible arrangements shoots up very sharply as the number of amino acids is increased. By the time you get to ten different amino acids, there are more than 3,500,000 possibilities and with twenty amino acids, almost 2,500,000,000,000,000,000 arrangements. (This seems unbelievable, but it is so. If the reader is doubtful, let him try listing the different arrangements for only 6 amino acids. He will probably give up long before he has run out of arrangements.)

In the case of our average protein with 50 amino acids, even though the 500 are not all different, the number of possible arrangements is so large that it can only be expressed by a 1 followed by 600 zeroes. This is a far, far greater number than the number of all the atoms in the universe. You may understand why this should be if you will imagine taking the 26 letters of the alphabet and counting the number of words you can make out of them. Not only the real words now, but words with any number of letters up to 500, and especially including all the unpronounceable ones.

Remember that each one of these amino-acid arrangements is a slightly different protein. It is no wonder, then, that the body can design different proteins to accomplish different tasks without any danger of ever running out of new varieties. No wonder, too, that out of a type of molecule such as this, life can be built.

Notice that the publisher of The Chemicals of Life *(and of several other books I have quoted from) is Abelard-Schuman. Even while I was writing* The Chemicals of Life, *Henry Schuman merged his publishing firm with Abelard, a publishing firm owned by Mr. Lou Schwartz, and it was with Mr. Schwartz and the editors who worked for him that I dealt with when the book came to be published.— And for the publication of a dozen books after that, too, including the popularization of Dr. Boyd's book on genetics.*

It was Henry Schuman, though (who has since died), who started me in the business of popular nonfiction.

One can't help overlapping if one insists on writing many books. For instance, I discussed uranium fission in Inside the Atom, *in* Understanding Physics, *Volume 3, in* The Neutrino, *and in* The Intelligent Man's Guide to Science.

Sometimes, in cases of such multiple repetition, I even use one book as a guide to what I am saying in another book (I do try to use shortcuts, when that turns out to be possible).

The repetition is never total, of course. Each book appeals to a different audience or has the item inserted in a different setting. Thus, Understanding Physics *is narrower and more detailed than* The Intelligent Man's Guide to Science, *so in the former book I can deal with uranium fission in a more leisurely and thorough manner.* The Neutrino *is still more detailed but is aimed somewhat off-center as far as uranium fission is concerned and is at a somewhat less specialized level. And another book of mine on that subject,* Inside the Atom, *is intended for teen-agers and is the simplest of the four.*

In each case, I handle the matter differently and this makes the repetition less dull for me than it might otherwise be. But "less dull" is not actually "non-dull" and at the present time if I were asked to write another book in which I had to make a big deal about the discovery and development of the ideas of uranium fission, I would heave a big sigh and try to refuse.

Naturally, then, I try, on occasion, to pick a subject far removed from anything I have previously handled. Not only does this allow me to avoid the feeling of déjà vu, which does come when I go around the same merry-go-round the half-dozenth time, but I can indulge in my continuing penchant for self-education.

After all, it's ridiculous to suppose that I know enough concerning every subject I write books about, to write a book about it. On occasion, I agree to write a book on a subject I know little about. Then I have to learn about it before I can write the book.

This can be very nerve-racking. I can be skimming along happily, learning and teaching simultaneously, so to speak, with the learning process staying one chapter ahead of the teaching—when I suddenly come up against a phase of the subject I have trouble understanding. You get that momentary feeling that a whole book is going to swirl down the drain.

I've never actually had to wash out a book entirely, because of midway failure to learn, but there are places where I have to skate delicately over very thin ice. In Volumes 1 and 3 of Understanding Physics, *for instance, I felt on reasonably firm ground throughout, but in Volume 2 there are a couple of places where I'm not entirely sure I really knew what I was talking about.*

But the risks I take are small compared to the pleasure of diving into new areas—

Thus in the early days of 1965, Mr. Arthur Rosenthal of Basic Books *asked me about the importance of the noble gas compounds which had recently been discovered, and which had created quite a sensation. I gave some vague answer, for I had only followed the matter superficially, when an idea struck me full-blown. I said, "Hey, Arthur, do you want me to write a book about it?"*

That, it turned out, had been the idea in his mind all along. It was why he asked me the question in the first place. So I wrote a book about it.

Naturally, as is my wont, I started at the beginning and didn't get to the noble gas compounds till the last chapter, but so what! It was delightful to be breaking new ground and, fortunately, that new ground was solid all the way. Since I had a thorough chemical background, there was no trouble in going through the necessary self-educative project.

And, of course, the greatest fun in such a book are the sidelines you might explore. I concentrated on the noble gases (helium, neon, argon, krypton, xenon, and radon) but the compounds some of them form are usually with fluorine. I stopped, therefore, to give a quick review of the history of chemical knowledge of fluorine, which has its dramatic moments—

from THE NOBLE GASES (*1966*)

This history begins with the miners of early modern times. In 1529, the German mineralogist George Agricola (1490–1555) described the uses of a certain mineral in ore smelting. The mineral itself melted easily, for a mineral, and, when added to the ore being smelted in a furnace, caused it to melt more easily, thus bringing about a valuable saving of fuel and time.

Agricola called the mineral *fluores* from the Latin word meaning "to flow," because it liquefied and flowed so easily. In later years, it came to be called *fluorspar*, since *spar* is an old German word for a mineral; a still newer name is *fluorite*, since "ite" is now the conventional suffix used to denote a mineral.

In 1670, a German glass cutter, Heinrich Schwanhard, found that when he treated fluorspar with strong acid, a vapor was produced that etched his spectacles. This was most unusual, for glass is generally unaffected by chemicals, even by strong ones. Schwanhard took advantage of this property to develop a new art form. He covered portions of glassware with protective varnish and exposed it to the vapor, ending with clear figures on a cloudy background. Naturally, Schwanhard did not know the chemical details of what was happening, but the process of etching was dramatic enough, and the artwork he produced was unusual enough to attract continuing interest.

The Swedish chemist Karl Wilhelm Scheele (1741–1786) was the first to study the vapor of acidified fluorspar in some detail, in 1771. He was able to show, for instance, that the vapor was an acid, and he called it "fluoric acid." As a result, Scheele is commonly given credit for having discovered the substance.

It was probably a tragic discovery, for Scheele had a bad habit of sniffing and tasting any new substances he discovered. "Fluoric acid" was one of several of his discoveries that most definitely should not be treated in this manner. He died at the early age of forty-four, after some years of invalidism; in all probability, his habit of sniffing and sipping unknown chemicals drastically shortened his life. If so, "fluoric acid" (and other chemicals) had its first famous chemical victim. Scheele was by no means the last.

Once Scheele had established that the vapor produced from acidified fluorspar was an acid, a misconception at once arose as to its structure. The great French chemist Antoine Laurent Lavoisier had decided at just that time that all acids contained oxygen, and it was difficult to break away from that view in the face of so famous a proponent.

In 1810, however, the English chemist Humphry Davy (1778–1829) was able to show that "muriatic acid," a well-known strong acid, contained no oxygen. He decided that a green gas that could be obtained from muriatic acid was an element; he named it *chlorine* from a Greek word for "green." "Muriatic acid" then was a compound, Davy demonstrated, of hydrogen and chlorine—but no oxygen— and could be called *hydrogen chloride* in its gaseous state, or *hydrochloric acid*, when dissolved in water.

By 1813, Davy was convinced that Scheele's "fluoric acid" was another example of an acid without oxygen. The French physicist André Marie Ampère suggested that the molecule consisted of hydrogen plus an unknown element. Since "fluoric acid" had certain similarities to the newly renamed hydrochloric acid, it seemed very likely to both Davy and Ampère that the unknown element was very like chlorine. Indeed, they decided to call it *fluorine;* the first syllable coming from "fluorspar," while the suffix was chosen to emphasize the similarity of the new element to chlorine. "Fluoric acid" became *hydrogen fluoride* in its gaseous form, hydrofluoric acid in solution.

What chemists wanted to do, once the existence of fluorine came to be so strongly suspected, was to settle all doubts by isolating the element.

Hydrogen chloride (HCl) could, after all, be treated with oxygen-containing chemicals in such a way that the hydrogen atom was snatched away and attached to oxygen to form water. The chlorine atoms, left behind, combined to form chlorine molecules (Cl_2).

Could not hydrogen fluoride (HF) be similarly treated, so that molecular fluorine (F_2) would be formed? Unfortunately, it could not. As we now know, oxygen is more electronegative than chlorine and can snatch hydrogen's electron (along with the rest of the hydrogen atom) from chlorine. Oxygen is, however, less electronegative than fluorine and is helpless to remove hydrogen from the hydrogen fluoride molecule.

Indeed, as no chemical reactions sufficed to liberate fluorine gas from its compounds, it became clear to nineteenth-century chemists that fluorine atoms held on to the atoms of other elements with record strength. Once free, those same fluorine atoms would recombine with other atoms with immense vigor. It came to be suspected, therefore, that fluorine was the most active of all elements and the most difficult to liberate. That, of course, made the task of liberation all the more of a challenge.

Davy himself had shown that it was not necessary to use chemical reactions in order to liberate a particular element from its compounds. An electric current, passing through a molten compound, can, under proper circumstances, separate the elements composing the compound. He demonstrated this in the case of the alkali metals and alkaline earth metals. The atoms of these elements are the most active in giving up electrons, and they therefore form compounds readily and are released from those compounds only with great difficulty. Prior to Davy's time, these elements had not been isolated, but in 1807 and 1808, using an electric current, Davy isolated and named six metals: sodium, potassium, magnesium, calcium, strontium, and barium.

It seemed natural that fluorine-containing compounds could be split up and free fluorine gas liberated by some electrical method; beginning with Davy, chemist after chemist tried. The attempts were dangerous in the extreme, for hydrogen fluoride is a very poisonous gas and free fluorine, once liberated, is more poisonous still. Davy was badly poisoned by breathing small quantities of hydrogen fluoride and this may have contributed to his later invalidism and his death at the age of only fifty-one.

Other prominent chemists of the time were also poisoned, and their lives made miserable and undoubtedly shortened by the same source. One notable Belgian chemist, Paulin Louyet, was actually killed, as was the French chemist Jérôme Nicklès. And yet the danger of the work seemed but to add to the challenge and excitement of the problem.

The usual starting substance in the attempt to obtain fluorine was fluorspar, which by the nineteenth century was understood to be *calcium fluoride* (CaF_2). To pass an electric current through fluorspar, one had to melt it first and then maintain it at a comparatively high temperature throughout the experiment. Fluorine was more active than ever at such high temperatures.

It was probably formed by the current, but as soon as it was, it promptly attacked everything in sight. It corroded the electrodes through which the electric current entered the fluorspar, even when they were composed of such comparatively inert materials as carbon, silver—even platinum.

A French chemist, Edmond Frémy (1814–1894), a student of the martyred Louyet, repeated the work with fluorspar in 1855, with the usual unsatisfactory results. It occurred to him that it might be preferable to pass an electric current through hydrogen fluoride. Hydrogen fluoride was a liquid at room temperature, and at this lower temperature, fluorine might be easier to handle. Unfortunately, until Frémy's time, hydrogen fluoride was available only in water solution. If there was any water about, fluorine reacted with it at once, tearing the hydrogen atoms out of the water molecule with such force that oxygen was liberated in the energetic form of ozone. One ended with hydrogen fluoride again.

Frémy therefore worked out methods for producing *anhydrous hydrogen fluoride,* that is, hydrogen fluoride that was pure and water-free, by acidifying potassium hydrogen fluoride (KHF_2). Unfortunately, he found himself stymied. Anhydrous hydrogen fluoride would not pass an electric current.

In the end, he, too, gave up. As the 1880's dawned, fluorine was still victor. It had defeated the best efforts of many first-class chemists for three-quarters of a century. (But Frémy, at least, took sufficient care of himself in the course of his experiments to live to be eighty—no mean feat for a fluorine chemist.)

Frémy had a student, Ferdinand Frédéric Henri Moissan, who took up the battle. He tried everything. He formed phosphorus trifluoride and tried to combine it with oxygen. Oxygen and phosphorus held together particularly tightly, and in this case, Moissan felt, the oxygen might be able to compete successfully with fluorine. Not entirely. The battle ended in a draw and Moissan ended with a compound in which phosphorus was combined with both oxygen and fluorine.

He then tried to pass phosphorus trifluoride over red-hot platinum. Platinum combines with fluorine only weakly and it also combines with phosphorus; perhaps it would combine only with the phosphorus and liberate the fluorine. No such luck. Both phosphorus and fluorine combined with the platinum.

Moissan decided to try electrical methods again. He began with arsenic fluoride and abandoned that after beginning to detect in himself signs of arsenic poisoning. He then turned to hydrogen fluoride, and eventually underwent four different episodes of poisoning with that gas, which undoubtedly helped cause his death at the age of fifty-four.

Moissan made use of Frémy's anhydrous hydrogen fluoride, but decided to add something to it to make it possible for it to carry an electric current. He had to add something that would not make it possible for some element other than fluorine to be liberated at the positive electrode. (If any element other than fluorine could be liberated, it would be—fluorine was last in line.) Moissan added potassium hydrogen fluoride to the hydrogen fluoride. The liquid was simply a mixture of fluorides and now it would carry a current.

Furthermore, Moissan made use of equipment built up out of an alloy of platinum and iridium, an alloy that was even more resistant to fluorine than platinum itself. Finally, he brought his entire apparatus to a temperature of $-50°$ C., where even fluorine's activity ought to be subdued.

And yet the experiment failed. Moissan considered and noted that the stoppers that held the electrodes had been corroded. Something was needed for the stopper that would not conduct a current, so that platinum-iridium alloy was eliminated. What else? It occurred to him that fluorspar itself did not carry a current, and could not be attacked by fluorine, either (it already held all the fluorine it could). Moissan carefully carved stoppers out of fluorspar and repeated the experiment.

On June 26, 1886, he obtained a pale yellow-green gas about the positive electrode. Fluorine had finally been isolated, and when Moissan later repeated the experiment in public, his old teacher, Frémy, watched.

Moissan went on, in 1899, to discover a less expensive way of producing fluorine. He made use of copper vessels. Fluorine attacked copper violently, but after the copper was overlaid with copper fluoride, no further attacks need be expected. In 1906, the year before his death, Moissan received the Nobel Prize in chemistry for his feat.

Despite all this, fluorine remained a most ticklish problem for another generation. It could be isolated and used, but not easily and not often. Most of all, it had to be handled with extreme care—and few chemists cared to play with it.

It isn't often one can joke about science. To do so well, one has to know quite thoroughly what it is one is joking about, and in my case, chemistry is the only subject I know so well, I can play games with it.

Back in 1947, when I was working for my Ph.D. I was making use of catechol in my research. This is a white organic compound which is supplied in tiny feathery crystals. Catechol dissolves very rapidly and the tiny crystals disappear the instant they hit the top of the water. Watching that happen one day, I thought: What if they disappeared just a fraction of a millimeter above the top of the water?

Since the forthcoming write-up of my Ph.D. dissertation was much in my mind, it was the work of a moment to begin a solemn dissertation containing all the stigmata of academic turgidity about a substance which dissolved in water 1.12 seconds *before* you added the water.

Once it was done, I showed it to John Campbell of Astounding Science Fiction. He laughed and offered to publish it. I cautiously asked him to let me use a pseudonym, as the article might come out before I had my Ph.D. safely tucked away in my inner jacket pocket and the faculty members who met to decide on my fitness might take it amiss if I showed irreverence for the holy name of chemical research.

John promised, but forgot, and the article appeared in the March, 1948, issue of Astounding, not long before my doctor's orals were due, and with my very own personal name blazoned all over it. The article had a mock-solemn title, "The Endochronic Properties of Resublimated Thiotimoline," a palsied style, and a list of fake references to nonexistent journals.

It was an utter success, and I understand the New York Public Library was pestered for days by eager youngsters trying to find the nonexistent journals so they could read more on the subject.

This did not assuage my agony at all, for I thought I was through. I was sure that I would be tossed out of the oral examination by the united thrust of eight indignant academicians. Fortunately, the Columbia chemistry department was far less stuffy than I imagined and they saw nothing wrong with a little irreverence. Not only did they treat me with kindness in the course of the orals, but when it was drawing to a close and I was half dead with suspense and tension (as doctoral candidates invariably are— doctor's orals being one of the more sadistic rituals of academic life), Professor Ralph S. Halford asked solemnly, "Asimov, can you tell us something about the endochronic properties of resublimated thiotimoline?"

That broke me up entirely. I was completely unable to say another word, for laughing and gasping, and they led me out in the hall to recover, while they spent twenty minutes swapping dirty jokes and pretending they were discuss-

*ing my case. (I've been at the other end of doctor's orals
since that day in May of 1948, so I know.)*

—Oh, I made it, by the way.

*There are a number of chemists, to this day, I think, who
know nothing about my writings except for thiotimoline.
I wrote three articles altogether on this mysterious subject.
In the third I abandoned scientific-paper jargon and presented the subject as a pretended speech to a nonexistent
scientific society. It appeared in the early years of the space
age and that is reflected even in the title: "Thiotimoline and
the Space Age." I'm presenting it here in full:*

"Thiotimoline and the Space Age" (1960)

*(Transcript of a speech delivered at the 12th annual meet-
ing of the American Chronochemical Society.)*

Gentlemen:

I have been called the founder of chronochemistry and
in response I cannot resist a certain sense of pride. To have
originated a new science is a privilege given to very few.

I can still remember, quite clearly, that day in 1947 when
I first dropped a pinch of thiotimoline into water and
thought I noticed something odd. To be sure, it dissolved
rapidly; but I was used to that. It always seemed to vanish
the instant it touched the water.

But I had never handled a sample of thiotimoline quite
as pure as the pinch I had obtained that July day and, as I
watched the white powder drop toward the water, I distinctly remember myself thinking: Why, that dissolved *before* it hit the water.

Well, it's an old story to you, I know, though I still like
to linger on the thrill of the slow awakening of certainty;
of the measurements taken; of the first crude timings by
eye; of the more delicate work of the original endochronometer—the same instrument now at the Smithsonian.

The announcement of endochronicity, of the fact that a
substance existed which dissolved in water 1.12 seconds
before the water was added created a stir. You all remember it, I'm sure. And yet, somehow, the impression arose
that thiotimoline was a hoax. There was a distinct air of

amusement in many of the comments in the learned journals. Private communications reaching me showed a distressing tendency to describe experiments which obviously lacked all scientific validity and which, I could but conclude, were meant as some sort of joke. Perhaps the final proof of the damage this has done is that after twelve years of existence, the American Chronochemical Society can muster an audience of exactly fifteen people to hear this talk.

It has been an expensive joke, gentlemen, one that has cost us our lead in the race for space. For while American researchers have, but with difficulty, obtained grants to continue their investigations of thiotimoline and have been starved into small-scale experiments, while withering under the genial air of disbelief on the part of their colleagues, the Soviet Union has established the town Khruschevsk in the Urals, whose popular nickname of "Tiotimolingrad" will well describe the nature of the activities that go on behind the walls of the modern and well-equipped scientific laboratories that have been established there.

That the Soviet Union has taken thiotimoline seriously and has done something about it is as sure as can be, and yet we remain sunk in complacency. No important political figure has viewed the matter with alarm. If they have said anything at all for publication, it is simply, "What's thiotimoline?" I intend now to explain to these nearsighted politicos just what thiotimoline means to our space effort.

Thiotimoline research graduated from what we might now call the "classic" stage, to the "modern" with the development of the "telechronic battery" by Anne McLaren and Donald Michie of the University of Edinburgh. If you have read about it anywhere, you can only be clairvoyant, for the popular press and much of the learned press maintained a stubborn silence. In fact, the original paper appeared only in the small though highly respected *Journal of Irreproducible Results,* edited by that able gentleman Alexander Kohn. Let me describe the telechronic battery.

A simple endochronometer—with which we are all acquainted—is a device which will automatically deliver water into a small tube containing thiotimoline. The thiotimoline will dissolve 1.12 seconds before the water is delivered.

Imagine the endochronometer so connected with a second similar unit that the solution of the thiotimoline in the first activates the water-delivering pipette of the second. The thiotimoline of the second unit will dissolve 1.12 seconds before that water is delivered, and therefore 2.24 seconds before the water is delivered to the first unit.

An indefinite number of endochronometers can thus be hooked up, the thiotimoline of each of the series dissolving 1.12 seconds before the preceding member. A battery consisting of about 77,000 such units would yield a final sample of thiotimoline which dissolved a full day before the initial quantity of water was delivered.

Such batteries have now been developed both at Edinburgh and in my own laboratories in Boston in extremely compact models, through use of printed circuits and advanced miniaturization. A device of not more than a cubic foot in volume can afford a twenty-four hour endochronic interval. There is strong, if indirect, evidence that the Soviet Union possesses even more sophisticated devices and is turning them out in commercial quantities.

The obvious practical application of the telechronic battery is that of water prediction. In other words, if the first element of a battery is exposed to the air in such a way that rain, if any, will fall upon it, the final element will dissolve the day before and thus offer a foolproof method of predicting rain—or lack of rain—one day ahead.

I trust you will all see, gentlemen, that the telechronic battery can be used for generalized predictions as well.

Suppose, to take a frivolous example, you were interested in a particular horse race. Suppose you intended to place a wager that a particular horse would win that race. Twenty-four hours in advance of the race, you could make up your mind quite firmly that if the horse were to win the next day, you would, immediately upon receiving the news, add water to the first element of a telechronic battery. If it did not win, you would not.

Having made that decision, you need then but observe the last element. If the thiotimoline in the last element dissolves—followed by a chain of solutions all along the battery at 1.12 second intervals, with which you need not be concerned—you will know that the horse will win beyond doubt. You might even, if you were in a flamboyant mood, allow the solution of the final element to activate a flashing light, a fire gong, a charge of explosive; anything that will unmistakably attract your attention.

You laugh, gentlemen, and yet can this system not be applied, without change, to the launching of a satellite?

Suppose that four hours after launching, an automatic device on board the satellite telemeters a signal to the launching base. Suppose, next, that this radio signal is designed to activate the first element of a telechronic battery.

Do you see the consequences? The sending of the signal four hours after launching can only mean that the satellite is safely in orbit. If it were not, it would have plunged to destruction before the four hours had elapsed. If then, the final element of the telechronic battery dissolves today, we can be certain that there will be a successful launching tomorrow and all may proceed.

If the final element does not dissolve, the launching will not be successful and there must, therefore, be something wrong with the satellite assembly. A team of technicians will begin checking the device and at the moment when the defective item is corrected, the telechronic battery will operate. The launching will then be scheduled in the full expectation of success.

Do you still laugh, gentlemen?

Is this not the only feasible explanation for the consistent Soviet successes as compared with our own very spotty record? It is customary, of course, to attribute the appearance of unfailing success of Soviet launchings to the fact that they have been deliberately hiding many failures, but does this stand up? Have they not, with remarkable consistency, managed to score successes at such time as would most profit themselves?

Sputnik I went up within a month of the hundredth birthday of Tsiolkovsky, the Soviet rocket pioneer. Sputnik II went up to celebrate the fortieth anniversary of the Russian Revolution. Lunik II went up just before Khrushchev's visit to the United States. Lunik III went up on the second anniversary of Sputnik I.

Coincidence? Or did they simply have the foreknowledge of their telechronic batteries? Have they tested a number of possible rocket assemblies and selected that one for which success was forecast? How else can one explain that the United States has not yet succeeded in launching any of their many rockets on some significant day.

Nor, remember, do the Soviets invariably hold their announcements back until they are certain they have achieved success, as some have suggested. In at least one case, they announced an achievement in advance.

When Lunik III was on its way to circle the Moon, the Soviet scientists confidently announced it would take pictures of the hidden side of the Moon as it progressed around that body in its orbit. As far as the orbit of Lunik III was concerned, they were safe. From its motion and from the positions of Earth, Moon, and Lunik, the orbit of Lunik III could be calculated with absolute precision.

How could the Soviet scientists, however, be so sure that the intricacies of the camera assemblage would work to perfection? Could it be that the successful completion of the camera task was set to activate a telechronic battery at the launching base? Could its activation have allowed them to make their announcement a day before the pictures were taken with the full knowledge that success and a prestige victory would result?

I say the answer is: Obviously, yes.

And what of future attempts to send a man into space? Suppose the man were to agree to send a signal, manually, after a certain time had elapsed after firing. A telechronic battery would then tell us, while the astronaut was still on the ground and unlaunched that not only would he be in orbit but that he would be alive and at least well enough to send the message.

If the telechronic battery remains inactive, the man will not be sent up. It is as simple as that. Since it is the chance of harm to an astronaut that is the deciding factor holding back the step of "man into space," it seems certain that the Soviet Union will achieve this goal first, thanks to our government's obtuseness with respect to thiotimoline.

Presumably, one can extend the principle to all manner of scientific and nonscientific investigations. Gigantic megabatteries can even be built—in theory—to predict the result of an election to be held the following year—but I have labored the point long enough. Let me, instead, make a few remarks concerning the great dangers as well as the great benefits, which are involved in thiotimoline research.

These begin with the oldest of all paradoxes of thiotimoline—the paradox of fooling. In other words, the chance of having thiotimoline dissolve and then being fooled by a refusal to add the water. The original argument against such a notion, as elucidated in my laboratory, involved the theory of the endochronic atom—which has since been confirmed by half a dozen other investigators. One pair of the bonds of one or more of the carbon atoms in the thiotimoline molecule are forced, through supersteric hindrance, to a point in the temporal plane. One bond extends 1.12 seconds into the past and one extends 1.12 seconds into the future. When the future end of a thiotimoline molecule dissolves and drags the rest of the molecule with it, it is therefore not predicting a possible future event. It is recording an actual future event.

Nevertheless, it has been shown that fooling thiotimoline is possible in theory. Using Heisenberg's principle of uncertainty, it can be demonstrated that one cannot say with certainty that an individual molecule of thiotimoline will dissolve before the water is added and that, in fact, the probability of its not doing so is quite appreciable.

That is undoubtedly true—for an individual molecule. When, however, quintillions of molecules are involved as is the case with even the most microscopic samples of thiotimoline actually used in the individual units of even the most sophisticated telechronic batteries, the chance that all of those quintillions, or even a detectable fraction of them, will fail to dissolve is infinitesimal.

To be sure, in setting up a telechronic battery, in which many thousands of units are involved, the failure of the instrument will depend on the failure to dissolve of any one of those units. The chance of "Heisenberg failure," as it is called, can be calculated and some estimates at least seem to show that a battery will give a false positive one time out of rather more than a million.

In such a case, the final unit in a telechronic battery will dissolve even though water is not added to the first. Somewhat more often, the converse will be true; that the final unit will not dissolve in advance even though water is added to the first. Naturally the former alternative is more interesting from the theoretical viewpoint, the question arising: Then where did the water come from?

An attempt was made in my laboratories to actually record such a false negative involving solution without subsequent addition of water. The possibility of creation of matter out of nothing existed and this would be of great importance in connection with the Gold-Hoyle theory of the steady-state universe.

The principle involved in the attempt was simple. One of my students would set up a battery adjusted for the manual addition of water the next day, intending in all honesty to allow the experiment to take its course. The final unit would, theoretically, dissolve. I would then place the first student at a different task and put a second student in charge of the battery with instructions not to add water.

Our first great surprise was to find that the final unit actually dissolved, under these circumstances, about once in twenty efforts. This was a far greater incidence than could possibly be explained by "Heisenberg failure." But, as it rapidly turned out, the thiotimoline was not "fooled." Something, in every case, brought about the addition of water. In the first case, the original student returned to add the water and did so before he could be stopped. In another case, there was accidental spillage. In another, a janitor—

But it would be tedious to describe the manner in which thiotimoline, so to speak, refused to be fooled. Suffice it that we did not have one true case of "Heisenberg failure."

With time, of course, we began to guard against ordinary accidents and the incidence of "pseudofailure" declined. For instance, we placed the battery in closed, desiccated vessels; but, during pseudofailure, these cracked and broke.

In our final experiment we thought that surely we had a "Heisenberg failure" but in the end, the experiment was not reported in the literature. I tried instead, and without success, to report the implications of it to appropriate officials. Let me describe the experiment to you now.

We placed the battery in a welded steel container after it had registered solution.

And as we waited for the moment when the water should be added but would not, Hurricane Diane struck New

England. That was in August of 1955. The hurricane had been predicted, its course had been followed and we were ready for it. There had been several hurricanes in New England in '54 and '55 and we were hardened to it.

At one point, though, the Weather Bureau announced the danger to be passed, the hurricane was blowing out to sea. We all sighed with relief as we waited for zero minute.

However, if any of you were in New England that day you will remember that the Weather Bureau announced later that it had "lost" the hurricane; that the backlash struck surprisingly; that five inches of rain or more fell in many places within an hour; that rivers rose and extensive flooding began.

I watched that rain; it was a deluge. I watched the small river running across our campus become a torrent and begin to spread up and out across the lawns while the lines of shrubbery seemed to grow out of roiled sheets of water.

I shouted for an ax. One of my students brought one, remarking afterward that I sounded so wild he was almost afraid I had turned homicidal maniac.

I smashed that steel container. I removed the telechronic battery and in the flickering gray light of that storm-lashed day, I filled a beaker of water and waited for zero minute, ready to douse the battery at the proper moment.

As I did so, the rain slackened, the hurricane moved off.

I do not say we caused the hurricane to return and yet— water had to be added to that battery somehow. If the stainless steel container had to be floated away on a rising flood and smashed by wind and water to have that done, it would be done. The original solution of the final unit predicted that; or else it predicted my deliberate subversion of the experiment. I chose the latter.

As a result of all this, I can envisage what I can only call a "peace bomb." Enemy agents working within a particular nation, can assemble telechronic batteries, operate them until a case occurs in which the final unit dissolves. That battery can then be encased in a steel capsule and placed near a stream well above high-water mark. Twenty-four hours later, a disastrous flood is bound to occur, since only so can water reach the container. This will be accompanied by high winds since only so can the container be smashed.

Damage will undoubtedly be as great in its way as would result from an H-Bomb blast and yet the telechronic battery would be a "peace bomb" for its use will not bring on retaliation and war. There would be no reason to suspect anything but an act of God.

Such a bomb requires little in the way of technology or expense. The smallest nation, the smallest of revolutionary or dissident groups could manage it.

Sometimes in my more morbid moments, I wonder if perhaps Noah's flood—the prototype of which actually has been recorded in Mesopotamian sediments—was not brought about by thiotimoline experiments among the ancient Sumerians.

I tell you, gentlemen, if we have one urgent task ahead of us now it is to convince our government to press for international control of all sources of thiotimoline. It is boundlessly useful when used properly; boundlessly harmful when used improperly.

Not a milligram of it must be allowed to reach irresponsible hands.

Gentlemen, I call you to a crusade for the safety of the world!

By the time "Thiotimoline and the Space Age" had been written, Astounding Science Fiction in whose pages so many of my stories had appeared had changed its name to Analog Science Fact-Fiction. But the stubbornness of the human heart is strange. The magazine has been Analog for a decade but it will always be Astounding to me.

Since I have been talking about my Ph.D., I am reminded of the paper I had to write as part of my task in qualifying for the degree. It was elaborate indeed. It eventually made a sixty-seven-page booklet, complete with tedious mathematics and sixty-six equations, seven tables, four graphs, four appendices, a list of references—all the paraphernalia, in short.

It was published in 1948 and copies are buried in Columbia's archives and in my own library and, as far as I know, nowhere else in the world. A shortened version of the dissertation was published in 1950 in the Journal of the American Chemical Society (Volume 70, page 820, if you're curious enough to check) but that's not the same thing at all.

You might notice, by the way, that this was published be-fore my textbook, Biochemistry and Human Metabolism, *and so were a few other strictly scientific papers. I don't count these papers as my earliest nonfiction, however, for they weren't written in my capacity as writer. They were a concomitant of my role as scientist, and nothing more—like dropping beakers.*

Yet my dissertation is the rarest item in my personal library, and I ought to preserve it here. Not the whole thing of course; even I couldn't endure that. Just the sum-mary—for flavor. And note the title, which is even more ridiculous than the one I plastered on the first thiotimoline article, and quite authentic besides:

from "The Kinetics of the Reaction Inactivation of Tyrosinase during its Catalysis of the Aerobic Oxidation of Catechol" (*1948*)

1—The aerobic oxidation of catechol, as catalyzed by the enzyme, tyrosinase, during the first 140 seconds of reaction has been carefully reinvestigated, utilizing buffered enzyme-catechol systems containing limited quantities of ascorbic acid (the chronometric method). It has been found that during that early part of the reaction, the relationship of total quinone formed (Q) to the observed time of chrono-metric endpoint (T), is better expressed by the equation:

$$Q = \frac{a(T - M)}{b + T - M} \qquad \text{MODIFIED CHRONOMETRIC EQUATION}$$

than by a similar relationship previously used, in which the value, M, was ignored. In this expression, a and b are con-stants, characteristic of the particular enzyme-substrate system employed. The value of M, here introduced as a necessary correction factor, has been shown to be constant with time for a given set of experimental conditions. Its value varies from one system to another inversely as the degree of agitation of the reaction mixture is varied, and M has been interpreted, therefore, as a measure of the time of mixing. An algebraic method for determining the values of a, b, and M has been described.

2—It has also been found that during that early part of the reaction (140 seconds) the reaction course is equally well expressed by an equation of the type:

$$Q = a' (1 - e^{(M-T)/b'}) \qquad \text{MODIFIED FIRST-ORDER EQUATION}$$

where a' equals 0.65a and b' equals 0.69b.

3—For reaction times greater than 140 seconds, the reaction course has been followed through the utilization of buffered enzyme-catechol systems containing an excess of ascorbic acid; the extent of reaction being measured by determining the residual ascorbic acid at various reaction times. It has been found by this method that the experimentally observed reaction course approximates (within experimental error) that predicted by the Modified Chronometric Equation for periods up to eight minutes, during which 95% of the enzyme is inactivated. The reaction course predicted by the Modified First-Order Equation departs widely from the experimentally observed course after only a little over 2 minutes of reaction.

4—An analysis of the kinetic implications of the Chronometric Equation has been presented and the results are consistent with the experimental observation that the half-life of the enzyme is independent of the original enzyme concentration. However, the analysis also indicates that the specific inactivation rate of the enzyme is not constant, but decreases with time. Several possible interpretations of these kinetic implications are inspected and arguments are presented against the possibility that this decrease in specific inactivation rate with time is due to the protective effect of compounds formed during the enzyme reaction or to the existence of a "reversible inactivation" phenomenon.

5—A kinetic model is proposed in which tyrosinase is considered as inactivating in stepwise fashion through a series of decreasingly active and increasingly stable intermediates. It is shown that such a model can explain all experimental data reported in this communication, and is not inconsistent with previously known facts concerning the relationship of enzyme stability to types of enzyme activity.

A general equation derived from this kinetic model is presented, and it is suggested that the Modified Chronometric Equation is merely an empirical simplification thereof.

PART 6
BIOLOGY

ONE CRITICISM of The Chemicals of Life *(my first non-fiction book for the general public) was important and jus-tified. I had made a vital omission.*

The book dealt with proteins and with the smaller mole-cules that worked along with them and the implication was clear that these were the substances crucial to life. The title said as much. And not once, anywhere in the book, was there any mention of the nucleic acids.

The trouble was that the true significance of nucleic acids, their central importance to life chemistry, was only becoming clear in the early 1950's, and I wasn't sharp enough to get it in time for the book.

I had a chance to correct the omission six years later when Mac Talley came to me with a title. It was The Well-springs of Life *and he wanted a book that would fit. Since he was always excellent at talking me into books, I agreed and talked about all kinds of wellsprings of life. I began, for instance, by discussing it in the most immediate fashion —where did babies come from?*

from THE WELLSPRINGS OF LIFE *(1960)*

The question of the beginning of life almost forces itself on mankind. What child can be so dead to curiosity as not to wonder, on occasion, where he came from, and how? The innocent question is almost traditional. Parents whose children never asked, "Where do babies come from?" would probably feel uneasy and, I think, rightly so.

Even if a youngster were not dimly aware that he had not always been on the scene and if he were not, therefore, curious (or even apprehensive) concerning his own origin, there would still be the drama of birth all about him. The arrival of a younger brother or sister would be preceded by months of excitement and suspense, the mystery of which he himself would only vaguely share and which would consequently pique and frustrate him. There would be a disquieting and frightening change, both physical and temperamental, in his mother. Finally, there would follow such a revolution in family procedure (usually to his own disadvantage in terms of loss of attention received) that he must brood about it all and, eventually, ask.

And if he remained an only child, there would still be friends who would go through this traumatic experience. A new baby would appear out of nowhere, and the friend would have a possession he himself would not have.

Moreover, this question, "Where do babies come from?" though traditionally asked and rarely unexpected, is also traditionally embarrassing and difficult to answer. Modern mothers may frequently launch into some bowdlerized version of the biological background of birth, but rarely do they do so with poise. And in most cases, even today, the earliest explanations of the process leave the child with the thought that children are found either under cabbage leaves or under a hospital bed, and that they are brought either by a stork or in a doctor's little black bag.

Such explanations would satisfy all but the most formidable youngster, since he would have no reason to suspect that there is anything inherently improbable in the creation of a baby out of nothing. When, later in life (and, perhaps, thanks to the folk wisdom of the gutter, not very much later in life), he learns that the baby originated as a result of the activities of the father and the mother, this activity is what he may find difficult to believe.

But believe it he must, eventually. The life of the baby, he must finally admit, is the product of the life of the parents; human life arises from human life.

If the child is brought up on a farm, he is apt to gain an accurate insight into the process of baby-making much earlier than the city child, since he will undoubtedly have a chance to observe the behavior of livestock on the farm. He will learn soon enough that calves, colts, and chicks are the products of their parents, and he will learn in detail the indispensable (if transient) role of the bull, the stallion, and the rooster in the process.

Then again, the crop that is laboriously grown and triumphantly harvested springs not from the sterile earth, but from the seeds produced by the crops of yesteryear. Life comes only from life in the case of every animal man herds and of every plant man cultivates.

All this, which each child must discover for himself, either through observation or explanation, with greater or lesser trauma, had to be discovered by mankind as a whole at some early stage of culture. Probably the discovery proved no easier for mankind than for the individual child.

The question, "Where do babies come from?" was often answered by primitive man with tales equivalent to those of the stork and cabbage leaves. In Greek legends, for instance, there are stories of mares which turn their backs to the fructifying east wind and are made pregnant thereby, bearing foals of extraordinary speed. This may have been merely symbolic to later, more sophisticated Greeks, but it may well reflect an early stage where it was actually believed that the wind could be responsible for babies.

The numerous legends of god-born heroes in Greek myths may also reflect the early period when men were honestly uncertain of what brought about pregnancy—perhaps a god, perhaps a ritual prayer, perhaps sitting under a sacred tree. The fertility rites in primitive agricultural societies may have originated, in part, from the same uncertainty.

And the truth, when finally learned, may well have proved as embarrassing for mankind generally as for each child individually. Some people have seen a reflection of this momentous discovery in the biblical legend of the forbidden fruit which Adam and Eve ate and which brought sin and mortality into the world.

Yet, trauma or not, by the time any society had grown sophisticated enough to develop writing (an invention that marks the boundary between the prehistoric and the historic), they had also grown sophisticated enough to know where babies came from. The supernatural and mystic were put aside, and the baby was accepted as the product of the sexual activity of the mother and father. And this, with appropriate modifications, served to explain where lambs, pups, kittens, goslings, and fruit tree saplings came from.

It would seem that, having discovered this about man and having made the extension to various plants and animals, it would be simple and easy to make a further extension to all plants and animals, to suppose that all young of whatever kind were the product of parents.

And yet that next step (which to us, out of the wisdom of hindsight, seems so natural) was not taken until modern times.

After all, if we try to put ourselves in the place of our ancestors, we will notice that there are animals and plants which survive despite the fact that they are not cared for by man. They survive, in fact, despite all man can do to wipe them out.

It is exasperating. Useful domestic animals must be carefully guarded and watched over if they are to remain alive and healthy, yet creatures such as mice, rats, mosquitoes, and flies flourish and multiply, though unrestricted and merciless war is declared on them. The tender grass is nurtured with love and plant food, while dandelions are poisoned and torn up; but it is the grass that perishes and the dandelions that rise triumphant over adversity.

Where do the vermin and weeds come from?

It is only too easy to fall into the exasperated belief that they spring up from the soil itself; that they are formed of mud and corruption; that their birth, in short, is a kind of conspiracy on the part of inanimate nature to spite man by turning itself into noxious forms of life.

Thus, in *Antony and Cleopatra* (Act II, Scene 7) Shakespeare has the Roman, Lepidus, say, "Your serpent of Egypt is bred now of your mud by the operation of your sun; so is your crocodile."

Lepidus was half-drunk at the time, and even when sober, he was not (as pictured by Shakespeare) a great brain. His drinking companions, Antony and Octavius, who knew better, gravely went along with the gag.

Obviously, Shakespeare himself believed no such thing and introduced the statement as a piece of comedy, but it is quite certain that many in his audience found sufficient humor in the drunken byplay and were quite content, otherwise, to believe that the corrupting mud of the river Nile would indeed bring forth serpents and crocodiles to plague mankind.

The Egyptians themselves (and reasonable foreign ob-
servers, such as Herodotus) knew very well that serpents
and crocodiles laid eggs and that only from those eggs
were new serpents and crocodiles produced.

But then, serpents and crocodiles are sizable creatures
and their eggs are large and easily noticeable. Smaller vermin can be more misleading. Field mice may make their
nests in holes burrowed into stores of wheat, and those
nests may be lined with scraps of scavenged wool. The
farmer, coming across such nests, from which the mother
mouse has had to flee, and finding only naked, blind, and
tiny infant mice, may come to the most natural conclusion
in the world: he has interrupted a process in which mice
were being formed from musty wheat and rotting wool.

Which goes to prove that many a false theory is firmly
grounded on the best evidence of all: "I saw it with my
own eyes!"

Let meat decay and small wormlike maggots will appear
in it. Eventually those maggots become flies. Out of dead
meat come live worms and insects. This is no vague theory.
This is eyewitness evidence, as any man can prove for himself with nothing more than a piece of decaying meat.

The greatest and clearest mind of the ancient world,
that of Aristotle of Stagira, believed this, as indeed he had
to, on the evidence he had. He believed in the ability of
nonliving matter to give rise to certain types of living creatures as a matter of constant and everyday occurrence. This
is called the doctrine of *spontaneous generation.*

This doctrine was accepted and taken for granted by all
learned men throughout ancient times, throughout the Middle Ages, and into early modern times.

The first crack in the doctrine appeared in 1688, when
an Italian physician and poet named Francesco Redi
thought he would supplement the evidence of his eyes by
arranging an experiment. (By and large, the ancient thinkers were content to observe Nature as it existed and un-
folded. They did not try to experiment; that is, to interfere with the natural course of events and thus force Nature to give an answer to some question. This failure to
experiment, more than anything else, set narrow bounds to
the advance of Greek science.)

Redi noticed that decaying meat not only produced flies

but also attracted them. Others before him must have noticed this, too, but Redi was the first to speculate that there
might be a connection between the flies before and the flies
after; at least he was the first to test such a speculation.

He did this by allowing samples of meat to decay in
small vessels. The wide openings of some vessels he left untouched; others he covered with gauze. Flies were attracted
to all the samples but could land only on the unprotected
ones. Those samples of decaying meat on which flies
landed produced maggots. The decaying meat behind the
gauze, upon which the foot of fly had never trod, produced
no maggot at all, although it decayed just as rapidly and
made just as powerful a stench.

Redi's experiments showed plainly that maggots, and
flies after them, arose out of eggs laid in decaying meat by
an earlier generation of flies. It was just as with serpents
and crocodiles, but because the flies' eggs were so small,
they went unobserved and so arose the misapprehension.

*But that was just a beginning. I traced the origin of life
back in time a few billion years and down to the molecular
level as well. That brought in nucleic acids in the last two
chapters.*

*In 1953, you see, Francis Crick and James Watson,
working at Cambridge University in England, had elucidated the structure of DNA (deoxyribonucleic acid) and
showed how it could form replicas of itself over and over
again. That was the biochemical analogue of reproduction.
But it was in 1953 that I had been writing* The Chemicals of
Life *and I had missed it.*

Naturally, I put it into The Wellsprings of Life *which I
wrote in 1959 and published in 1960. But then in 1961—*

*The next question was how the nucleic acid molecule
was connected with protein manufacture. It was the detailed structure of the nucleic acid in the chromosomes
which established the particular chemistry of the cell, but
it was still the proteins that did the actual chemical work.
There had to be some connection.*

*I advanced one theory as to that connection near the
end of* The Wellsprings of Life *but it turned out to be an
utterly wrong one. And in 1961, the year after the book*

was published, the correct theory was worked out. Watson and Crick received the Nobel Prize in 1962 for their breakthrough and Marshall Nirenberg who sparked the second received his in 1968.

So a second time, I was left high and dry with a book that was crucially out-of-date as soon as it was published. You simply have no idea how frustrating that is.

I finally managed to patch up the end of The Wellsprings of Life to include the genetic code (for that is what the nucleic acid/protein interconnection is called) in the fourth printing of the paperback version, which appeared in 1967, but the hard-cover edition still remains untouched.

However, all is not bitter. The Wellsprings of Life brought me my favorite sentence of all the sentences that have appeared in all the reviews of all my books. Professor George G. Simpson of Harvard University reviewed The Wellsprings of Life for Science, and in the course of the review, he said, "Asimov is one of our natural wonders and national resources."

I have read that sentence and ruminated over it maybe a thousand times and have enjoyed it every time. I won't go so far as to say that I agree with it, you understand, but I will defend with my life Professor Simpson's right to say it.

Anyway, back to my subject. In the midst of my chagrin over my outdated books, Mac Talley phoned me in early 1962 to ask if I would write a book on the genetic code, which was now much in the news thanks to Nirenberg's breakthrough. I said, sorrowfully, that I dared not because the field was advancing so rapidly that any book I wrote would be obsolete at once. (I had been bitten twice, and I did not want to make it thrice.)

Six weeks later, Walter Bradbury, who was then at Harper's, wrote to ask me the same question. Well, I can resist once (if I'm lucky) but never twice. When two people ask me, human flesh and blood must fail.

I explained to Brad, however, that Mac had asked me first and that if I did do the book I would have to let Mac get the first crack at it. (I have a very simplistic code of ethics inflicted upon me by a father trained in the precepts of the Talmud, and it complicates my life unbearably.)

I suggested that Mac at New American Library sign me up for the book and do the soft-cover and that Mac then arrange with Brad to have Harper's do the hard-cover first. Brad reluctantly demurred; Harper's would not do a hard-cover by way of a contract with anyone but the author himself.

I saw Harper's point of view but I was very abashed. I was very anxious to do a book for Brad (whom I finally landed three years later with The Neutrino) and yet there was no way I could argue with the fact that Mac had asked me first. So I told Brad that I was in a dilemma from which there was no escape but, alas, not to do the book at all.

Brad asked what the dilemma might be and I explained my problem as to the Right Thing To Do by my father's lofty principles—and Brad laughed and said he gave me permission to do it with Mac, and he would catch me next time around. So all was well.

I am afraid I get into these inter-publisher complications now and then. I make an honest attempt to please them all and try never to give any of them reasonable cause for grievance—but the more publishers I get and the more books I write, the harder it is.

For instance, at this writing, I haven't yet told Doubleday I am doing this book for Houghton Mifflin. It was Houghton Mifflin who suggested doing it, so I can't do it for anyone else; but Doubleday is my oldest publisher and has published more books of mine than any other, and they may well consider that the Hundredth Book ought to have been theirs. And this may occur to them at precisely the time when I ask for formal permission to quote from various Doubleday books in this Houghton Mifflin one.

Well, I shall break the news to them later this month and to keep them happy (I hope) I shall accompany it with a suggestion that may please them and which will restore the balance.

But I digress once again . . .

In the end, The Genetic Code found a hard-cover publisher in Orion Press, and in it I had the pleasure of going into careful detail on the 1961 breakthrough.

Since 1962, more has been learned about the details of the genetic code, but there has been no breakthrough like the ill-timed (for me) Watson-Crick breakthrough of 1953 *or the Nirenberg breakthrough of 1961. The Genetic Code can and should be updated but there is nothing in it that sounds medieval.*

Perhaps I shouldn't complain. One advantage of writing a large number of books on a large variety of sometimes-overlapping subjects is that you can correct yourself as you go along and pretty painlessly, too. When readers write to me asking me for more up-to-date information than is contained in one of my books, I can sometimes simply refer them to another of my books.

Thus I took up the question of the origin of life in The Wellsprings of Life *as I understood it in 1960. In* The New Intelligent Man's Guide to Science, *I stretched it to incorporate what scientists had learned by 1965. Then in* Photosynthesis, *which I recently wrote for Basic Books, I could follow it through 1968.*

from PHOTOSYNTHESIS (*1968*)

The first to suggest seriously that life might have had its start in an atmosphere other than the present one was the English biochemist John B. S. Haldane. In the 1920's he pointed out that if life was responsible for the oxygen in the atmosphere, it ought to have started when there was no oxygen in it and when carbon dioxide was present instead . . .

In 1936 a Russian biochemist, Alexander Ivanovich Oparin, published a book called *The Origin of Life*. In it he reasoned that Earth's original atmosphere contained methane and ammonia and suggested that it was in this that life had made its beginning.

In either case, the molecules that served as raw material were small ones. Yet the end result, if life were to be produced, must be enormous molecules of such substances as protein and nucleic acid.

Put in its simplest form, then, the creation of life involved the formation of large molecules out of small ones, and this requires an input of energy.

There are at least four important sources of energy on the primordial Earth: 1) the internal heat of the Earth, 2) the electrical energy of thunderstorms, 3) the radioactive breakdown of certain isotopes in the Earth's crust, and 4) the ultraviolet radiation from the Sun. All four sources were probably present in greater quantity in the distant past than today.

The first who actually tried to imitate primordial conditions in a laboratory experiment was Melvin Calvin. He chose as his raw materials carbon dioxide and water vapor. As his energy source Calvin decided to use the fast-flying particles emitted by radioactive isotopes.

Calvin exposed his mixture of water and carbon dioxide to radiation from radioactive isotopes and, after a while, tested the mixture to see if anything new had formed. He found that some simple organic molecules had appeared, molecules somewhat larger and more complex than the original ones. He found, for instance, molecules of formaldehyde ($HCHO$) and of formic acid ($HCOOH$).

This was a promising beginning. Simple molecules could be made more complicated by energy input of a type available on the primordial Earth . . .

In 1953, Stanley Lloyd Miller placed a mixture of ammonia, methane, and hydrogen in a large glass vessel. In another, he boiled water. The steam that formed passed up a tube connecting the two vessels and into the gas mixture. The gas mixture was pushed by the steam through another tube back into the boiling water. The second tube passed through a surrounding bath of cold water so that the steam condensed into liquid before dripping back into the boiling water. The gas mixture bubbled through the boiling water and around the course again, driven always by freshly formed steam.

Naturally, Miller made very certain that everything he used was completely sterile; that there were no living cells in the system to form complicated compounds. If complicated compounds formed, it would have to be in the utter absence of life.

It would have been reasonable to use ultraviolet light as the energy source, but ultraviolet light is easily absorbed by glass and this raised the problem of getting enough energy through the glass and into the gas mixture. Miller therefore decided to try the use of an electric spark that would serve as an imitation of the kind of energy made available by lightning. Through the gas in one portion of the system, he set up a continuing electric spark.

Things began to happen at once. The water and gases were colorless to begin with, but by the end of one day the water had turned pink. As the days continued to pass, the color grew darker till it was a deep red.

After a week Miller was ready to subject his mixture to analysis. Like Calvin, he found simple organic molecules in his mixture. One of these was the formic acid which Calvin had detected. Other compounds, related to formic acid, but still more complicated, were also present. These included acetic acid (CH_3COOH), glycolic acid ($HOCH_2COOH$), and lactic acid ($CH_3SHOHCOOH$), all of which were substances that are intimately associated with life.

The presence of ammonia in the starting mixture meant that nitrogen atoms were also available for the buildup of more complex molecules, and Miller found nitrogen-containing compounds too in his final mixture. There were present hydrogen cyanide (HCN), for instance, and urea (NH_2CONH_2).

Most important of all, though, Miller discovered among his products two different amino acids. (Amino acids are the relatively small building blocks out of which the giant protein molecules are built up.) There are nineteen different amino acids that commonly appear, in varying numbers, in protein molecules and the two detected happened to be the two simplest: glycine and alanine.

Miller's experiment was significant in several ways. In the first place, these compounds had formed quickly and in surprisingly large quantity. One-sixth of the methane with which he had started had gone into the formation of more complex organic compounds, yet the experiment had only been in operation for a week.

How must it have been, then, on the primordial Earth, with its vast warm ammoniated ocean stirred by winds of methane, all baking under the Sun's ultraviolet radiation for many millions of years? Uncounted tons of complex compounds would surely have been formed and the oceans must have become a kind of "warm soup" of them.

Then, too, the kind of organic molecules formed in Miller's experiments were just those present in living tissue. The path taken by the simple molecules, as they grew more complex, seemed pointed directly toward life. This point-

ing-toward-life continued consistently in later, more elaborate experiments. At no time were molecules formed in
significant quantity that seemed to point in an unfamiliar,
nonlife direction.

Thus, Philip Hauge Abelson, working at the Carnegie
Institution of Washington, followed Miller's work by trying a variety of similar experiments with starting materials
made up of different gases in different combinations. It
turned out that as long as he began with molecules that
included atoms of carbon, hydrogen, oxygen, and nitrogen,
amino acids of the kind found normally in proteins were
formed.

Nor were electric discharges the only source of energy
that would work. In 1959, two German scientists, W. Groth
and H. von Weyssenhoff, designed an experiment in which
ultraviolet light could be used after all, and they got amino
acids also.

It is important to progress farther and go beyond the
very simplest products. One way of doing so would be to
start with larger samples of raw materials and subject them
to energy for longer periods. This would produce increasing numbers of more and more complicated products; but
the mixtures of these products would become increasingly
complex and would be increasingly difficult to analyze.

Instead, chemists began with later stages. The products
formed in earlier experiments would be used as new raw
materials. Thus, one of Miller's products was hydrogen
cyanide. At the University of Houston, the Spanish-born
biochemist J. Oro added hydrogen cyanide to the starting
mixture in 1961. He obtained a richer mixture of amino
acids and even a few compounds consisting of individual
amino acids hooked together in short chains in just the
same way in which they are hooked together within the
protein molecules.

He also formed purines, compounds containing a dou-
ble-ring system of carbon and nitrogen atoms, and which
are found within the various nucleic acid molecules. A particular purine called "adenine" was obtained, one that is
found not only in nucleic acids but in other important compounds associated with life.

In 1962, Oro used formaldehyde as one of his raw materials and produced two five-carbon sugars, ribose and

deoxyribose, both of which are essential components of nucleic acids.

In 1963, the Ceylon-born biochemist Cyril Ponnamperuma, at Ames Research Center in California, working with Ruth Mariner and Carl Sagan, began with adenine and ribose as his raw materials and exposed them to ultraviolet light. They linked up to form "adenosine" in the same fashion in which they are hooked together in nucleic acid molecules.

If phosphates were also included with the starting mixture, they too were added on to the adenosine to form "adenylic acid," one of the "nucleotides" that form the building blocks of nucleic acids. Indeed, by 1965, Ponnamperuma was able to announce that he had formed a double nucleotide, a structure in which two nucleotides are combined in exactly the same manner in which they are combined in nucleic acid molecules.

In short, the raw materials of Atmosphere I, exposed to almost any reasonable energy source (particularly to ultraviolet light) built up rapidly into more and more complicated molecules aimed directly at proteins and nucleic acids.

Experimenters in the laboratory have not yet formed natural proteins and nucleic acids in the complete absence of life, but the direction is unmistakable. Eventually, molecules sufficiently complicated to show the properties of life would be formed on the primordial Earth.

Thus, nucleic acids would surely develop finally, possessing molecules sufficiently complex to be capable of bringing about the production of other molecules exactly like themselves out of the raw materials all about. Such nucleic acid molecules maintain and multiply themselves, and this is the minimum one could expect of a living thing. They would represent the first and simplest manifestation that we could call life.

When can all this have happened? Calvin has isolated complex hydrocarbons (molecules made up of carbon and hydrogen atoms only) imprisoned in rocks that are up to three billion years old. These are probably the remnants of very simple living things, living when the rock was first formed.

Considering that the Earth's crust may not be much

over three and a half billion years old, this means that the "chemical evolution" which preceded the actual formation of life may have run its course in as little as half a billion years. This is not too surprising, when we think that small-scale chemical experiments have produced so much in experiments that lasted merely days and weeks.

In fact, "blind" chemical processes are not so blind. Given certain raw materials and a supply of energy, the changes that take place are just those that are most probable in the light of known chemical and physical laws, and these changes prove to be inevitably in the direction of life. Life is therefore the result of high-probability changes that are next to impossible to avoid if the conditions are right. By this view, life is no "miracle" at all.

The most ambitious books I ever wrote on biological subjects were a pair of interconnected ones: The Human Body *and* The Human Brain. *These were the first of my books to be handled by the adult division of Houghton Mifflin, as opposed to the juvenile division. The editor was David Harris, who is also editor of this book.*

In the case of The Human Body, *I broke one of my own rules—and I must say it was one of my silliest rules. For some reason, I usually don't let experts (that is, people who happen to know more concerning a particular subject than I do) see my manuscripts. If my publishers wish to check them with such experts, I never object; I am even secretly relieved. But I rarely take that precaution on my own.*

This is not because I can't use such refereeing, because I most certainly can. I have made enormous howlers in my time and a few have even survived into print.

For instance, in The Realm of Numbers, *I casually spoke of an equilateral right triangle (all three sides equal in length) instead of an isosceles right triangle (two sides equal in length). There is no such thing as an equilateral right triangle and I know that very well. The mistake was carelessness rather than ignorance, and somehow that makes it more reprehensible. And what is most reprehensible is that I never caught it in revision, in galley proof, in page proof, or even in the final book. It had to be pointed out to me by numerous young readers.*

The most embarrassing letter of all came from a thirteen-

year-old who had an argument with his teacher over the matter and who said, "If Isaac Asimov says it's so, then it's so," and sent me a letter demanding I write to his teacher. It stands out in my memory as a really rotten moment when I sat down to write him that when Isaac Asimov says it's so, he sometimes makes an egregious ass of himself.

Perhaps the reason I don't have my manuscripts checked is that I have some dim notion that I am playing some sort of game. I am trying to be accurate and my readers are trying to catch me out in errors, and if I have myself checked, that's cheating. Such an attitude would be quite irrational, of course, but there you are.

Yet in the case of The Human Body, I didn't dare try to play that game. After all, I was a member of the faculty of a medical school which was crawling with the usual number of anatomists. If I made a dumb mistake in anatomy, I would have them buzzing about my ears like animated stilettos.

So I handed the manuscript to Dr. Elizabeth Moyer, a Junoesque anatomist whose special talent it is to say exactly what is on her mind to dean and freshman alike. She pointed out quite a few mistakes, which I hastily corrected, and she was very blunt indeed over the fact that I had placed the spleen on the wrong side of the body. The whole school knew about it within forty-eight hours and even now, five years later, when time hangs heavy on her hands, she looks me up and tells me again.

But one thing she said particularly astonished me. She said, "I was almost afraid to read your chapter on reproduction. I thought you'd be impossible. But actually I found it the best chapter in the book."

Imagine! I admit that in my socializing I tend to notice the existence of the ladies. As a friend of mine once said, I take advantage of the known eccentricity of writers in general and allow ribald nuances to creep into my conversation.

But that's only in life. In my writing, things are entirely different. Nowhere in my books, fiction or nonfiction, is there a sentence designed (to use a delightful Victorian phrase) to bring the blush of shame to the cheek of innocence.

Therefore I will resist the impulse to include that chap-

ter on reproduction here, because my readers are as pure as I am. Or, if they are just a shade less pure, they can buy the book.

The Human Body *contains nothing on the brain, nerves, sense organs, or ductless glands. They were the hardest parts so I left them out, promising the publishers I would take care of them in a separate book.*

The publishers calmly went ahead and published the first book on the assumption that I would really do the second. Both Houghton Mifflin and New American Library had had specific experience with the way I started writing one book and made two (or a dozen) out of them.

Deep in my bosom, however, I wasn't at all sure I could do The Human Brain *and I was in high hopes that perhaps the world would suddenly come to an end and I wouldn't have to try.*

The world did not come to an end and eventually, I had to sit down at the typewriter and begin The Human Brain. *It turned out to be one of the hardest books I ever had to write. Like* Understanding Physics, *Volume 2, I skated on thin ice trying to get the information into my head so that I could ladle it out for the readers. There were times when the only relief I could get from the unbearable tension that resulted was to yell at my children.*

I managed, I think. At least, after the book was published, I got a call from the interviewer on some radio talk show asking me to come on their program as a brain expert and answer questions from the audience. I said, "Heavens! I'm no brain expert."

He said, "But you wrote a book on the brain."

So I said, with artless honesty—as is my way, "Yes, but I studied up for the book and put in everything I could learn. I don't know anything but the exact words in the book, and I don't think I can remember all those in a pinch. After all," I went on, a little aggrieved, "I've written books on dozens of subjects. You can't expect me to be expert on all of them just because I've written books about them."

He absorbed that and then said with what I thought was a trace of contempt, "You mean you're not an expert on anything?"

"Well," I said, "I'm an expert on one thing."

"Oh?" he said. "What's that?"

"On sounding like an expert," I said, cheerfully. "Do you want me to show up on your program to answer questions on that?"

—But he didn't.

PART 7
WORDS

MY ADVANCE into new writing areas has usually been the result of circumstances, rather than through some deliberate plan on my part. As I said at the start of the book, I never plan anything. As in the case of "The Man of La Mancha" (whom I suspect I resemble in some ways), I let the wild winds of fortune carry me onward whithersoever they blow.

For instance, writers must be, of necessity, interested in words. These are, after all, the tools of their trade. And a writer, who is also a chemist, ought to be particularly interested in chemical words—in the names of the elements, as example. Why is there an element named ruthenium? Or praseodymium?

I rarely wonder about such things without deciding to make the matter the subject of some piece of writing or other. In 1956, when this particular gnat began buzzing in my ear, I was writing science articles for Astounding Science Fiction. *Consequently, I wrote a letter to John Campbell, asking if he would like an article on the derivations of the names of the elements.*

By the time I had done that much, though, I was burning with a hard, gemlike flame and could not be headed off. I began the article (which I called "Names, Names, Names"), without waiting for an answer, on April 29, 1956. By the time I finished, a few days later, I still hadn't received an answer, so I mailed it off.

—You guessed it. A few hours after I mailed the article, I received a letter from John. He didn't like the idea.

Embarrassed at the thought of sending an article where it wasn't wanted, I sent off another letter at once (airmail this time), explaining what had happened, and asking him to place the article into a return envelope without bothering to read it.

On May 17, I called home from school to ask if there were any interesting mail. (I used to do that routinely in the days when I was at the school every day.)

"Yes," said my wife, "there's a check."

Now I can't be fooled that way. At any given moment, I know exactly what checks are on their way or should be on their way and I was expecting nothing particular that day.

So I said, rather sharply, "For what?"

And my wife answered, knowing very well she was being unresponsive, "For two hundred twenty-five dollars."

It turned out to be from John. Before putting my article in the return envelope, he had decided to read it, and then he had decided to buy it. —Passing strange are the ways of editors.

Two months later, I was having lunch with Lillian McClintock of Abelard-Schuman at Locke-Ober's. The question under discussion was my next book for A-S and I was bubbling over with a novel idea. Why not prepare a collection of the science essays I had been writing for Astounding. —I did not then foresee that the day would come when year after year I would be writing science essays for Fantasy and Science Fiction and year after year publishing collections of them with Doubleday.

Lillian was a little dubious at first but my eloquence won her over and it was agreed that I was to send over tear sheets of my articles for a reading by one of the A-S editors.

Naturally, the article I sent over with greatest eagerness was "Names, Names, Names" which was so fresh it had not yet been published. (I don't know why it is, but it always seems to me that whatever it is that I have last written is best and most exciting. Logic tells me this cannot possibly be true all the time, but I don't try to interfere with this irrational and purely emotional feeling. It keeps me writing in a constant state of high delight at all times.)

By November, it was decided to do the book, which eventually appeared as Only a Trillion and from which I quoted the introduction earlier in this book. There was one modification, though. Abelard-Schuman did not want "Names, Names, Names." They asked me to write other material as replacement, and I did. But my rejected article *grew all the dearer to me as I brooded over editorial obtuseness.*

A new chance came a year later. I had met Austin Olney of Houghton Mifflin in connection with the small task of writing an introduction to an English translation of an originally French book on computers.

Once that was out of the way, the conversation swung around, as it somehow often does, to the possibility of my writing a book. On December 26, 1957, I had the first of many such lunch sessions over prospective books.

Austin advanced the notion of my writing a book on mathematics for youngsters—a book which later turned out to be Realm of Numbers *(from which I quoted earlier).*

I was about to agree when an unaccustomed bolt of shrewdness struck my usually artless brain. My eyes narrowed with a kind of transparent cunning and I said, "I'll do a book for you, Austin, if you'll let me do a book for me."

Naturally, he wanted to know what I had in mind and I never thought faster in my life. I had to invent a book on the spot that would incorporate the essence of "Names, Names, Names," so that my hurt brainchild might be healed at last.

I babbled on wildly and what came out was the plan for a book to be entitled Words of Science *in which the background of various scientific terms would be explained in a series of one-page essays, arranged alphabetically, and including, of course, the names of all the elements.*

Austin, good-hearted soul that he is, agreed, and by March 28, 1958, the book was done.

It proved much more successful than I had expected it to be, and was therefore the precursor of others of what I came to call the "Words" books. Indeed, I have done two more books in the precise format of Words of Science. *These are* Words on the Map *and* Words from History. *The titles are self-explanatory, and here are some samples from each:*

from WORDS OF SCIENCE (*1959*)

HELIUM

In 1868, a total eclipse was visible in India and, for the first time, the Sun's atmosphere (best observed during eclipses) could be studied by the new technique of spectroscopic analysis. This had been developed only nine years earlier and consisted of passing the light radiated from a white-hot substance through a glass prism. The light is split up into lines of different colors, and each element forms its own characteristic pattern of colored lines in fixed positions.

The French astronomer Pierre J. C. Janssen allowed the light of the solar atmosphere to pass through the prism during the Indian eclipse and noticed that among the familiar lines of earthly substances, a yellow line was produced which he could not identify. The British astronomer Sir Norman Lockyer compared the position of this line with those of similar lines produced by various elements, and decided that this new line was produced by an element in the Sun that was not present, or had not yet been discovered, on Earth. He called it *helium*, from the Greek word for the Sun, "helios."

For decades that was how matters stood. Helium remained an oddly colored line in sunlight and nothing more. Few chemists took it seriously.

In 1888, the American chemist William F. Hillebrand found that a uranium mineral named uraninite, when treated with strong acid, gave off bubbles of gas. He studied this and decided it was nitrogen. To be sure, some of the gas was nitrogen, but Hillebrand unfortunately ignored the fact that, when heated, some of its spectrum lines were not those of nitrogen.

The Scottish chemist Sir William Ramsay read of this experiment and was dissatisfied. He used another uranium mineral, cleveite, and, in 1895, repeated the experiment. He and Lockyer studied the spectral lines of the gas, and almost at once they realized what they had. Fully twenty-seven years after helium had been discovered in the Sun, it was finally located on Earth.

IDIOT

It is perhaps only human that there are a great many different words used to express mental deficiency, most of them slang; the vocabulary of insult is always great. Psychologists, however, have tried to make objective use of three of them to indicate various grades of mental deficiency.

A *moron* is only mildly deficient. He is capable of doing useful work under supervision. The term was adopted in 1910 by psychologists, and is derived from the Greek "moros" (stupid).

More seriously retarded is an *imbecile*, who cannot be trusted to do useful work even under supervision, but is capable of connected speech. Whereas *moron* has always applied to mental deficiency, *imbecil*e referred originally to physical deficiency since the word is derived from the Latin "in-" (not) and "baculum" (staff); that is, it refers to a person too weak to get along without a staff. In the modern meaning, it is the mind that cannot get along without help.

Most seriously retarded is the *idiot*, one who is not capable of connected speech or of guarding himself against the ordinary dangers of life. This word has the oddest history of the three. The ancient Greeks were the most political of people. Concerning oneself with public business was the pet hobby of everyone. The Greek word "idios" means "private" so a Greek who, despite all this, was odd enough to concern himself only with his private business rather than with public business was an "idiotes." The Greek view concerning such a person is obvious since "idiotes" and "idiot" are the same word.

Of the more colloquial words, *fool* comes from the Latin "follis," meaning "bellows," obviously implying that a fool is someone whose words, though many and loud, are so much empty air. The slang expression "windbag" is the exact equivalent. *Stupid* is from the Latin "stupere" (to be stupefied; to be rendered speechless). Here the implication is of someone without words. Apparently, for one to be intelligent, his words must be neither too few nor too many, and in my opinion that's not a bad way of putting it.

RH NEGATIVE

There is a common Indian monkey, given the name of *rhesus* by the French naturalist Jean Baptiste Audebert in 1797. Audebert insisted that the name was simply made up and meant nothing and yet . . .

In 1900, the Austrian physiologist Karl Landsteiner discovered that human blood might contain one of two substances, or neither (or, as was discovered two years later, both). The substances were called simply A and B so that four blood types—A, B, O, and AB—were possible. Blood also contained antibodies (see ANTIBODY) for the substance or substances it did not possess, so that B blood, for instance, could not be added to A blood or vice versa without causing the blood corpuscles to stick together and grow useless. It was only after Landsteiner's discovery, therefore, that blood *transfusion* (from the Latin "trans," meaning "over," and "fundere," meaning "to pour") became practical; and physicians knew enough to "pour over" blood from a well person to a patient that needed blood without killing the patient.

Blood substances not interfering with transfusion also exist. One was discovered in 1940 by Landsteiner and the American physician Alexander S. Wiener in the blood of a rhesus monkey. The new substance was therefore called *Rh* from the first letters. Some eight varieties of this factor are known today. No natural antibodies can exist against Rh, but in the case of all but one variety, antibodies can be developed artificially. The exceptional variety is called *Rh negative,* the others, *Rh positive.*

It sometimes happens that a mother with Rh negative blood is carrying an unborn child who has inherited Rh positive from the father. Some of the child's Rh positive may filter across to the mother's blood, which may then develop antibodies against it. If these antibodies filter back into the child's blood, they may ruin enough red corpuscles to allow a very sick baby to be born. Physicians then have to replace the baby's blood with fresh blood quickly and, to be prepared for that possibility, expectant mothers are routinely typed for Rh these days, so that at least one third of the madeup name *Rhesus* has become very significant indeed.

from WORDS ON THE MAP (*1962*)

NEW JERSEY

In 1066, William II, Duke of Normandy, set sail for England, defeated and killed the English king, Harold, and became William I, King of England. His descendants ruled both England and Normandy, plus other sections of France from time to time. Gradually, over the centuries, however, the English-ruled portions of France were taken by the French armies. Finally in 1958, the English lost their last foothold in continental France.

Of the Norman inheritance, however, they retained one last remnant, a few islands off the coast of France. Because they are in the English Channel, they are called the *Channel Islands*.

The largest of these islands was called, in Roman times, "Caesaria insula," (Caesar's island"). During the Middle Ages, when the Latin language was garbled by barbarians, "Caesaria" became tongue-twisted to *Jersey*.

A successful British naval officer of the seventeenth century, George Carteret, was born on the island of Jersey. During the English Civil War, Carteret was a Royalist fighting for the king. When Charles I was beheaded in 1649, Carteret held out in Jersey for two years before he was forced to retreat to France.

The son of Charles I visited Jersey before the surrender and, in gratitude, granted Carteret land in America. In 1660, this son regained the throne as Charles II and when, in 1664, the Dutch possessions in America were captured, part was given to Carteret in fulfillment of the promise.

Carteret named his territories after the island of his birth which he had so well defended and it is still known as *New Jersey*, though before 1702 it existed in two sections, *West Jersey* and *East Jersey*.

New Jersey was one of the thirteen original states of the United States and was the third to ratify the Constitution.

PHILADELPHIA

After the time of Alexander the Great, there were lines of Macedonian monarchs over Egypt and Asia who kept largely to one or two names. For instance, all the Egyptian kings of the period were called Ptolemy, while the kings of western Asia were called, for the most part, Seleucus or Antiochus.

In order to distinguish one monarch from another, the kings would adopt a second name, which was usually very flattering. For instance the first Ptolemy was Ptolemy Soter ("preserver"). Next were Ptolemy Philadelphus ("loving his sister"), Ptolemy Euergetes ("benefactor"), Ptolemy Philopater ("loving his father"), and so on.

About 260 B.C., Ptolemy Philadelphus rebuilt a city in Palestine that had suffered in recent wars and renamed it *Philadelphia* after himself. It is the modern *Amman,* the capital of Jordan.

In western Asia Minor, another line of Macedonian kings were called Attalus. Of these, the second was Attalus Philadelphus and, about 150 B.C., he founded a city which he called *Philadelphia* also. This Philadelphia is mentioned in the Bible, in Chapter 3 of Revelation, as a city that was faithful to Christianity under trying circumstances. Many centuries later, in 1390, it was the last city in Asia Minor to fall to the Turks. It is now called *Alasehir,* from Turkish words meaning "red city," because of the color of its soil.

The name of the old Macedonian kings traveled to the Americas in modern times. In 1681, a city was founded in the new colony of Pennsylvania by the pious William Penn. To him, *Philadelphia* seemed perfect on two counts. First, it reminded one of the old city of Asia Minor that was faithful to Christianity, and secondly, the word could be translated "brotherly love." So it is that the largest city in Pennsylvania and the fourth largest in the United States is called *Philadelphia,* and is sometimes referred to as the "City of Brotherly Love."

VIRGIN ISLANDS

East of Puerto Rico, there is a chain of small islands that curves down to the South American continent. The most northerly of the group were discovered by Columbus in 1493, during his second voyage, and were named by him in honor of Saint Ursula and her companions, who were supposed to have died about 450, defending themselves against the Huns. They were all virgins and the islands are therefore the *Virgin Islands*.

The Virgin Islands have had an unusually mixed history as far as European colonization is concerned. The Dutch, British, Spanish, and French have all, at one time or another, established themselves there. The largest island, a little south of the rest of the group, bears the name of *St. Croix* (sant-kroy) or *Santa Cruz* (san'tuh-krooz), both (the former French, the latter Spanish) meaning "Holy Cross."

In 1753, Denmark purchased St. Croix from the French and also occupied two islands to the north, which bear the names of *St. Thomas* and *St. John*, after two of the apostles. This was one of Denmark's very rare excursions into colonization outside the Arctic. These three islands were lumped under the name of *Danish West Indies*.

In 1917, the United States was worried lest Germany might win World War I, then raging, and force weak Denmark to cede the islands, thus gaining a foothold in the western hemisphere. Playing it safe, the United States bought the islands from Denmark. The official title is now the *Virgin Islands of the United States*. (They are usually called simply Virgin Islands, but this is inaccurate because a couple of dozen small islands to their east are also part of the group, but belong to England. Those are called the *British Virgin Islands*.)

Marks of a century and a half of Danish ownership remain on the map of the islands, however. Since the fifteenth century, Denmark has been ruled by kings that have alternately borne the names of Frederik and Christian. Well, the two chief towns on St. Croix are *Frederiksted* and *Christiansted*, meaning "Frederik's town" and "Christian's town" respectively.

from WORDS FROM HISTORY (*1968*)

BLOODY SHIRT

In 1689, the English overthrew their monarch James II, and put in his place his daughter Mary II, and her husband William III, in a joint reign. This change met the approval of most Englishmen, but the case was different in Scotland. James II was the representative of a Scottish dynasty and within three months of James' ejection, the Scots rose in an unsuccessful revolt.

William tried to placate them and offered to call a truce with every clan that tendered its submission to him before December 31, 1691. There would be no reprisals for earlier acts of rebellion. By that day, all the clans had given their submission except the Macdonalds of Glencoe (in west-central Scotland). Their leader stubbornly waited till the last minute and then it was too late. A sudden snowstorm delayed him and it wasn't till January 5, 1692, that he could find a proper official with whom he could register his submission.

The Campbell clan was the sworn enemy of the Macdonalds, and here was a chance to take advantage of the letter of the law, for the Macdonalds by failing to meet the deadline had become outlaws. The Campbells came to Glencoe, accepted Macdonald hospitality for twelve days, and then at five in the morning, the Campbells (with the king's writ giving them permission) slaughtered all the Macdonalds they could find, and did so with revolting brutality.

After the massacre, so goes the tale, those wives who survived displayed the bloody shirts of their stabbed husbands to arouse compassion and spur on vengeance. This may be the origin of "to wave the bloody shirt," meaning to rouse, deliberately, a passion for revenge.

This played a role in American history. After the Civil War, the Republicans kept the Democrats out of national power for a quarter of a century by waving the *bloody shirt* of the Civil War, keeping the blame for that carnage fixed firmly upon them.

MOB

It is natural for those who consider themselves among the "better classes" to look down on the people generally and to have insulting names like "rabble" for them.

There is often a tinge of fear added to contempt in the aristocrats' view of the people. The common folk, through much of history, have been ignorant and without proper leadership. When they feel uncommonly ill-used, they sometimes rise in blind wrath and destroy anything they can reach. Almost invariably, however, they are beaten down before long by the well-organized forces of government and society and are slaughtered mercilessly in revenge. An example is to be found in the Peasant's Revolt in Germany in 1524.

What's more, crowds of people can be swayed by clever orators. Once they are ignited, the excitement of the moment and the mutual encouragement of individuals among them can lead them out of control. Shakespeare records in *Julius Caesar* how Mark Antony cleverly turned the people against Caesar's assassins. It is no wonder that Roman writers referred to the "mobile vulgus" (the "fickle multitude").

Sometimes the roused people, under capable leadership, can make their rebellion stick, for a while at least. Thus, in Great Britain, the people carried through a rebellion to the point of executing King Charles I in 1649. When Charles II, his son, was reinstated as king in 1660, his supporters felt considerable resentment against the "fickle multitude," which now cheered the return of the new Charles as loudly as it had cheered the killing of the old.

At the aristocratic Greenribbon Club, there was frequent contemptuous talk of the "mobile vulgus" until, finally, through frequent use, the term was shortened to its first syllable, *mob*. The word is now used for any dangerous and disorderly crowd of people. More recently, it has been applied to an organized group of gangsters.

POTEMKIN VILLAGE

In 1745, a young German princess, Sophia of Anhalt-Zerbst, married Peter, the nephew of the Russian empress.

The 16-year-old bride adopted the Russian religion and took the Russian name of Ekaterina (Catherine). Peter succeeded to the throne in 1762, but was half-mad and was quickly murdered, probably with the connivance of Catherine.

The German princess became the Russian empress Catherine II (also called Catherine the Great), reigned for thirty-four years, and was one of the ablest monarchs Russia ever had.

She was most notorious among her contemporaries because of her lovers. But then, it was taken for granted that eighteenth-century kings have their mistresses—why should not an eighteenth-century queen do the equivalent?

Her most famous lover was a Russian soldier named Gregory Potemkin. He had distinguished himself in the war fought against Turkey from 1768 to 1774, in which Crimea and other lands in the western and southern Ukraine were absorbed into Russia.

Both Catherine and Potemkin were seriously interested in improving Russia's economy, but this could not be done without more reform than Catherine was willing to see. Potemkin tried to reorganize the Ukraine and carry through a huge colonization venture. Corruption and bad planning spoiled matters and when Catherine demanded to see the results, he had to do considerable faking. In a tour of the south in 1787, he cleverly managed to have Catherine see only what he wanted her to see. He is even supposed to have built false-front villages, carting "happy villagers" from one to the other just ahead of her.

For that reason, *Potemkin villages* has come to mean a fake with which government officials delude people into thinking all is well. More generally, a Potemkin village is anything which looks good—but on the outside, only.

PART 8
HISTORY

ACTUALLY, I wrote three other "Words" books as well, but not in the same format. In Words from the Myths, for instance, I told, in connected fashion, the tales of the Greek myths and stopped periodically to point out how certain words and phrases in the English language arose from them—words like jovial, hermetic, and Achilles' heel, for instance.

This, naturally, gave me the idea for a companion book and in December, 1963, I brought in Words from Greek History. In it, I told Greek history in more or less connected fashion, as I had told the Greek myths, stopping whenever I wanted to point out word derivations (laconic, marathon, philippic, and so on.)

The trouble was it was too long, and Austin handed it back to me and told me that he had very lightly pencil-marked the passages he thought might be cut, without harm to the book. I looked through it with some dismay and said, "But Austin, you're cutting out all about the words."

And he said, "I guess the history parts were more interesting."

I said, "Let me take this home and think about it."

Tumultuous emotions were tumbling about inside me. What Austin didn't know and what no one knew except me, for that matter, was that in college it had been only after some hesitation that I had decided to major in chemistry. There had been a strong impulse to major in history. What finally swung me to chemistry was my feeling that as a history major all I would be able to do in later life would be to teach and engage in library research, whereas chemistry could lead to active experimentation in the laboratory. (It was only in later life that I discovered I would rather teach than do lab work and would rather do library research than either. —And so it goes.)

My interest in history stayed on even when I moved into chemistry. In 1944 and 1945, years before I had published a single book, I began gathering notes for what was intended to be a massive history of World War II. It never came to anything, of course, but I gathered roughly a million words of notes before the enchantment left me.

Now, nearly twenty years later, here was Austin incautiously telling me that he found the historical portions of a book interesting. What's more, I remember that Austin had once said to me as follows, and I quote him precisely: "Isaac, any time some publishing house asks you to do a specific book and you feel like doing it, go ahead. But if you ever write a book strictly because it's your own idea, bring it to us and we'll publish it."

I placed Words from Greek History *aside, therefore, and began all over with a completely new book. (Of course, that did not mean that* Words from Greek History *remained a total loss. No, indeed, the material within it was incorporated to a considerable extent in the eventual* Words from History. *I try not to let anything go to waste.)*

The new book I called The Greeks *and it was an overall history of Greece—plain history, no "words"—from 2000 B.C. to A.D. 1964. I brought it in and said to Austin, "Here's the revision of* Words from Greek History *and I wrote it strictly because it's my own idea. So publish it."*

And Houghton Mifflin published it as my first "straight history" book. Of course, it was primarily intended for nonhistorians, as my science books are primarily intended for nonscientists.

from THE GREEKS (*1965*)

THE SPARTAN WAY OF LIFE

The Messenian wars cost Sparta a high price also. A half-century of war, so hard-fought, had ground the military life deep into the Spartan consciousness. It seemed to them they never dared relax, especially when there were so few Spartans and so many helots (slaves). Surely if the Spartans ever relaxed, even slightly, the helots would rise at once.

Furthermore, the Messenian wars had developed the

role of the heavily armed foot soldier, or hoplite. Military training had to be particularly hard to inure the soldier to wearing heavy armor and wielding heavy weapons. Fighting was not a trade for weaklings as the Spartans practiced it.

For that reason, the Spartans dedicated their lives to warfare. Spartan youngsters were inspected at birth to see if they were physically sound. If they were not, they were abandoned and allowed to die. At the age of seven, they were taken from their mothers and were brought up in barracks.

They were taught to endure cold and hunger, were never allowed to wear fine clothes or eat good food, were trained in all military arts and were taught to endure weariness and pain without complaint.

The Spartan code was to fight hard, follow orders without questions, and to die rather than retreat or surrender. To run away, a soldier had to throw down his heavy shield, which would otherwise slow him down; if he died, he would be carried home, in honor, upon his shield. Therefore, Spartan mothers were supposed to instruct their sons to return from war "with their shields or on them."

The Spartan adults ate at a common table, everyone bringing his share, all contributing from the substance produced from his lands by the labor of his helots. (If a Spartan lost his land for any reason, he was no longer entitled to a place at the table, which was a great disgrace. In later centuries fewer and fewer Spartans were entitled to such a place as land became concentrated in fewer and fewer hands. This was a source of weakness for Sparta but only toward the end of her history did she try to reform the situation.)

The food at the common table was designed to fill a person and keep him alive, but nothing more. Some non-Spartan Greek, having tasted the porridge that Spartans ate in their barracks, is supposed to have said that he no longer wondered why Spartans fought so bravely and without the slightest fear of death. Such porridge made death welcome.

In later centuries, the Spartans maintained that this way of life originated with a man named Lycurgus (ligh-kur′gus) who lived, according to their tradition, sometime about 850 B.C., long before the Messenian wars. However, this is almost certainly not so and it is even doubtful that Lycurgus existed at all.

The proof of this is that down to about 650 B.C. Sparta does not seem to have been very much different from the other Greek states. She had her art, her music, her poetry. During the seventh century, a musician from Lesbos named Terpander (tur-pan'der) came to Sparta and did well there. He is supposed to have improved the lyre and is called the "Father of Greek music."

Most famous of all Spartan musicians was Tyrtaeus (tur-tee'us). By tradition, he was an Athenian but he may well have been a native Spartan. In any case, he lived during the Second Messenian War and his music was said to have inspired the Spartans to new feats of bravery when their ardor flagged.

It was only after the Second Messenian War that the deadly hand of utter militarism completely shut off all that was creative and human in Sparta. Art, music, and literature came to a halt. Even oratory (and all Greeks have loved to talk from ancient times to the present day) was stopped, for Spartans practiced speaking very briefly and to the point. The very word "laconic" (from Laconia) has come to mean the quality of speaking pithily.

By 1964, Austin knew my deplorable habit of making several books grow where one had been planted. When he agreed to publish The Greeks *he said, with commendable editorial caution, "Look, Isaac, will you do me a favor? Don't write a history of Rome until we see how* The Greeks *does."*

That was only fair. The Greeks *was published in June, 1965, and on August 2, I visited the Houghton Mifflin offices and asked how the book was doing. "Pretty well," Austin said. I asked if the reviews were all right and he said they were.*

So I said, "Are you willing to risk publishing a history of Rome?"

He said, "Yes! You can go home and start it, and we'll prepare a contract."

I said, "You can prepare a contract, but I don't have to go home. Here is the manuscript."

What I had done, you see, was gamble that The Greeks

*would do reasonably well and had prepared another his-
torical manuscript just in case.*

*I did another thing about the history of Rome, too. The
Greeks had proven too long and Austin had gently maneuvered the cutting of some ten thousand words or so. I was
determined to avoid that sort of thing in the future. (It so
happens that amputating ten thousand glorious words is a
painful operation and, unlike the more ordinary kinds of
operations such as the mere hacking off of a right arm, no
one has developed an anesthetic for it.)*

*So I only wrote half the history of Rome and thus made
sure it wouldn't be too long. I called it* The Roman Re-
public *and it was obvious there would have to be* The
Roman Empire *following it—and so there was.*

*Of course, I have particular fun when I see something,
or think I see something, which is not brought out in the
usual history books. There is the case, for instance, of
Pompey, a popular Roman general of the first century
B.C., and the Temple at Jerusalem, and here is what I said
about that:*

from THE ROMAN REPUBLIC (*1966*)

South of Syria was the land of Judea. A century before,
Judea had revolted against the Seleucid Empire and had
gained its independence under a line of rulers known as
the Maccabees (mak'uh-beez). Judea prospered under them
at first, but eventually its history came to be largely that of
the quarrels among different members of the ruling family.

When Pompey arrived, two brothers of the Maccabee
family were fighting a civil war. One was Hyrcanus II
(her-kay'nus) and the other Aristobulus (uh-ris"toh-byoo'-
lus)—both Jews despite their Greek-sounding names.
Each brother tried to win the all-powerful Roman to his
side.

Pompey demanded that all fortresses in Judea be sur-
rendered to him. This was denied him, and Jerusalem refused to allow him to enter. For three months Pompey laid
siege to it, and then the always stiff-necked Jews reluctantly
gave in.

Pompey took the city and, out of curiosity, entered the

Holy of Holies of the Temple at Jerusalem—the most sacred chamber of the Temple which only the High Priest might enter and then only at the Day of Atonement.

No doubt many Jews must have expected Pompey to die on the spot as a result of divine displeasure, but he emerged completely unharmed. Nevertheless, it is an interesting fact that from that point on, from the time of his violation of the Temple, Pompey's successes came to an end. The rest of his life was one long frustrating failure.

About this time, Austin was promoted into the higher reaches of the hierarchy (though he remains as accessible as ever) and I came to be more closely associated with Walter Lorraine and Mary K. Harmon. This means that my lunches can be with any of six different combinations of these three, including an occasional lunch with all three, as was true when this book was first planned.

I am now doing history books fairly regularly and am delighted to be doing so. All are put out in uniform design so it is clear they form a series. Houghton Mifflin is just egging me on by doing that, whether they know it or not. It is now my intention, while life and breath hold out, to write history after history, dealing with different periods, different regions, different aspects. With sufficient ingenuity I can manage to do this for decades and produce an indefinite number.

And when I cautiously hint at this to Mary K., who is the sweetest lady editor one could possibly encounter, she says, without batting an eyelash, "That's fine, Isaac."

Well, if I'm going to write a million histories, I can't resist quoting a couple of short passages.

from THE EGYPTIANS (*1967*)

Gnosticism was a pre-Christian philosophy that stressed the evil of matter and the world. To the Gnostics, the great abstract God, who was truly real, good, and the omnipotent ruler of all, was a personified Wisdom (or, in Greek, *gnosis*, hence "Gnosticism").

Wisdom was utterly divorced from the universe—unreachable, unknowable. The universe was created by an inferior god, a "demiurge" (from a Greek word meaning "worker for the people"—a practical ruler, an earthly sort of being rather than a divine god above and beyond matter). Because the ability of the demiurge was limited, the world turned out to be evil, as was all in it, including matter itself. The human body was evil, and the human spirit had to turn away from it, and from matter and the world, in an attempt to strive backward to spirit and Wisdom.

Some Gnostics found themselves attracted to Christianity and vice versa. The outstanding leader of this line of thought was Marcion (mahr'shee-on), a native of Asia Minor, and supposedly the son of a Christian bishop.

Writing during the reigns of Trajan and Hadrian, Marcion held that it was the God of the Old Testament who was the demiurge—the evil and inferior being who had created the universe. Jesus, on the other hand, was the representative of the true God, of Wisdom. Since Jesus did not partake of the creation of the demiurge, he was pure spirit, and his human shape and experiences were merely a deliberate illusion taken on to accomplish his purposes.

The Gnostic version of Christianity was quite popular in Egypt for a time, since it fitted in well with the anti-Jewish feeling in the land. It made of the Jewish God a demon, and made of the Jewish scriptures something that was demon-inspired.

Gnostic Christianity, however, did not endure long, for the mainstream of Christianity was firmly set against it. Most of the Christian leaders accepted the God of the Jews and the Old Testament as the God spoken of by Jesus in the New Testament. The Old Testament was accepted as inspired scripture and as the necessary preface to the New Testament.

Nevertheless, though Gnosticism passed away, it left behind some dark strains. There remained in Christianity some feeling concerning the evil of the world and of man, and with it an anti-Jewish feeling that was stronger than before.

What's more, the Egyptians themselves never abandoned a kind of Gnostic view with regard to Jesus. They consistently interpreted the nature of Jesus in such a way as to minimize its human aspect. This not only contributed to a continuing debilitating internal struggle among the

Christian leaders but was an important factor, as we shall see, in the eventual destruction of Egyptian Christianity.

Another, more joyful, influence of Egyptian ways of thought on Christianity involved the lovely Isis, Queen of Heaven. She was surely one of the most popular goddesses, not only in Egypt but in the Roman Empire, and it was fairly easy to transfer delight in beauty and gentle sympathy from Isis to the Virgin Mary. The important role played by the Virgin in Christian thought lent to the religion a warmly feminine touch that was absent in Judaism, and certainly the existence of the Isis cult made it easier to add that aspect to Christianity.

This was the easier still because Isis was often shown with the infant Horus on her lap. In this aspect Horus, without the hawk head, was known to the Egyptians as Harpechruti ("Horus, the Child"). He had his finger on his lips as a sign of infancy—an approach to sucking his thumb, so to speak. The Greeks mistook the sign as one that asked for quiet, and in their pantheon he became Harpocrates (hahr-pok′ruh-teez), god of silence.

The popularity of Isis and Harpocrates, mother and child, was transferred to Christianity, too, and helped make popular the idea of the Virgin and Christ Child that had captured the imagination of millions upon millions in the Christian centuries.

from THE NEAR EAST (*1968*)

One important factor in Assyria's favor was that its iron supplies increased . . . The Assyrian army was the first to really exploit the new metal in quantity, and it entered a two-century career of conquest that was to make it the terror of the world.

Nor was it only a matter of iron. The Assyrians were the first to make a science of the siege of cities. From very early times, cities had learned that by building walls about themselves they could hold off an enemy most effectively. From the top of the walls it was easy to fire a hail of arrows down upon the enemy, while the enemy in turn could do little damage in shooting arrows up to the tops of the walls.

A siege became an endurance contest, therefore. Those

laying siege avoided attempts to fight their way in and take the city "by storm." Instead they were content to isolate the city and prevent food supplies from entering. In this way, the city could be starved into surrender. The city under siege held out as long as possible in the hope that the besieging army would succumb to boredom, attrition, and disease. It was generally a long pull and often, with both sides suffering, some compromise arrangement was made in which the city agreed to pay tribute but preserved itself intact.

The Assyrians, however, at this period of history, began to devise methods for beating down the wall. They built heavy devices that could not be pushed over, placed them on wheels so that they could be moved easily against the wall, armored them to protect the men within, and equipped them with battering rams to beat down the wall. Once a breach was made in the wall and the besieging army poured in, it was usually all over.

This form of siege warfare introduced a new element of horror. As long as battles were mainly army against army, bloodshed was limited. A defeated army could run away, and even fleeing soldiers could turn and defend themselves. However, when a city was taken by storm, its population was pinned against its own wall and could not flee. It was filled with material goods for looting, and with helpless women and children who might be abused without fear of reprisal. In the fury of war and the excitement of victory, the sack of a city involved cruelties beyond description.

Oddly enough, long before I began to write actual history books, my interest in history showed up in my fiction. Or, come to think of it, why should that be odd; isn't it natural that should be so?

In the 1940's, you see, I wrote a series of stories about the fall of the Galactic Empire, the thousand-year Dark Age that followed, and the rise of the Second Galactic Empire. What I had in mind was the fall of the Roman Empire, of course, and I was very free in making analogies, although the imitation was never slavish.

The stories involved the deliberate establishment of two Foundations of scientists toward the end of the days of the First Empire. It seems that the science of "psychohistory" (an invented term of my own, which deals with the study of quantitative sociology so that the sweeping changes of history can be foreseen in advance and foretold) had been perfected. The Foundations were therefore located in such places and in such fashion as would serve to reduce (according to the predictions of psychohistory) the length and disastrousness of the Dark Age interregnum.

My stories were intended to follow the working out of that plan, but I never finished. How I started the series and why I never finished I outlined a couple of years ago for the fellow members of one of my professional societies, The Science Fiction Writers of America. Here is what I said, in part:

from "There's Nothing Like a Good Foundation" (*1967*)

The Foundation Series had its origin in 1941, in the course of a subway ride to see John W. Campbell, Jr., editor of *Astounding Science Fiction*. In those days, I visited him frequently and always brought with me the plot of a new s.-f. story. We discussed it and I went home and wrote it. Then he would sometimes accept it and sometimes not.

On this subway ride, I had no story idea to present him with so I tried a trick I still sometimes recommend. I opened a book at random, read a sentence, and concentrated on it till I had an idea. The book was a collection of the Gilbert and Sullivan plays which I just happened to have with me. I opened it to *Iolanthe* and my eye fell on the picture of the fairy queen kneeling before Private Willis of the Grenadier Guards.

I let my mind wander from the Grenadiers, to soldiers in general, to a military society, to feudalism, to the breakup of the Roman Empire. By the time I reached Campbell I told him that I was planning to write a story about the breakup of the Galactic Empire.

He talked and I talked and he talked and I talked, and when I left I had the Foundation Series in mind. It lasted for seven years, during which I wrote eight stories, ranging in length from a short story to a three-part serial . . .

But there are disadvantages to a series of stories. There is, for one thing, the bugaboo of self-consistency. It is annoying to be hampered, in working out a story, by the fact that some perfectly logical development is ruled out since, three stories before, you had to make such a development impossible because of the needs of the plot of *that* story . . .

Before I could write a new Foundation story I had to sit down and reread all the preceding ones, and by the time I got to the eighth story that meant rereading 150,000 words of very complicated material. Even so, my success was limited. In April, 1966, a fan approached me with a carefully made out list of inconsistencies in dates, names, and events that he had dug out of the series by dint of close reading and cross-reference.

Furthermore, in designing each new Foundation story, I found I had to work within an increasingly constricted area, with progressively fewer and fewer degrees of freedom. I was forced to seize whatever way I could find without worrying about how difficult I might make the next story. Then, when I came to the next story, those difficulties arose and beat me over the head.

Then again, I had to start each story with some indication of what had gone before, for those readers who had never read any of the earlier stories. When I wrote the eighth story, I was forced to begin with a long introduction which I had to disguise as an essay my adolescent girl-heroine was writing for class. It was not at all easy to make such an essay interesting. I had to introduce a number of human-interest touches and interrupt it by action at the first possible opportunity . . .

The eighth story had carried me only one-third of the way through the original plan of describing one thousand years of future history. However, to write a ninth story meant re-reading the first eight, starting with a longer prologue than ever, working in a narrower compass than ever, and so on. So I quit—permanently . . .

The Foundation Series were first published in book form in three volumes in the early 1950's [*Foundation, Foundation and Empire, Second Foundation*] and they have never gone out of print. As book-club selections, in paperback form, in foreign editions, in hard-cover reissues, and paperback reissues, they seem to have an indefinite number of lives . . .

No week passes without some piece of fan mail referring to the Foundation stories and usually asking for more. And at the 24th World Science Fiction Convention, held in Cleveland in 1966, the Foundation Series was awarded a Hugo as the All-Time Best Series.

What more can I ask for having opened a book in the subway twenty-five years ago?

Here's a passage, then, from one of the Foundation stories, one which was originally called "The Dead Hand" and which was eventually included in Foundation and Empire, *the middle book of the trilogy. It deals with Cleon II, Galactic Emperor, and while I wrote it, I had in mind Roman history. There was a little bit of Justinian and Belisarius of the sixth century and a little bit of Tiberius and Sejanus of the first century and so on.*

from "The Dead Hand" (*1945*)

Cleon II was Lord of the Universe. Cleon II also suffered from a painful and undiagnosed ailment. By the queer twists of human affairs, the two statements are not mutually exclusive, nor even particularly incongruous. There have been a wearisomely large number of precedents in history.

But Cleon II cared nothing for such precedents. To meditate upon a long list of similar cases would not ameliorate personal suffering an electron's worth. It soothed him as little to think that where his great-grandfather had been the pirate ruler of a dust-speck planet, he himself slept in the pleasure palace of Ammentetick the Great, as heir of a line of Galactic rulers stretching backward into a tenuous past. It was at present no source of comfort to him that the efforts of his father had cleansed the realm of its leprous patches of rebellion and restored it to the peace and unity it had enjoyed under Stanel VI; that, as a consequence, in the twenty-five years of his reign, not one cloud of revolt had misted his burnished glory.

The Emperor of the Galaxy and the Lord of All whimpered as he lolled his head backward into the invigorating plane of force about his pillows. It yielded in a softness that did not touch, and at the pleasant tingle, Cleon relaxed a bit. He sat up with difficulty and stared morosely at the distant walls of the grand chamber. It was a bad room to be alone in. It was too big. All the rooms were too big.

But better to be alone during these crippling bouts than to endure the prinking of the courtiers, their lavish sympathy, their soft, condescending dullness. Better to be alone than to watch those insipid masks behind which spun the tortuous speculations on the chances of death and the fortunes of the succession.

His thoughts harried him. There were his three sons; three straight-backed youths full of promise and virtue. Where did they disappear on these bad days? Waiting, no doubt. Each watching the others; and all watching him.

He stirred uneasily. And now Brodrig craved audience. The lowborn faithful Brodrig; faithful because he was hated with a unanimous and cordial hatred that was the only point of agreement between the dozen cliques that divided his court.

Brodrig—the faithful favorite, who had to be faithful, since unless he owned the fastest speed ship in the Galaxy and took to it the day of the Emperor's death, it would be the atom chamber the day after.

Cleon II touched the smooth knob on the arm of his great divan, and the huge door at the end of the room dissolved to transparency.

Brodrig advanced along the crimson carpet and knelt to kiss the Emperor's limp hand.

"Your health, sire?" asked the Privy Secretary in a low tone of becoming anxiety.

"I live," snapped the Emperor with exasperation, "if you can call it life where every scoundrel who can read a book of medicine uses me as a blank and receptive field for his feeble experiments. If there is a conceivable remedy; chemical, physical, or atomic, which has not yet been tried; why then, some learned babbler from the far corners of the realm will arrive tomorrow to try it. And still another newly discovered book, or forgery more-like, will be used as authority.

"By my father's memory," he rumbled savagely, "it seems there is not a biped extant who can study a disease before his eyes with those same eyes. There is not one who can count a pulsebeat without a book of the ancients before him. I'm sick and they call it 'unknown.' The fools! If in the course of millennia, human bodies learn new methods of falling askew, it remains uncovered by the studies of the ancients and uncurable forevermore. The ancients should be alive now, or I then."

The Emperor ran down to a low-breathed curse while Brodrig waited dutifully. Cleon II said peevishly, "How many are waiting outside?"

He jerked his head in the direction of the door.

Brodrig said patiently, "the Great Hall holds the usual number."

"Well, let them wait. State matters occupy me. Have the Captain of the Guard announce it. Or wait, forget the state matters. Just have it announced I hold no audience, and let the Captain of the Guard look doleful. The jackals among them may betray themselves." The Emperor sneered nastily.

"There is a rumor, sire," said Brodrig, smoothly, "that it is your heart that troubles you."

The Emperor's smile was little removed from the previous sneer. "It will hurt others more than myself if any act prematurely on that rumor. But what is it *you* want? Let's have this over."

Brodrig rose from his kneeling posture at a gesture of permission and said, "It concerns General Bel Riose, the Military Governor of Siwenna."

"Riose?" Cleon II frowned heavily. "I don't place him. Wait, is he the one who sent that quixotic message some months back? Yes, I remember. He panted for permission to enter a career of conquest for the glory of the Empire and Emperor."

"Exactly, sire."

The Emperor laughed shortly. "Did you think I had such generals left me, Brodrig? He seems to be a curious atavism. What was the answer? I believe you took care of it."

"I did, sire. He was instructed to forward additional information and to take no steps involving naval action without further orders from the Imperium."

"Hmp. Safe enough. Who is this Riose? Was he ever at court?"

Brodrig nodded and his mouth twisted ever so little. "He began his career as a cadet in the Guards ten years back. He had part in that affair off the Lemul Cluster."

"The Lemul Cluster? You know, my memory isn't quite —Was that the time a young soldier saved two ships of the line from a head-on collision by . . . uh . . . something or other?" He waved a hand impatiently. "I don't remember the details. It was something heroic."

"Riose was that soldier. He received a promotion for it," Brodrig said dryly, "and an appointment to field duty as captain of a ship."

"And now Military Governor of a border system and still young. Capable man, Brodrig!"

"Unsafe, sire. He lives in the past. He is a dreamer of ancient times, or rather, of the myths of what ancient times used to be. Such men are harmless in themselves, but their queer lack of realism makes them tools for others." He added, "His men, I understand, are completely under his control. He is one of your *popular* generals."

"Is he?" the Emperor mused. "Well, come, Brodrig, I would not wish to be served entirely by incompetents. They certainly set no enviable standard for faithfulness themselves."

"An incompetent traitor is no danger. It is rather the capable men who must be watched."

"You among them, Brodrig?" Cleon II laughed and then grimaced with pain. "Well, then, you may forget the lecture for the while. What new development is there in the matter of this young conqueror? I hope you haven't come merely to reminisce."

"Another message, sire, has been received from General Riose."

"Oh? And to what effect?"

"He has spied out the land of these barbarians and advocates an expedition in force. His arguments are long and fairly tedious. It is not worth annoying your Imperial Majesty with it at present, during your indisposition. Particularly since it will be discussed at length during the session of the Council of Lords." He glanced sidewise at the Emperor.

Cleon II frowned. "The Lords? Is it a question for them,

Brodrig? It will mean further demands for a broader interpretation of the Charter. It always comes to that."

"It can't be avoided, sire. It might have been better if your august father could have beat down the last rebellion without granting the Charter. But since it is here, we must endure it for the while."

"You're right, I suppose. Then the Lords it must be. But why all this solemnity, man? It is, after all, a minor point. Success on a remote border with limited troops is scarcely a state affair."

Brodrig smiled narrowly. He said coolly, "It is an affair of a romantic idiot; but even a romantic idiot can be a deadly weapon when an unromantic rebel uses him as a tool. Sire, the man was popular here and is popular there. He is young. If he annexes a vagrant barbarian planet or two, he will become a conqueror. Now a young conqueror who has proven his ability to rouse the enthusiasm of pilots, miners, tradesmen, and such-like rabble is dangerous at any time. Even if he lacked the desire to do to you as your august father did to the usurper, Ricker, then one of our loyal Lords of the Domain may decide to use him as his weapon."

Cleon II moved an arm hastily and stiffened with the pain. Slowly he relaxed, but his smile was weak, and his voice a whisper. "You are a valuable subject, Brodrig. You always suspect far more than is necessary, and I have but to take half your suggested precautions to be utterly safe. We'll put it up to the Lords. We shall see what they say and take our measures accordingly. The young man, I suppose, has made no hostile moves yet."

"He reports none. But already he asks for reinforcements."

"Reinforcements!" The Emperor's eyes narrowed with wonder. "What force has he?"

"Ten ships of the line, sire, with a full complement of auxiliary vessels. Two of the ships are equipped with motors salvaged from the old Grand Fleet, and one has a battery of power artillery from the same source. The other ships are new ones of the last fifty years, but are serviceable, nevertheless."

"Ten ships would seem adequate for any reasonable undertaking. Why, with less than ten ships my father won his first victories against the usurper. Who *are* these bar-barians he's fighting?"

The Privy Secretary raised a pair of supercilious eye-brows. "He refers to them as 'the Foundation.'"

PART 9
THE BIBLE

IN A WAY, none of my books has done badly. By that I mean that none has lost money for its publisher and none has had to be remaindered.

On the other hand, not one of my Hundred Books has ever hit the best-seller lists or even come close to doing so. Nor do I expect any of my future books to do so. I'm rather resigned to that. After all, my books don't contain those little items that have a broad general appeal: no sex to speak of, very little violence and, indeed, not much sensationalism of any sort.

I don't mean to sound aggrieved, or to give the impression that I feel I am maintaining integrity and virtue against difficulties. Not at all. It never occurs to me to add sensationalism of any sort, and if I tried to do so I almost certainly couldn't do it convincingly and would merely ruin the book. What's more, to do everyone justice, not one editor of the many with whom I have dealt, has ever once by as much as a word indicated that I ought to stick in a little sex or violence for the sake of additional sales.

Despite all this resignation and contentment, I will admit that I get a little rattled when one of my books manages to get into the black with a narrower margin than usual. Two of my "words" books didn't do as well as the rest, for instance. These were Words in Genesis *and* Words from the Exodus, *which, together, covered the first five books of the Bible and searched out their contribution to English vocabulary.*

This was particularly frustrating, for I had hoped to continue all the way through the Bible in similar fashion, and now I was too abashed to do so. ·

Yet the matter of the Bible nagged at me and nagged at me until some time in 1965 I wondered if I might not do a big book on the whole Bible. It would be a book that dealt

*with the historical background to the events of the Bible
rather than merely with word derivations, for I had begun
my history series by then and I was all of a history-fire.
Then, too, I thought of doing it at the adult level rather
than aiming it at youngsters primarily.*

As it happened, I had done a big book, Asimov's Biographical Encyclopedia of Science and Technology *the year
before for Doubleday and it was doing considerably better
than, in my heart of hearts, I had thought it would. It
seemed to me that Doubleday might be receptive to another
book.*

*They were! In no time at all, I was sending samples to
Lawrence P. Ashmead, the Doubleday editor with whom I
am currently working most closely. He is a young man of
incredible industry, gentleness, and charm, and I am delighted with him.*

*Eventually the book was all done, all 400,000 words of
it, stretching from Genesis to Revelation, and Doubleday
decided to put it out in two volumes, published in successive Octobers. The first volume dealt with the Old Testament and the second volume with—but you've guessed it.*

*My greatest difficulty with the book was the title. Gen-
erally, I make up a direct and simple title, and it stays, like*
The Neutrino *or* Photosynthesis. *Or the editor makes one
up either to begin with or as an alternative and that stays, as*
The Wellsprings of Life *or* The Intelligent Man's Guide to
Science.

*Not so in the case of my Bible book. My working title
when I first broached the subject to Doubleday was* It's
Mentioned in the Bible. *That was vetoed at once.*

*So I worked along with the manuscript under the work-
ing title of* Background to the Bible. *Once the manuscript
began to go through the publishing mills, Larry called me
up to say that he didn't think* Background to the Bible *had
enough oomph, and he suggested* The Intelligent Man's
Guide to the Bible.

*I was intrigued at the thought of the book as a compan-
ion piece for* The Intelligent Man's Guide to Science *but
said at once that we would have to get permission from
Basic Books. Titles are pretty much up for grabs and there
are countless books that duplicate some other books' titles.
Indeed* The Intelligent Man's Guide to Science *itself bears
an uncomfortable similarity to George Bernard Shaw's* The

Intelligent Woman's Guide to Socialism. *Still, there's my fetish for playing it square with all my publishers and Larry Ashmead is naïve enough to share my views on ethics anyway.*

So we asked Basic Books, certain that was merely the formality of the courteous approach, and to our discomfort, Basic Books vetoed the notion very firmly.

That was it! I at once abandoned that title, to make Basic Books happy, and tried to think of a still better title for Doubleday to make them happy. I pointed out to Larry, therefore, that science might be for intelligent men, but that the Bible was supposed to be for everybody. Why not name the book, then, Everyman's Guide to the Bible? Larry thought that was fine and the galley proofs came out with that title.

But then the Doubleday salesmen got into the act. There was an "Everyman's Library" put out by another publishing house and besides, Asimov's Biographical Encyclopedia of Science and Technology was, as I said earlier, doing better than expected. Why not, then, Asimov's Guide to the Bible?

I objected that it would sound like egregious arrogance on my part whereupon the editorial staff of Doubleday united in a soothing effort designed to assure me that my reputation for modesty was worldwide and nobody would object to my name in the title. So I let myself be soothed.

I'm not sure, though, that my reputation for modesty is really worldwide because there is a well-known story at Doubleday that goes as follows: Time magazine printed two very complimentary columns on me in their July 7, 1967, issue and one Doubleday editor came running to Larry Ashmead when the issue came out, asking if he had seen it and volunteering the information that it was full of "delightful Asimovian immodesties."

Anyway, I thought I would test them. When the book came out, the book jacket was tasteful, conservative, and yet interestingly designed. Across the top is "Isaac Asimov" in pale blue. Underneath, "Asimov's Guide to the" still in pale blue, and finally "Bible" in larger letters (with a particularly large "B") in a subdued red.

I took one look at it and said with a perfectly straight face, "How come the Bible gets top billing?"

You think they all laughed, knowing that Asimov, with

his worldwide reputation for modesty, was just kidding?

Not at all. They began to assure me that my name appeared twice and that that more than made up for the fact that "Bible" was in larger letters.

But never mind. A good part of the fun in the Bible book was my chance to discuss a million and one items at will. For instance, when Balaam is trying to curse the children of Israel immediately before their invasion of Canaan, he refers to the unicorn. So I got a chance to talk about the unicorn:

from ASIMOV'S GUIDE TO THE BIBLE (*1968*)

Balaam's inability to curse continued at all stations. From Mount Pisgah, Balaam praised God, saying:

> Numbers 23:22. *God brought them out of Egypt; he* [Israel] *hath as it were the strength of an unicorn.*

The Bible mentions the unicorn on several other occasions, notably in the Book of Job:

> Job 39:9. *Will the unicorn be willing to serve thee, or abide by thy crib?*

The Hebrew word represented in the King James Version by "unicorn" is *re'em*, which undoubtedly refers to the wild ox (*urus* or aurochs) ancestral to the domesticated cattle of today. The *re'em* still flourished in early historical times and a few existed into modern times although it is now extinct. It was a dangerous creature of great strength and was similar in form and temperament to the Asian buffaloes.

The Revised Standard Version translates *re'em* always as "wild ox." The verse in Numbers is translated as "they have as it were the horns of the wild ox," while the one in Job is translated "Is the wild ox willing to serve you?" The Anchor Bible translates the verse in Job as "Will the buffalo deign to serve you?"

The wild ox was a favorite prey of the hunt-loving Assyrian monarchs (the animal was called *rumu* in Assyrian, essentially the same word as *re'em*) and was displayed in their large bas-reliefs. Here the wild ox was invariably shown in profile and only one horn was visible. One can well imagine that the animal represented in this fashion would come to be called "one-horn" as a familiar nickname much as we might refer to "longhorns" in speaking of a certain breed of cattle.

As the animal itself grew less common under the pressure of increasing human population and the depredations of the hunt, it might come to be forgotten that there was a second horn hidden behind the first in the sculptures and "one-horn" might come to be considered a literal description of the animal.

When the first Greek translation of the Bible was prepared about 250 B.C. the animal was already rare in the long-settled areas of the Near East, and the Greeks, who had had no direct experience with it, had no word for it. They used a translation of "one-horn" instead and it became *monokeros*. In Latin and in English it became the Latin word for "one-horn"; that is, "unicorn."

The Biblical writers could scarcely have had the intention of implying that the wild ox literally had one horn. There is one Biblical quotation, in fact, that clearly contradicts that notion. In the Book of Deuteronomy, when Moses is giving his final blessing to each tribe, he speaks of the tribe of Joseph (Ephraim and Manasseh) as follows:

> Deuteronomy 33:17. *His glory is like the firstling of his bullock, and his horns are like the horns of unicorns . . .*

Here the word unicorn is placed in the plural since the thought of a "one-horn's" single horn seems to make the phrase "horns of a unicorn" self-contradictory. Still, the original Hebrew has the word in the singular so that we must speak of the "horns of a unicorn," which make it clear that a unicorn has more than one horn. In addition, the parallelism used in Hebrew poetry makes it natural to equate "unicorn" and "bullock," showing that the unicorn is something very much resembling a young bull. The Revised Standard Version has, in this verse, the phrase "the horns of a wild ox."

And yet the fact that the Bible speaks of a unicorn seemed, through most of history, to place the seal of divine assurance upon the fact that a one-horned animal existed. The unicorn is therefore commonplace in legends and stories.

This is especially so since travelers in Greek times spoke of a one-horned beast that existed in India, and assigned great powers to the single horn of that animal. For instance, a cup made out of the horn of such a beast rendered harmless any poisonous liquid that might be poured into it.

There is, indeed, a one-horned beast in India (as well as in Malaya, Sumatra and Africa) and this is the rhinoceros (from Greek words meaning "nose-horn"). The horn on its snout is not a true horn but is a concretion of hair; nevertheless, the concretion looks like a horn and fulfills the purpose of one. It is very likely that the rhinoceros is the Greek unicorn, although its horn scarcely possesses the magic qualities attributed to it in legend.

Since the rhinoceros is one of the largest land animals still alive, and is possessed of enormous strength, it might be thought to fit the description in the Bible. Some Latin translations of the Bible therefore convert the Greek *monokeros* into "rhinoceros." But this is farfetched. It is very unlikely that the Biblical writers knew of the rhinoceros and they certainly knew of the wild ox.

The unicorn entered European legend without reference to the rhinoceros, which was as unknown to the medieval Westerner as to the Biblical Israelite. The shape of the unicorn was, to the European, whatever fancy pleased to make it, and it is most familiar to us now as a rather horselike creature with a single long horn on its forehead. In this shape, two unicorns were depicted as supporting the royal arms of Scotland. When Scotland and England were combined under the House of Stuart in 1603, the Scottish unicorns joined the English lions on the coat of arms of what now became Great Britain.

The old enmity between the two nations is reflected in the nursery rhyme "The lion and the unicorn were fighting for the crown." The fact that it is an English rhyme and that England usually won the wars, though never conclusively, is signified by the second line, "The lion beat the unicorn all around the town."

The most distinctive feature of this modern unicorn is its horn, which is long, thin, slowly tapering, and a straight helix. It has precisely the shape and dimensions, in fact, of the single tooth of the male of a species of whale called the narwhal. This tooth takes the shape of a tusk, sometimes twenty feet long.

Undoubtedly, sailors occasionally obtained such tusks and then sold them to landlubbers for great sums by claiming each to be the horn of a unicorn with all the magical virtue of that object.

Getting involved in the Bible leads me to alter my other fields of writing perceptibly. For instance, I couldn't resist using my increased familiarity with Biblical details as a background to one of my F & SF articles:

"Twelve Point Three Six Nine" (*1967*)

Once in junior high school, my English teacher gave the class the assignment of reading and pondering Leigh Hunt's poem "Abou ben Adhem." Perhaps you remember it.

Abou ben Adhem awoke one night from a deep dream of peace and found an angel making a list of the names of those who loved God. Ben Adhem naturally wanted to know if he was included and was told he wasn't. Humbly he asked to be included as one who loved his fellow men, at least.

The next night the angel reappeared "And show'd the names whom love of God had bless'd/And lo! Ben Adhem's name led all the rest."

I knew the poem and had a pretty good notion as to the course of the class discussion planned for the next day by the teacher. There would be little homilies about how to love God meant to love mankind and vice versa. I agreed with that, but thought it would be rather dull to spend time on so self-evident a proposition. Could not some alternate meaning be wrenched out of the miserably unsubtle poem? I could find none.

The next day, our English teacher, with a kindly smile, asked, "Now, class, who will volunteer to tell me why Abou ben Adhem's name led all the rest?"

Blinding inspiration struck me. I raised my hand violently and when the teacher nodded at me, I said, with a beatific smile, "Alphabetical order, sir!"

I didn't really expect him to be grateful for this new light I was shedding on Leigh Hunt's poem, so I wasn't surprised when he pointed his thumb quietly at the door. I left (knowing the way, for I had been ejected for obstreperous behavior on several previous occasions) and the class discussion went on without me.

But, as I discovered afterward, Abou ben Adhem had been effectively punctured and the teacher had gone on to discuss other matters, so I suppose I won out.

If I get weary of the lack of subtlety in "Abou ben Adhem" you can imagine how desperate I get at those who maintain the entire Universe to be equally unsubtle.

Naturally I get most desperate when the unsubtlety is of a sort to which I feel myself to be (in secret) deeply attracted. For instance, there are those who, having noted some simple and hackneyed relationships between numbers or between geometrical figures, promptly suppose that the structure of the Universe is designed merely to show off those relationships. (And, to my self-disgust, I always find this sort of thing interesting.)

Mystics have been guilty of such simple-mindedness, I am sure, in every society complicated enough to have invented arithmetic, but the best early examples known today are to be found among the Greeks.

For instance, Pythagoras of Samos, about 525 B.C., plucked taut strings and listened to the notes that were produced. He observed that pleasant-sounding combinations of notes were heard when strings were of lengths that bore a simple arithmetical ratio to one other: 1 to 2 or 3 to 4 to 5. It was that, perhaps, which led him and his followers to believe that the physical world was governed by numerical relationships, and simple numerical relationships at that.

It is true, of course, that numerical relationships are of importance in the Universe, but they are not always simple by any means. For instance, a fact of apparently fundamental importance is the ratio of the mass of the proton to the electron—which is 1836.11. Why 1836.11? No one knows.

But we can't blame the Pythagoreans for their lack of knowledge of modern physics. Let us rather consider with astonishment a pupil of Pythagoras by the name of Philolaus of Tarentum. As far as we know, he was the first man in history (about 480 B.C.) to suggest that the Earth moved through space.

Let's try to trace his reasoning. As the Greeks could see, the starry heavens revolved about the Earth. However, seven particular heavenly objects—the Sun, the Moon, Mercury, Venus, Mars, Jupiter, and Saturn—moved independently of the fixed stars and of each other. One might suppose, therefore, that there were eight concentric (and transparent) spheres in the heaven, revolving about the Earth. The innermost contained the Moon affixed to itself, the next Mercury, then Venus, then the Sun, then Mars, Jupiter, Saturn. The eighth and outermost contained the host of stars.

Philolaus was not content with this arrangement. He suggested that the eight spheres did not move about the Earth but about some "central fire." This central fire was invisible, but its reflection could be seen as the Sun. Furthermore, the Earth itself was also fixed in a sphere that revolved about the central fire. And, in addition, there was still *another* body, the "counter-Earth," which we never saw because it stayed always on the side of the Sun opposite ourselves, and that counter-Earth was in still another sphere that revolved about the central fire.

So a total of ten revolving spheres are allowed for in Philolaus' system: the eight ordinary ones, plus a ninth for the Earth, and a tenth for the counter-Earth.

However did Philolaus arrive at that? To be sure, two centuries after his time, Aristarchus of Samos also suggested the Earth moved—but he insisted it moved around the Sun. This was considered absurd at the time, but at least Aristarchus made use of bodies perceptible to the senses. Why did Philolaus invent an invisible central fire and an invisible counter-Earth?

The probable answer rests with the *number* of spheres. If the Earth revolved about the Sun, you would have to add a sphere for the Earth, but subtract one for the now stationary Sun and the total would still be eight. If you keep both Earth and Sun moving about an invisible center and added a counter-Earth, you would have ten.

And why ten spheres? Well, the Pythagoreans thought ten was a particularly satisfactory number because $1 + 2 + 3 + 4 = 10$, something which lent itself to involved reasoning that ended in ten as a perfect number. If, then, we argue that the Universe has to be perfect and that its notion of perfection had to agree with that of the Pythagoreans, and if it were further granted that the Universe had no reason for existence but to exhibit that perfection—then the total number of spheres has to be ten (even though two of the spheres have to be kept secret for some arcane reason).

Unfortunately the trouble with all such irrefutable arguments based on the mystical properties of numbers is that no two people can ever quite bring themselves to believe in the same mystique. The Pythagorean notion went out of the window and astronomers contented themselves with eight spheres. Indeed, since the starry sphere was dismissed as mere background, the magic number became seven.

Arguments concerning the structure of the Universe, based on simple arithmetic (and worse) did not die out with the Greeks, by any means.

In 1610 Galileo, using the telescope, discovered that Jupiter had four lesser bodies circling it. This meant that there were eleven bodies (excluding the fixed stars themselves) that circled the Earth according to the old Greek system—or eleven bodies circling the Sun, according to the new-fangled Copernican system.

Great was the opposition to this new discovery, and the arguments against it by one adversary will live forever in the history of human folly.

It was not necessary, explained the learned scholar, to look through the telescope. The new bodies could not be there, since there could only be seven bodies circling the Earth (or Sun) and no more. If the additional bodies were seen, it had to be because of a defect in the telescope, because the new bodies *could not* be there.

And how could one be sure they could not be there? Easy! As there are seven openings in the head—two eyes, two ears, two nostrils, and a mouth—so there must be seven planetary bodies in the heavens.

Thus, it seemed, it was necessary to so order the entire Universe as to make some sort of permanent record in the heavens as to the number of openings in the human head. It was as though God needed crib notes that would enable him to keep the figure in mind so that he wouldn't create Man with the wrong number of openings. (I'm sorry if that sounds blasphemous, for I don't mean it to be so. The blasphemy is on the part of those men, past and present, who try to make it appear that God is a kindergarten infant, playing with number blocks.)

Such folly dies hard. In fact, it never dies.

Astronomers, having accepted the Copernican notion of bodies circling the Sun rather than the Earth, now recognized two classes of bodies in the Solar System.

There were bodies that revolved directly about the Sun; these were the planets and in 1655, six were recognized— Mercury, Venus, Earth, Mars, Jupiter, and Saturn. Then, there were bodies that revolved not about the Sun directly, but about one of the planets. These were the satellites and there were five of them recognized at the time: our own Moon and the four satellites of Jupiter, which Galileo had discovered (Io, Europa, Ganymede, and Callisto).

But in 1655 the Dutch astronomer Christian Huygens discovered a satellite of Saturn which he named Titan. That meant the Solar System consisted of six planets and six satellites. Huygens was a first-class scientist and a great figure in the history of astronomy and physics, but he wasn't proof against the symmetry of six and six. He announced that the total was complete. No more bodies remained to be found.

Alas, in 1671 the Italian-French astronomer Giovanni D. Cassini discovered another satellite of Saturn and spoiled the symmetry. Huygens lived to see it, too. Indeed, he lived to see Cassini discover three more satellites of Saturn.

Then we have Johann Kepler, who was not content with merely working out the number of heavenly bodies on the basis of simple arithmetic. He went a step further and tried to work out the relationships among the distances of those bodies from the Sun by interconnection with simple geometry.

There are five and only five regular solids (solids with all faces equal and all angles equal—as is true, for instance, of the cube, the most familiar of the five).

Why not reason as follows, then? The regular solids are

perfect and so is the Universe. There are just five regular solids and, since there are six planets, there are just five interplanetary gaps.

Kepler therefore attempted to nest the five regular solids in such a way that the six planets moved along the various boundaries in the proper relationship of distances. Kepler spent a lot of time trying to adjust his solids and failed. (The acid test, that makes Kepler a great deal more than a crackpot, is that, having failed, he promptly dropped the notion.)

During the last week of 1966, however, I discovered something about Kepler I had not known before.

I was attending a meeting of the American Association for the Advancement of Science and was listening to papers on the history of astronomy. One particularly interesting paper included the statement that Kepler had felt that there ought to be just 360 days in a year. The Earth was rotating faster than it should have been, which was what made the number of days in the year 365¼. (If the day were 24 hours and 21 minutes long, there would be just 360 days in the year.)

This too-fast rotation of the Earth, in Kepler's view, somehow carried over to the Moon, forcing it to revolve a bit too quickly about the Earth. Obviously the moon should be revolving about the Earth in just $\frac{1}{12}$ of a year; that is, in about 30⅖ days. Instead, it revolved in only about 29½ days.

If the Earth revolved about the Sun in 360 days of 24⅓ hours apiece (naturally, the hours and its subdivisions would be slightly lengthened to make just 24 hours to the slightly longer day), how convenient that would be. After all, 360 is such a pleasant number, being exactly divisible by 2, 3, 4, 5, 6, 8, 9, 10, 12, 15, 18, 20, 24, 30, 36, 40, 45, 60, 72, 90, 120, and 180. No other number approximating its size is evenly divisible in so many different ways.

And if each lunar month were equal to 30 days of a little over 24 hours each, there would be exactly 12 lunar months in a year. The number 12 is evenly divisible by 2, 3, 4, and 6; and 30 by 2, 3, 5, 6, 10, and 15.

Nor is it just a matter of tricks of numbers. With 30 days to the lunar month and 12 lunar months to the year, a beautifully simple calendar could be devised.

Instead, what do we have? About 29½ days to a lunar month, about 365¼ days to a year, and about 12⅜ lunar months to the year. And the result of this farrago of fractions? Nearly five thousand years of fiddling with calendars that has ended with one that is *still* inconvenient.

My thoughts might have ended there, but the lecturer at the AAAS meeting gave the number of lunar months in the year in decimal form rather than fractions. He said, "Instead of 12 lunar months to a year, there are 12.369." *

My eyebrows raised in astonishment at once. Indeed? Are there really 12.369 lunar months in a year? My mind began fitting notions together and at the conclusion of the lecture I raised my hand to ask a question. I wanted to know if Kepler had tried to draw a certain simple deduction from that figure. No, said the lecturer, it sounds like something Kepler might have done, but he didn't.

Excellent! Excellent! That left me free to indulge in a little mysticism of my own. After all, every one knows I am in love with figures, and I could easily design the Universe in order to show off first-grade arithmetic. What's more, I happen to be interested in the Bible, so why not show that the design of the Universe is connected with certain elementary statistics involving the Bible?

(I am not without precedent here. Isaac Newton was an indefatigable Biblical student who produced nothing worthy of note; and the Scottish mathematician John Napier, who first worked out logarithms, also worked out a completely worthless system for interpreting the Book of Revelation.)

Let me, therefore, go along with Kepler. Let us suppose that the whole purpose of the rate of Earth's rotation about its axis, the Moon's revolution about the Earth, and the revolution of the Earth/Moon system about the Sun, is to present mankind with pretty numbers and a symmetrical calendar.

What, then, went wrong? Surely God knew what he was doing and would not make a careless mistake. If the year were more than 360 days long there would have to be a reason for it; an exact reason. The error would be no error

* Actually, this is wrong, I think. According to the best figures I can find, the number of lunar months in a year is closer to 12.368. It is 12.36827, to be exact. But let's not spoil my chapter.

but would be something designed to instruct mankind in the simple-minded manner that mystics seem to like to consider characteristic of God.

There are 365¼ days in a year so that the excess over 360 (the "right" number) is 5¼ or, in decimal form, 5.25. You must admit now that 5.25 is an interesting number since 25 is the square of 5.

Let's reason like a mystic. Can 5.25 be a coincidence? Of course not. It must have meaning and that meaning must be in the Bible. (After all, God is the center about which the Bible revolves as the Sun is the center about which the Earth revolves. What is more natural than to find in the revolving Bible the reasons for the details of the revolving Earth.)

The Old Testament, according to tradition, is divided into three parts: the Law, the Prophets, and the Writings. All are holy and inspired, but the Law is the most sacred portion and that is made up of the first five books of the Bible: Genesis, Exodus, Leviticus, Numbers and Deuteronomy.

Why, then, are there five days beyond the "proper" 360? Surely in order to mark the five books of the Law in the very motions of the Earth. And why the extra quarter day beyond the five? Why, to make the excess not merely 5 but 5.25. By squaring the 5 and emphasizing it in that fashion, the Law is demonstrated to be not only holy, but particularly holy.

Of course, there is a catch. The length of the year is not really precisely 365.25 days. It is a bit short of that, and is 365.2422 days long. (To be even more precise it is 365.242197 days long, but 365.2422 is close enough, surely.)

Does that mean that the whole scheme falls to the ground? If you think so, you don't know how the mind of a mystic works. The Bible is so large and complex a book that almost any conceivable number can be made to have a Biblical significance. The only limit is the ingenuity of the human mind.

Let's, for instance, take a look at 365.2422. The excess over the "proper" 360 is 5.2422. The figures to the right of the decimal point can be broken up into 24 and 22 and the average is 23. What, then, is the significance of the 23?

We have settled that the 5 represents the five books of the Law. That leaves the Prophets and the Writings. How many books are contained in those? The answer is 34.*

That doesn't seem to get us anywhere—but wait. Twelve of the books are relatively short prophetic works: Hosea, Joel, Amos, Obadiah, Jonah, Micah, Nahum, Habakkuk, Zephaniah, Haggai, Zechariah and Malachi. For convenience, in ancient times, these were often included in a single roll which was referred to as the Book of the Twelve.

Thus, in the apocryphal book of Ecclesiasticus (accepted as canonical by the Catholics) the author—writing about 180 B.C.—lists the great men of Biblical history. After mentioning the major prophets individually, he lumps the minor prophets together:

> Ecclesiasticus 49:10. *And of the twelve prophets let the memorial be blessed* . . .

Well, then, if the twelve minor prophets be included as a single book—as there is ample precedent for doing—how many books are there in the Prophets and Writings together by the Jewish/Protestant count? Why, 23.

We can therefore say that of the number of days in the year (365.2422), 360 days represent the "correct" figure, 5 days represent the Law, and 0.2422 represent the Prophets and the Writings. The days of the year thus become a memorial to the Old Testament.

That takes us to the number of lunar months in the year, which is 12.369, the number that first attracted my attention.

If the days in the year represent the Old Testament, then surely the lunar months in the year must represent the New Testament. Any mystic will tell you that this is self-evident.

Well, then, what can we say would be a central difference between the Old Testament and the New Testament? We might try this: In the Old Testament, God is treated as a single entity while in the New Testament, He is revealed as

---

* At least according to Jews and Protestants. The Roman Catholic version of the Bible includes eight additional books considered apocryphal by Jews and Protestants.

a Trinity. Consequently if this is so, and if the number of lunar months in a year represents the New Testament, that number should somehow be related to the number 3.

And if we look at 12.369, we see that it is neatly divisible by 3. Hurrah! We are on the right track, as any fool can plainly see (provided he *is* a fool, of course).

Let us, then, divide 12.369 by 3, and we come out with 4.123. Surely that is a highly significant number, consisting, as it does of, the first four integers.

And what connection do the first four integers have with the New Testament? Why the answer is obvious and springs to the mind at once.

The four gospels, of course! The four separate biographies of Jesus by Matthew, Mark, Luke and John.

It so happens that Gospels 1, 2 and 3—Matthew, Mark and Luke—give essentially the same view of Jesus. Many of the incidents found in one are found in the others and the general trend of events is virtually identical in all. These are the "synoptic Gospels," the word "synoptic" meaning "with one eye." Gospels 1, 2 and 3 all see Jesus with the same eye, so to speak.

Gospel 4, that of John, is quite different from the other three; differing, in fact, on almost every point, even quite basic ones.

Therefore, if we are going to have the number of lunar months in the year signify the Gospels, would it not be right to group 1, 2 and 3 together and keep 4 separate? And is this not precisely what is done in a number like 4.123?

If you had doubts before, would you not admit we were on the right track now?

We can say then that of the number of lunar months in a year, 12.369, the 12 represents the Gospel of John (4 times 3, for the Trinity) and the 0.369 represent the Synoptic Gospels (123 times 3).

But why is the Fourth Gospel first? Why is a third of the number of lunar months in a year 4.123, rather than 123.4?

This is a good and legitimate question and I have an answer. If the central fact of the New Testament is the Trinity, we must ask how the matter of the Trinity is handled in the various Gospels.

The first evidence of the existence of all three aspects of

God together is at the time of Jesus' baptism by John the Baptist (who, of course, is *not* the John who wrote the Fourth Gospel). In Mark, the oldest of the Gospels, the incident at the baptism is described as follows:

> Mark 1:10. *And . . . he* [Jesus] *saw the heavens opened, and the Spirit like a dove descending upon him:*
> Mark 1:11. *And there came a voice from heaven, saying, Thou art my beloved Son, in whom I am well pleased.*

Here Father, Son and Holy Spirit are all present at once. Nothing in this account, however, would make us necessarily think that this manifestation was apparent to anyone outside the Trinity. There is nothing to make us suppose, for instance (if Mark only is considered), that John the Baptist, who was present at that moment, was also aware of the descent of the Spirit, or heard the voice from heaven.

Similar accounts are given in Matthew 3:16–17, and in Luke 3:22. Neither in Matthew nor in Luke is it stated that anyone outside the Trinity was aware of what was happening.

In John's Gospel, however, the Fourth, the account of the descent of the Spirit is placed in the mouth of John the Baptist.

> John 1:32. *And John bare record, saying, I saw the Spirit descending from heaven like a dove, and it abode upon him.*

Since, in Gospel 4, the first manifestation of the Trinity is described as clearly apparent to man, something that is not so in Gospels 1, 2 and 3, then obviously the number *ought* to be 4.123, rather than 123.4.

What more can anyone want?

Now let me emphasize something I hope has been quite apparent to everyone. I am merely playing with numbers. What I have presented here in connection with the days and months in the year has been made up out of my head, and I am no more serious about it than I was, once long ago, about the alphabeticity of Abou ben Adhem.

And yet I would not be in the least surprised to find that some people were tempted to think there was something to all this nonsense. They might wonder if I had accidentally stumbled on a great truth without knowing it, even while I was imagining myself to be doing nothing more than playing silly games.

And I suppose that some people (maybe even the same people) would say: "Hey, I'll bet Abou ben Adhem's name led all the rest because the list *was* in alphabetical order."

PART 10
SHORT SHORTS

YOU CAN WELL IMAGINE that my writing very largely fills up my life.

Still when the large chunks; books, major articles, long-ish stories; are all put together, there are little chinks left in the interestices. I suppose I could use those little chinks to give me time to sit back and let my eyes glaze over, but I find it more restful to write small items. You might almost call them fillers.

For instance, every month I write a little 500-word arti-cle for Science Digest, *answering some question asked by a reader. It is placed in a department called "Isaac Asimov Explains." Since no limits are set on the questions (except for those imposed by my own finite knowledge and my own finite ingenuity in devising an answer that will fit into 500 words) I am sometimes forced to set myself some unusual and, therefore, interesting tasks.*

I have explained the meaning of relativity, for instance, also the significance of parity, the nature of time, and so on—and done each in 500 words. What's more, a question is angled at me, sometimes, that is clearly elicited by the fact that I am known to be a science-fiction writer. Here is one of them, as an example:

from "Isaac Asimov Explains" (*1968*)

In many science-fiction stories I read about "force fields" and "hyperspace." What are these and do they really exist?

Every subatomic particle gives rise to one or more of four different kinds of influences. These are the gravitational, electromagnetic, weak nuclear, and strong nuclear. Each influence spreads out from its source of origin as a "field" that, in theory, pervades the entire universe. Similar fields from large numbers of particles can add their separate influences and produce terrifically intense resultant fields. Thus, the gravitational field is by far the weakest of the four, but the gravitational field of the Sun, a body made up of so vast a number of particles, is enormous.

Two particles within such a field may be made to move toward each other or away from each other, depending on the nature of the particles and of the field and with an acceleration depending on how far apart they are. Such accelerations are usually interpreted as caused by "forces," so we speak of "force fields." In this sense, they really exist.

The force fields we know, however, always have matter as their source and don't exist in the absence of matter. In science-fiction stories, on the other hand, it is often useful to imagine the construction of strong force fields without matter. One can then have a section of vacuum which will serve as a barrier to particles and radiation just as though it were a solid piece of steel six feet thick. It would have all the interatomic forces but none of the atoms that give rise to those forces. Such "matter-free force fields" are a convenient science-fictional device but, alas, have no basis in the science we know today.

"Hyperspace" is another convenient science-fictional device; one intended to get around the speed-of-light barrier.

To see how it works, think of a large, flat sheet of paper on which there are two dots six feet apart. Next, imagine an extremely slow snail that can only travel a foot an hour. Clearly, it will take him six hours to travel from one dot to the other.

But suppose we bend the essentially two-dimensional sheet of paper through the third dimension, so as to bring the two dots close together. If they are now only a tenth of an inch apart and if the snail can somehow cross the air gap between the two ends of the piece of paper which have been curved toward each other in this fashion, he can go from one dot to the other in just a half minute.

Now for the analogy. If two stars are fifty light-years apart, then a spaceship going at maximum speed, that of light, will take fifty years to go from one to the other (relative to someone in either one of these star systems). This creates a great many complications, and science-fiction writers find they can simplify their plots if they pretend that the essentially three-dimensional structure of space can be folded through a fourth spatial dimension so that the stars are separated by only a small fourth-dimensional gap. The ship then crosses this gap and goes from one star to the other in a very short period of time.

It is customary for mathematicians to speak of objects with four dimensions by referring to analogous three-dimensional objects and adding the prefix "hyper," a Greek expression meaning "above," "over," or "beyond." An object whose surface is equally distant from the center in all four dimensions is a "hypersphere." Similarly, we can have a "hypertetrahedron," "hypercube," and a "hyperellipsoid." Using this convention, we can speak of the four-dimensional gap between the stars as "hyperspace."

But, alas, however convenient hyperspace may be to the science-fiction writer, there is nothing in the science we know to show that it exists as anything but a mathematical abstraction.

Since I have the final choice in answering questions, I sometimes elect to answer one not because it is important but because of some utterly extraneous reason.

For instance, on February 14, 1942, I met the young lady who was later to become my wife. (Yes, it was Valentine's Day, but that was thoroughly coincidental.) At the time I was quite young and totally impecunious. I had neither money, looks, presence, style, or any of the obvious qualities that would be expected to attract a girl who was the precise image of Olivia de Havilland.

I had to depend rather strongly on my possession of a high IQ. I felt, after all, that there might be two or three girls on Earth who would feel the stirrings of mad passion at a vision of intellect and—who knows—this might be one of them.

I therefore dropped casual hints to the effect that I was working toward my Ph.D., that I was writing and selling science fiction, and so on. It seemed to make little impact.

But once, on a rather unusually balmy April evening in 1942, when we were walking down Fifth Avenue, she asked me, "What happens if an irresistible force meets an immovable body?"

She may just have been making idle conversation or per-

*haps may have felt a perverse impulse to squelch my intel-
lectual arrogance. However, I answered her without hesitation and she said, "I never* dreamed *there was a sensible
answer to that."*

We were married on July 26, 1942.

*Naturally, when the question arose again in connection
with "Isaac Asimov Explains," I fell all over myself to
write an answer:*

from "Isaac Asimov Explains" *(1968)*

*What would happen if an irresistible force met an immov-
able body?*

This is a classic "puzzler" over which uncounted millions
of arguments must have rolled their wordy way.

Before I give you my solution, however, let's make a few
things clear. The game of exploring the universe by rational
techniques, like any other game, must be played according
to the rules. If two people are going to talk meaningfully
together, they must agree on what the symbols they use
(words or otherwise) are to be taken as meaning, and their
comments must make sense in terms of that meaning.

All questions that do not make sense in terms of the
definitions agreed upon are thrown out of court. There is
no answer because the question must not be asked.

For instance, suppose I asked the question, "How much
does justice weigh?" (I might be thinking, perhaps, of the
figure of a blinded Justice with scales in her hand.)

But weight is a property of mass and only material things
have mass. (Indeed, matter may be most simply defined as
"That which has mass.")

Justice is not a material thing, but an abstraction. By
definition, mass is not one of its properties, so that to ask
the weight of justice is to pose a meaningless question. It
requires no answer.

Again, it is possible, by a series of very simple algebraic
manipulations, to show that $1 = 2$. The only trouble is that
in the course of this demonstration, we must divide by zero.
In order to avoid such an inconvenient equality (to say
nothing of a number of other demonstrations that would
destroy the usefulness of mathematics) mathematicians

have decided to make division by zero inadmissible in any mathematical manipulation. The question then: "What is the value of the fraction 2/0?" violates the rules of the game and is meaningless. It requires no answer.

Now we are ready for our irresistible force and our immovable body.

An "irresistible force" is, by definition (if words are to have any meaning at all), a force that cannot be resisted; a force that will move or destroy any body it encounters, *however great*, without being perceptibly weakened or deflected. In any universe which contains an irresistible force, there can be no such thing as an immovable body, since we have just defined an irresistible force as capable of moving *anything*.

An "immovable body" is, by definition (if words are to have any meaning at all), a body that cannot be moved; a body that will absorb any force it encounters, *however great*, without being perceptibly changed or damaged by the encounter. In any universe which contains an immovable body, there can be no such thing as an irresistible force, since we have just defined an immovable body as capable of resisting *any* force.

If we ask a question that implies the simultaneous existence of both an irresistible force and an immovable body, we are violating the definitions implied by the phrases themselves. This is not allowed by the rules of the game of reason. The question, "What would happen if an irresistible force met an immovable body?" is therefore meaningless and requires no answer.

You might wonder if definitions can be so carefully made that no unanswerable questions can ever be asked. The answer, surprisingly enough, is "No!" Mathematicians have shown that it is impossible to devise any mathematical system that will not permit unanswerable questions. But that is another story.

Another category of brief in-betweens arises in connection with the introductions I write to other people's books. I get involved, usually, because someone asks me who is a friend of mine, or the friend of a friend, or the friend of a relative, or the relative of a friend. Apparently, these groups include nearly all the population of the globe and I've never worked out an efficient way to refuse friends, relatives, and their adjuncts.

I make up for it by trying to think up an introduction in which I manage to say something that strikes me as interesting. After all, I have to read the stuff as it comes out of the typewriter and I can't very well toss off something inconsequential and tepid as the least-effort way of fulfilling a commitment. I hate reading things that are inconsequential and tepid and, while a reader of a book can always skip the introduction, the writer of that introduction can't.

Here's one, for instance, that was placed in a science-fiction anthology entitled Future Tense, *edited by Richard Curtis:*

"On Prediction" (1968)

The matter of prediction is full of pitfalls.

For instance, if a new scientific theory is to prove a useful one, it ought to predict phenomena that are unexpected or even downright "impossible" by older theories. If the prediction is found to be accurate then that is a great point in favor of the new theory.

But is the prediction sufficient in itself to "prove" the new theory?—Not at all. Not if other aspects remain unacceptable.

For instance, I hereby propose a new theory to the effect that nylon is repelled by gravitational force and that anything made out of nylon will therefore fall upward. In line with this theory, I will predict that if you make a parachute of nylon and connect yourself to it by a harness and then jump from a plane, you will fall very slowly because gravitational repulsion will be pushing up against the nylon.

If you care to try the experiment you will find that this prediction is absolutely correct and goes flatly against old Galileo's statement that all objects fall at the same rate. Does that mean that nylon is *really* repelled by gravitation?

Of course not. What Galileo really said was that all objects fall at the same rate *in a vacuum* and, by taking air resistance into account, we can explain the parachute effect without postulating gravitational repulsion. Besides the one prediction that comes true is balanced by others that emphatically do not. A nylon object left to itself will *not* fall upward.

Or take the predictions of Immanuel Velikovsky. He advanced a theory that at the time of the Biblical Exodus, Jupiter expelled a comet which passed close to the Earth, caused the plagues of Egypt, stopped the Earth's rotation, affected its orbit, and did many more things before settling down to become the planet Venus. In line with all this, Velikovsky predicted that Venus would be found to be hotter than astronomers suspected and, by golly, he was right.

Does that mean that because of this correct prediction, we must accept the whole of Velikovsky's theories? Of course not. There remain many aspects of it (very many) which are extremely dubious in the light of modern theory. Astronomers will therefore try to explain Venus' temperature in various non-absurd ways before accepting Velikovsky, and it is my calm prediction that they will succeed.

But then if Velikovsky's theory is not correct, how did he know Venus was hot? Well, I know it's very frustrating, but coincidences can take place and if an intelligent, imaginative man makes many predictions, some of them are bound to be close enough to the truth (usually in a very primitive way), to cause innocents to suspect that all the other predictions are true, too.

For instance, the alchemists thought lead could be transmuted to gold and nineteenth-century chemists laughed at the whole idea. Twentieth-century chemists, however, succeeded in carrying through numerous transmutations of one element into another.

Aha!!! Can we not deduce from that that those old alchemists were smart cookies; that they knew what they were doing; that they had access to ancient secrets we have lost?

But how about telling the whole story. Alchemists thought lead could be transmuted to gold by ordinary chemical procedures like heating and distilling and mixing and muttering spells. We do it now by particle accelerators and nuclear reactors. The two sets of methods bear no relationship and merely to dream of a goal is no sign of preternatural knowledge of the eventually discovered methods of reaching that goal.

And so it is with predictions in fiction.

One can find lots of "predictions" in fiction if one looks assiduously enough and trustingly enough.

In the Greek myths, Daedalus invented feathered wings held together by wax, with which he and his son, Icarus, could fly through the air. Was that not a prediction of modern airplanes? Admittedly, we use metal and welding instead of feathers and wax but isn't the principle the same?

Again, in the Norse myths, the world was foreseen as coming to an end in the great Twilight of the Gods. And now science tells us that the world will come to an end when the Sun enters its red giant phase about eight billion years hence.

May we assume from that that the shaggy Norsemen of old had somehow figured out modern astrophysics?

Will anyone who believes that raise his hand?

And if we go through the fairy tales, we will come across flying carpets (helicopters?), seven-league boots (railroads?), magic (electronic instruments?), oracles (computers?), wicked demons (Nazis?), and anything else you want.

But, you know, the fantasts and mythmakers of the past were not trying for predictions. They were allegorizing or wishing.

Nowadays, though, we have science fiction, and what makes science fiction different from all previous types of fantasy literature, is that the science-fiction writer disciplines his imagination. Anything does *not* go. Only that goes that fits science as we know it today or as that science can be plausibly extrapolated. With that in mind, prediction really becomes prediction and not accident.

To be sure, it is not the first duty of the science-fiction writer to predict the future. His first duty is to write an entertaining story, which matches the structure of science or, at the very least, does not betray an ignorance of the structure of science.

In doing so, though, it is almost impossible for him not to draw a picture which is the equivalent of a prediction of some facet of future technology or sociology. And if an intelligent writer, with a competent understanding of science, does this, then, every once in a while, the prediction hews so close to the eventual course of history, as to come true.

This anthology is a sampling of stories in which the cloudy crystal ball cleared for a moment to allow a writer to look ahead and see what was to be—tanks, atomic bombs, television, communications satellites.

And as we read we must ask ourselves: What inventions or social phenomena being discussed in science fiction right now will come true a generation from now? Care to guess?

Still another grouping of short pieces comes under the heading of book reviews, a form of writing I never do willingly. There are three reasons for my reluctance, one of which is rather discreditable to myself. In the interests of frankness, I shall give all three, including the discreditable one.

First, I don't believe that a review should be written on the basis of what is said in the flap material or on what appears in the first five pages. I have read too many reviews of my own books which arrive at their inspiration in this way. I feel cheated in such cases and I feel prospective readers are cheated as well. This means that when I myself get a book for review, I must read the whole thing, and with reasonable care, too, and this means spending considerable time which I can often ill afford.

Second, I have some serious question as to the ethics of book reviewing. (I told you I have a troublesome and simpleminded set of ethics.) I quite understand that it is useful to warn the book-buying public in advance as to the contents and purposes of a book and even, in the opinion of the reviewer, its quality. (A review that tells certain readers enough about my books to let them know in advance they won't like them does me a favor. A reader who is conned into buying one of my books and hating it, not only will never buy another but he will be a constant source of word-of-mouth adverse opinion. Better not to make the sale in the first place.)

However, reviews of specialized books are often handed out to other individuals who specialize in that field. (Who else, after all, is competent to review?) When that happens, a reviewer finds himself compelled to speak either good or evil of a friend or rival. Can he ever be sure of objectivity? Will he be trying to do a friend a favor or a rival an injury? Will he lean over backward into reverse prejudice?

I'm as confident of my own integrity as it is reasonably possible to be but I see no reason to put it to unnecessary tests. For that reason, I have always refused to review science-fiction books, all of which are written by people who are simultaneously friends and rivals. Nonfiction I do review when pushed into it, but always with a twinge.

The third reason is the discreditable one. When I review a book favorably, passages from that review are often used in the promotional material for the book. And when that happens I get to feeling sorry for myself, since it seems unfair to me that I am boosting other peoples' books when my own are so very rarely reviewed under conditions of the slightest prominence.

This is thoroughly foolish of me, for since I turn out six to eight books a year I can scarcely expect to get the treatment accorded to someone whose book is an "event." I strongly suspect that most book-review editors have grown so calloused through watching my books come out every other month that they no longer see them. Besides, my books sell with nice regularity even without prominent reviews, so what is hurt except my own self-love?

Unfortunately, self-love is immune to rational arguments and I still get to feeling sorry for myself. About the only thing I can do to counter it is to write book reviews on occasion anyway on the principle that it is permissible to have silly weaknesses, but that it is not permissible to give in to them.

Naturally, though, I do try to pick books which I think will mean something to me so that when I review it I can also speak my mind, as, for instance, in the following review:

"An Uncompromising View" (*1968*)

Mechanical Man, The Physical Basis of Intelligent Life. Dean E. Wooldridge. McGraw–Hill Book Co., New York. 1968. 212 pp. $8.95.

This book is comparatively brief, not because it covers little ground, but because it covers a great deal with remarkable conciseness.

Its thesis rests in the proper interpretation of the ambiguous title. It deals not with the construction or theory of robots, but with the view that man himself—*you*, for instance—is a machine.

To make this point, Dr. Wooldridge moves systematically through the field of biology, passing from the abandoned outposts of vitalism, inward, ever inward, to the very heart of its still staunchly-manned core-fortress.

Addressing himself to the educated layman, he begins with proteins and nucleic acids and the great, if recent, victory over the genetic code. Having taken care of the molecules, he moves on to the cellular level and discusses the nervous system. From there, in unfaltering strides, he gives us a fascinating section at the organ level, for he takes up the brain. And in doing so, he takes up the computer, too, recognizing no fundamental difference between what the brain does and what the computer does (granting different levels of complexity *at present*). Then, on to the whole organism and its feeling of "consciousness," and to the final goal of society where such philosophical and sociological questions as free will and religion are considered.

The details are not new and at no point is the account so deep and detailed that one may feel educated in that particular aspect of biology. To present details or a biological education is clearly not the intent of the author.

What he is putting across, rather, is an attitude; and one that needs presentation, all the more so because it still rouses primitive fears and antagonisms.

The history of the intellectual progress of mankind can very nearly be made into an account of the slow abandonment of anthropocentrism. In astronomy, there is the successive abandonment of the Earth, then the Sun, as the center of the universe; in biology, there is the tardy realization that the plant and animal kingdoms were not primarily created for the service of man; in geology, there is the reluctant understanding that the physical Earth did not begin concurrently with human civilization; and so on, and so on, and so on.

Yet one harsh centric area remains. No matter how we gain knowledge concerning tropisms and reflexes—condi-

tioning and imprinting—most of us persist in thinking
that even if lower animals such as worms and insects can
be considered as acting in mechanical fashion and as
though they were being directed by (admittedly very complicated and successful miniaturized) computers—this is
not so in the case of the higher animals, and it is particularly not so in the case of man.

We have free will; *we* have consciousness; *we* decide
what to do of our own volition; *we* choose and select and
consider and ponder and create. It is almost an article
of faith that this goes beyond the purely mechanical fulfillment of blindly interlocking atoms and molecules and
that no machine can therefore be made into a man.

And yet the brain is made up of atoms and molecules
and nothing more. There is nothing in the most magnificent
human brain but the matter it contains. If there is something called a "mind" or "personality" or even "soul," it is
but a subjective interpretation of the consequences of the
working of that matter, and we can learn about these
mysterious words only by studying the matter.

At the 1967 AAAS meetings there was a ponderous
symposium discussing whether the human brain could be
understood in terms of the laws of physics and chemistry,
and the consensus was that it could not. This was an appall-
ing surrender to long-standing prejudice and, in my view,
represented a "failure of nerve." The coming century, I
trust, will demonstrate this, and Dr. Wooldridge's book—
cool, concise, and absolutely uncompromising in its material view of man's mind—reinforces that trust.

*Even in my fiction writing, I sometimes write a very short
piece to fill a scrap of time. I have written an occasional
"vignette" 500 words long or less. Such tiny pieces consist entirely of endings, to be sure, building up to the final
shock in the last line.*

*I myself am a devotee of the pun as final shock. This
penchant for punning and wordplay which I have induces
considerable unpopularity for myself at social gatherings,
you can well imagine. It was only two nights ago that I told
some friends of mine, Mr. and Mrs. Mamber, that if they
had a daughter they ought to name her Rebekah. Naturally,
they asked why, and I said that she would be known by*

the nickname, "Ree," and would then be "Ree Mamber."

I was ostracised for the rest of the evening.

Anyway, the first vignette I wrote depended for its effect on a perfectly deplorable pun in the last line, and one which makes its maximum impact on devotees of old-fashioned science fiction. I wrote it in such a way that the last line was by itself at the top of the final page of the manuscript, so that Anthony Boucher (who was then editor of F & SF *and who was an outstanding devotee of bad puns and campy science fiction) would not see in advance and find its impact deadened.*

It worked perfectly. He turned to the last page, not seeing what I was getting at, and the pun hit him dead center. Here is the vignette, in full:

"Dreamworld" (1955)

At thirteen, Edward Keller had been a science-fiction devotee for four years. He bubbled with Galactic enthusiasm.

His Aunt Clara, who had brought him up by rule and rod in pious memory of her deceased sister, wavered between toleration and exasperation. It appalled her to watch him grow so immersed in fantasy.

"Face reality, Eddie," she would say, angrily.

He would nod, but go on, "And I dreamed Martians were chasing me, see? I had a special death ray, but the atomic power unit was pretty low and—"

Every other breakfast consisted of eggs, toast, milk, and some such dream.

Aunt Clara said, severely, "Now, Eddie, one of these nights you won't be able to wake up out of your dream. You'll be trapped! Then what?"

She lowered her angular face close to his and glared.

Eddie was strangely impressed by his aunt's warning. He lay in bed, staring into the darkness. He wouldn't like to be trapped in a dream. It was always nice to wake up before it was too late. Like the time the dinosaurs were after him—

Suddenly, he was out of bed, out of the house, out on the lawn, and he knew it was another dream.

The thought was broken by a vague thunder and a shadow that blotted the sun. He looked upward in astonishment and he could make out the human face that touched the clouds.

It was his Aunt Clara! Monstrously tall, she bent toward him in admonition, mastlike forefinger upraised, voice too guttural to be made out.

Eddie turned and ran in panic. Another Aunt Clara monster loomed up before him, voice rumbling.

He turned again, stumbling, panting, heading outward, outward.

He reached the top of the hill and stopped in horror. Off in the distance a hundred towering Aunt Claras were marching by. As the column passed, each one of the Aunt Claras turned her head sharply toward him and the thunderous bass rumbling coalesced into words:

"Face reality, Eddie. Face reality, Eddie."

Eddie threw himself sobbing to the ground. Please wake up, he begged himself. Don't be caught in this dream.

For unless he woke up, the worst science-fictional doom of all would have overtaken him. He would be trapped, *trapped*, in a world of giant aunts.

PART 11
HUMOR

IN SOME WAYS, my most unexpected excursion (to myself, anyway) is into the realm of humor.

For many years, my writings were singularly free of humor, to my own astonishment and rather to that of others as well, for in my social life I am well known as an authentically funny fellow.

Good sense tells me not to say this myself, but I may as well indulge in one of my "delightful Asimovian immodesties"—one more won't kill me any deader than I am by now. The thing is that I am offhandedly witty, I am perfectly capable of telling jokes all evening without repeating myself (clean jokes, yet) and I can give an extemporaneous talk on any subject before any audience and have them in the aisles.

In fact, on those few occasions when I have addressed a scientific convention and given a legitimate scientific talk of the kind that later gets published in a solemn scientific journal—I still have them laughing.

So why is my writing so sober?

I'm not sure. Lack of self-confidence, perhaps. Every once in a while I did write what I considered to be a humorous science-fiction story. I invariably loved it and died laughing when I reread it. In each case I managed to sell it, and in each case a kind of solemn silence swallowed it up and it was never heard of again.

Fortunately, a turning point came in 1962, and it happened after this fashion:

It seems that every year at the annual World Science Fiction Convention, awards are handed out for a variety of categories, in imitation of the well-known Oscar awards of the movie industry. The science-fiction awards are called Hugos after Hugo Gernsback, the editor of the first magazine to be devoted entirely to science fiction. (It was Amaz-

ing Stories *and its first issue was* April, 1926.)

It occurred to Bob Mills, who had earlier been editor of F & SF, succeeding Tony Boucher, and who was now an author's agent, that an anthology of Hugo-winning short stories and novelettes ought to be prepared. As editor of that anthology, he felt, someone should be chosen who had never won a Hugo. The obvious candidate was myself since I had never won a Hugo and yet I was a perennial toastmaster at these Conventions (I told you I am a funny fellow) and had handed out more Hugos to other people than anyone else in the business.

Timothy Seldes, who was then my editor at Doubleday (he was Larry Ashmead's predecessor), was all for it and the proposal was put to me.

I was dubious for a very silly reason. I was already thinking of My Hundredth Book and was almost halfway to the goal. All the books I had written so far were really mine, for even when I published one as a collaboration, most or all of the writing chore was mine (except for the first edition of the biochemistry textbook). An anthology, however, would be primarily the work of others. Could I count a collection of other people's writings as a book of mine just because I had my name on it as editor?

Ordinarily, I might be able to argue that I had had to do a lot of reading and judging and that the book was my creation in that I had selected the stories and arranged them to make an organic whole. I couldn't even say that much in this case, however, since the stories which had won the Hugo were fixed and since they were to appear in chronological order.

So I agreed only on condition that I be able to write a longish introduction to each story and to the book as a whole and give it a kind of atmosphere that would make me feel justified in considering the book—to at least a certain extent—as a creation of my own.

And when I started working on these introductions, why, somehow, they turned out to be funny.

This time (aha!) it worked. At least I received a surprising number of letters from readers who flattered me by telling me that they thought the introductions were the best part of the book.

You can bet that was all the encouragement I needed. Prior to 1962, collections of my own stories appeared bare, *with no editorial comment. After 1962, collections of my stories tended to be surrounded by chatter, usually not-very-serious chatter, and this tendency has increased until it has reached an extreme (for now) in the very volume you are holding.*

So— Does this mean I can write a humorous science-fiction story after all? I decided to try again.

It came about because Esquire magazine was planning a special issue and asked me to contribute. I suggested a satir-ical piece (you see, it was beginning to go to my head) and they agreed, but when I sat down to write the article, it turned into a science-fiction story.

(I can't help it. I tell anyone who listens that there is a little man inside me that does the writing, that he is quite beyond my control, and that I just sit there at the type-writer and read what comes out in utter fascination.)

When I reread what I had written this time, however, I realized that it was a satire on The Double Helix, that excellent book written by James D. Watson, which tells the history of the discovery of the structure of DNA in ut-terly human terms.

The humor in my story depends partly on the reader having read The Double Helix or at least having read about The Double Helix, but so what? Anyone who is sufficiently interested in science fiction or in me to buy this rather heterogeneous mish-mash of a book you are now holding is bound to know about The Double Helix.

But when I sent the story to Esquire, it turned out that either they had never heard of The Double Helix or feared their readers hadn't—so they rejected it. (See, I even get rejects in the year 1968! I'm human!)

I didn't care. I sent it to Fred Pohl, and he took it for his magazine, If.

At least, he took it after a little hesitation. He wrote and said that he would like to cut it in half. (He must have had some obscure reason for that, but who knows what evil lurks in the hearts of editors.)

I wrote back, rather humbly, and said I didn't want to sound like Harlan Ellison (a tremendously talented science-fiction writer who is known throughout the field for his trigger-temper and his refusal to take any lip from any editor), but the story had to be published in toto for two reasons: (1) It was a satire on The Double Helix and the

*satirical point would be killed if it were cut, and (2) it
was the only story I had ever written in which I wrote as
ribaldly as I talk, and I might never do it again, so I didn't
want to lose one precious paragraph.*

*Consequently, said I, if he felt he had to cut it, would
he return the manuscript instead?*

*Whereupon Fred answered and said he would print it
in full and I did, too, sound like Harlan Ellison.*

Which was a terrible thing to say.

*Anyway, here's the story, which concludes the book in
symmetrical fashion. The first inclusion was a piece of the
very first science-fiction story I managed to write and sell;
and the last inclusion is the very latest (so far) science-
fiction story I managed to write and sell—thirty years later.*

"The Holmes-Ginsbook Device" (1968)

I have never seen Myron Ginsbook in a modest mood.

But then, why should I have? Mike—we all call him
Mike, although he is Dr. Ginsbook, Nobel Laureate, to a
reverential world—is a typical product of the twenty-first
century. He is self-confident, as so many of us are, and by
right should be.

He knows the worth of mankind, of society, and most
of all of himself.

He was born on January 1, 2001, so he is as old as the
century exactly. I am ten years younger, that much
farther removed from the unmentionable twentieth.

Oh, I mentioned it sometimes. All youngsters have their
quirks and mine had been a kind of curiosity about mankind's earlier history, concerning which so little is known
and so little, I admit, ought to be known. But I was curious.

It was Mike who rescued me in those days. "Don't," he
would say, leering at the girls as they passed in their bikini
business suits, and leaning over at intervals to feel the
material judiciously, "don't play with the past. Oh, ancient
history isn't bad, nor medieval times, but as soon as we
reach the birth of technology, forget it. From then on it's
scatology; just filth and perversion. You're a creature of
the twenty-first. Be free! Breathe deeply of our century's
clean air! It will do wonders for you. Look at what it's doing for that remarkable girl to your left."

And it was true. Her deep breathing was delightful. Ah, those were great days, when science was pulsing and we two were young, carefree and eager to grab the world by the tail.

Mike was sure he was going to advance science enormously and I felt the same. It was the great dream of all of us in this glorious century, still youthful. It was as though some great voice were crying: *Onward! Onward! Not a glance behind!*

I picked up that attitude from Paul Derrick, the California wizard. He's dead now, but a great man in his time, quite worthy of being mentioned in the same breath with myself.

I was one of his graduate students and it was hard at first. In college, I had carefully selected those courses which had had the least mathematics and the most girls and had therefore learned how to hemstitch with surpassing skill but had, I admit, left myself weak in physics.

After considerable thought, I realized that hemstitching was not going to help me make further advances in our great twenty-first-century technology. The demand for improvements in hemstitching was meager and I could see clearly that my expertise would not lead me to the coveted Nobel Prize. So I pinched the girls good-bye and joined Derrick's seminars.

I understood little at first but I did my best to ask questions designed to help Derrick demonstrate his brilliance and rapidly advanced to the head of the class in consequence. I was even the occasion for Derrick's greatest discovery.

He was smoking at the time. He was an inveterate smoker and proud of it, always taking his cigarette out and looking at it lovingly between puffs. They were girlie-cigarettes, with fetching nudes on the clear white paper—always a favorite with scientists.

"Imagine," he would say in the course of his famous lectures on Twenty-first-Century-Technological Concepts, "how we have advanced on the Dark Ages in the matter of cigarettes alone. Rumors reach us that in the ill-famed twentieth century, cigarettes were a source of disease and air-pollution. The details are not known, of course, and no one, I imagine, would care to find out, yet the rumors are convincing. Now, however, a cigarette liberates air-purifying ingredients into the atmosphere, fills it with a pleasant aroma, and strengthens the health of the smoker. It has, in fact, only one drawback."

Of course, we all knew what it was. I had frequently seen Derrick with a blistered lip, and he had a fresh blister that day. It impeded his speech somewhat.

Like all thoughtful scientists, he was easily distracted by passing girls, and on those occasions he would frequently place his cigarette in his mouth wrong-end-in. He would inhale deeply and the cigarette would spontaneously ignite, with the lit end in his mouth.

I don't know how many learned professors I had seen, in those days, interrupt their intimate conversations with secretaries to yell in agony as another blister was added to tongue or lip.

On this occasion, I said in jest, "Professor Derrick, why don't you remove the igno-tip before putting the cigarette in your mouth?" It was a mild witticism and actually, if I remember correctly, I was the only one who laughed. Yet the picture brought up by the remark was a funny one. Imagine a cigarette without its ignitable tip! How could one smoke it?

But Derrick's eyes narrowed. "Why not?" he said. "Observe!"

In front of the class, Derrick whipped out a cigarette, observed it carefully—his particular brand presented its girlies in lifelike tints—then pinched off the igno-tip.

He held it up between two fingers of his left hand and said again, "Observe!" He placed the unignitable residue of the cigarette in his mouth. A thrill went through us all as we observed from the position of the girlie that he had deliberately placed the cigarette in his mouth wrong-end-in. He inhaled sharply and nothing, of course, happened.

"The unblistering cigarette," he said.

I said, "But you can't light it."

"Can't you?" he said and, with a flourish, brought the igno-tip up against the cigarette. We all caught our breath. It was a sheer stroke of genius, for the igno-tip would light the safe outside end of the cigarette, *whichever end it was.*

Derrick inhaled sharply and the igno-tip flared into life, igniting the outer tip of the cigarette—and the tip of

Derrick's thumb and forefinger. With a howl, he dropped it and naturally, the entire class laughed with great cheerfulness this time.

It was a stroke of misfortune for me. Since I had suggested the miserable demonstration, he kicked me out of his class forever.

This was, of course, unfair, since I had made it possible for him to win the Nobel Prize, though neither of us realized it at the time.

You see, the laughter had driven Derrick to frenzy. He was determined to solve the problem of the unblisterable cigarette. To do so, he bent his giant mind to the problem full time, cutting down his evenings with the girls to five a week—almost unheard of in a scientist, but he was a notorious ascetic.

In less than a year, he had solved the problem. Now that it is over, of course, it seems obvious to all of us, but at the time, I assure you, it dumbfounded the world of science.

The trick was to separate the igno-tip from the cigarette and then devise some way of manipulating the igno-tip safely. For months, Derrick experimented with different shapes and sizes of handles.

Finally, he decided on a thin shaft of wood as ideal for the purpose. Since it was difficult to balance a cigarette-tip on the wood, he discarded the tobacco and paper and made use of the chemicals with which the cigarette tip had been impregnated. These chemicals he coated on the tip of the shaft.

At first, he lost considerable time trying to make the shaft hollow so that it could be sucked or blown through to ignite the chemicals. The resulting fire might then be applied to the cigarette. This, however, revived the original problem. What if one put the wrong end of the shaft in the hand?

Derrick then got his crowning idea. It would only be necessary to increase the temperature of the chemicals by friction, by rubbing the tip of the wood against a rough surface. This was absolutely safe for if, in the course of bestowing a fatherly kiss on the lips of a girl student intent on an A in her course at any hazard—a typical event in every scientist's life—one should rub the wrong end of the wood on a rough surface, nothing at all would happen. It was a perfect failsafe mechanism.

The discovery swept the world. Who, today, is without his package of igno-splints, which can be lit at any time in perfect safety, so that the day of the blistered lip is gone forever? Surely this great invention is a match for any other this great century has seen; so much a match, in fact, that some wags have suggested the igno-splints be called "matches." Actually, that name is catching on.

Derrick received his Nobel Prize in physics almost at once and the world applauded.

I returned then and tried to re-enroll in his class, pointing out that but for me he would never have earned that Nobel Prize. He kicked me out with harsh expletives, threatening to apply an igno-splint to my nose.

After that my one ambition was to win a Nobel Prize of my own, one that would drown out Derrick's achievement. I, John Holmes, would show him.

But how? How?

I managed to get a grant that would take me to England in order to study Lancashire hemstitching, but I had no sooner got there than I pulled every string I could to get into Cambridge, with its famous covey of girl students and its almost equally famous Chumley-Maudlin (pronounced Cholmondeley–Magdalen) Technological Institute.

The girl students were warm and exotic and I spent many an evening stitching hems with them. Many of the Cantabrigian scientists were struck with the usefulness of the pursuit, not having discerned earlier this particular advantage of sewing. Some of them tried to get me to teach them to hemstitch but I followed that old First Law of Scientific Motivation: "What's in it for me?" I didn't teach them a thing.

Mike Ginsbook, however, having watched me from a distance, quickly picked up the intricate finger-manipulations of hemstitching and joined me.

"It's my talent," he said with charming immodesty. "I have a natural aptitude at manipulation."

He was my man! I recognized at that moment that he would help me to the Nobel Prize. There remained only to choose the field of activity that would get it for us.

For a year our association produced nothing except for

a sultry brunette or two; and then one day I said to him lazily, "I can't help but notice, Mike, that your eyes are extraordinarily limpid. You're the only one on campus who doesn't have bloodshot sclera."

He said, "But the answer is simple. I never view microfilms. They are a curse."

"Oh?"

"I've never told you?" A somber look crossed his face and a clear stab of pain furrowed his brow. I had clearly activated a memory almost too sharp to bear. He said, "I was once viewing a microfilm with my head completely enclosed in the viewer, naturally. While I was doing that, a gorgeous girl passed by—a girl who won the title of Miss Teacher's Pet the next two years running, I might say—and I never noticed her. I was told about it afterward by Tancred Hull, the gynecologist. He spent three nights with her, the cad, explaining that he was giving her a physical checkup. Had pictures taken to prove it that were the talk of Cambridge."

Mike's lips were quivering. "From that time on," he said in a low, suffering voice, "I have vowed never to view a film again."

I was almost faint with the sudden inspiration that struck me. "Mike," I said, "might there not be some way in which microfilms can be viewed more simply? Look, films are covered with microscopic print. That print has to be enlarged for us to see it. That means bending over an immobile screen or encasing the head in a viewer.

"But—" and I could hardly breathe with the excitement of it—"what if the material on the film were enlarged until it could be seen with the naked eye and then a photograph of the enlarged print were taken? You could carry the photograph with you, looking at it at your leisure whenever you chose. Why, Mike, if you were looking at such a photo and a girl passed by, it would be the work of a moment to lift your head. The photo would not take up your attention as a viewer would."

"Hmm," said Mike, thoughtfully. I could see his giant mind spinning over every ramification of the subject. "It really might not interfere with girl-watching; less important, it might prevent bloodshot eyes. Oh, but wait, all you would have would be about five or six hundred words and you would be bound to read that through before the day was over. Then what?"

It was amazing to watch him pick unerringly the flaw in the project.

For a moment, I was daunted. I hadn't thought of that. Then I said, "Perhaps you could make a large series of small photographs and paste them together in order. Of course, that might be more difficult to carry."

"Let's see—" Mike's mind continued to work. He leaned back in his chair, closed his eyes, straightened suddenly and looked piercingly about in every direction to make sure there were no girls in the vicinity, then closed them again.

He said, "There's no question but that magnification is possible; photography is possible. If all of a typical microfilm is expanded and photographed, however, so that it could be read with the unaided eye, the resultant series of photographs would cover an area of—" Here he whipped out his famous girlie slide rule, designed by himself, with the hairline neatly and stimulatingly bisecting a buxom blonde. He manipulated it caressingly. "—An area of one hundred fifty square feet in area at least. We would have to use a sheet of paper ten feet by fifteen feet and crawl around on it."

"That would be possible," I muttered.

"Too undignified for a scientist unless, of course, he were pointing out something to a girl student. And even then she might get interested in reading whatever it was he was pointing out and that would kill everything."

We were both down in the dumps at that. We recognized that we had Nobel material here. Films had the virtue of being compact, but that was their only virtue.

Oh, if only you could fold a ten-foot-by-fifteen-foot piece of paper in your hand. You would require no electronic or photonic equipment to read it. You could read any part of it at will. You could go backward or forward without having to manipulate any controls. You would merely shift your eyes.

The whole thought was incredibly exciting. The technological advance involved in using eye muscles in place of expensive equipment was enormous. Mike pointed out at once that glancing back and forth over a large sheet of paper would exercise the eye muscles and equip a scientist better for the important task of not failing to observe the feminine parade.

It remained only to determine how best to make a large sheet of paper portable and manipulable.

I took a course in topology in order to learn folding techniques and many was the evening my girl friend of the day and I would design some order of folding. Beginning at opposite ends of the sheet of paper, we would come closer and closer as we folded according to some intricate formula, until we were face to face, panting and flushed with the mental and physical exertion. The results were enormously exciting but the folding procedures were never any good.

How I wished I had studied more mathematics. I even approached Prunella Plug, our harsh-voiced laundress, who folded bed sheets with aplomb and dignity. She was not about to let me into the secret, however.

I might have explained what I wanted the folding for, but I wasn't going to let *her* in on it. I meant to share the Nobel Prize with as few people as possible. The famous phrase of the great scientist Lord Clinchmore—"I'm not in science for my health, you know"—rang through my mind.

One morning I thought I had it. Oh, the exitement of it! I had to find Mike, for only his keen analytical mind would tell me if there were flaws in the notion. I tracked him down to a hotel room at last but found him deeply involved with a young lady—or popsie, to use the scientific term.

I banged away at the locked door until he came out, rather in a bad humor for some reason. He said, "Darn it, Jack, you can't interrupt research like that." Mike was a dedicated scientist.

I said, "Listen. We've been thinking in terms of two dimensions. What about *one* dimension?"

"How do you mean, one dimension?"

"Take the photos," I said, "and make them follow one after the other in a single line!"

"It would be yards and yards long." He worked out the figures with his finger on his colleague's abdomen, while I watched closely to make sure that he made no mistakes. He said, "It could easily be two-hundred feet long. That's ungainly."

"But you don't have to fold," I said. "You roll. You place one end on one plastic rod, and the other end on another. You roll them together!"

"Great Scott," said Mike, shocked into profanity by the thought. "Maybe you have it."

It was that very day, however, that the blow struck. A visiting professor from California had news. Paul Derrick, he said, was rumored to be working on the problem of a nonelectronic film. He didn't seem to know what that meant, but we did and our hearts sank again.

I said, "He must have heard of what we're doing here. We've *got* to beat him."

And how we tried! We took the photographs ourselves, pasted them side by side, rolled them on rods. It was a job of unimaginable complexity and delicacy that might well have used skilled artisans, but we were intent on allowing no outsider to see what we were doing.

It worked, but Mike was uncertain. He said, "I don't think it's really practical. If you want to find a particular place in the film, you have to roll and roll and roll, one way or another. It is very hard on the wrists."

But it was all we had. I wanted to publish, but Mike held back. "Let's see what Derrick has worked out," he said.

"But if he has this, he will have anticipated us."

Mike shook his head, "If this is all he's got, it doesn't matter. This isn't going to win the Nobel Prize. It isn't good enough—I just feel it, here."

He placed his hand on the girlie stitched on his shirt pocket so sincerely that I did not argue. Mike was a great scientist and a great scientist just knows what will get a Nobel Prize and what will not. That's what makes a scientist great.

Derrick did announce his discovery—and it had a flaw in it that an average high-school student would have spotted at once.

His nonelectronic film was simply our old two-dimensional sheets, but without even our efforts to fold them. It just hung down the side of a large wall. A movable ladder was supplied that was attached to a runner near the ceiling. One of Derrick's students climbed the ladder and read aloud into the microphones.

Everyone ooh-ed and ah-ed at the sight of someone reading with the unaided eye, but Mike, watching on television, slapped his thigh in amusement.

"The idiot," he said. "What about people with acrophobia?"

Of course! It leaped to the eye when Mike pointed it out. Anyone afraid of heights couldn't read under the Derrick system.

But I seized Mike's wrist and said, "Now wait awhile, Mike. They're going to laugh at Derrick and that's dangerous. As soon as this point about acrophobia comes out, Derrick will feel humiliated and he will turn every fiber of his magnificent brain to the project. He will then solve it in weeks. We've got to get there first."

Mike sobered up at once. "You are right, Jack," he said simply. "Let's go out on the town. A girl or two apiece will help us think."

It did, too, and then the next morning we thought about other things and got back to work.

I remember I was walking back and forth, muttering, "We've tried two dimensions; we've tried one dimension; what's left?" And then my eye fell upon Mike's girlie shirt with the nude on the breast pocket so cleverly hemstitched that strategic areas were distinctly raised.

"Heavens," I said, "we haven't tried *three* dimensions."

I went screaming for Mike. This time I was sure I had it and I could hardly breathe waiting for his judgment. He looked at me, eyes luminous. "We have it," he said.

It's so simple, looking back on it. We simply piled the photographs in a heap.

The heaps could be kept in place in any number of ways. They could be stapled, for instance. Then Mike got the idea of placing them between stiff cardboard covers to protect individual photographs from damage.

Within a month, we had published. The world rang with the discovery and everyone knew that the next Nobel Prize in physics would be ours.

Derrick, to do him justice, congratulated us and said, "Now the world can read without electronics and by the use of the unaided eyes, thanks to the Holmes-Ginsbook device. I congratulate those two dirty rats on their discovery."

That handsome acknowledgment was Science at its best.

The Holmes-Ginsbook device is now a household item. The popularity of the device is such that its name has been shortened to the final syllable and increasing numbers of people are calling them simply "books."

This eliminates my name, but I have my Nobel Prize and a contract to write a book on the intimate details surrounding the discovery for a quarter-million-dollar advance. Surely that is enough. Scientists are simple souls and once they have fame, wealth and girls, that's all they ask.

And that's it. You now have a more or less general once-over as far as my writing career is concerned, at the milestone of My Hundredth Book, and I must say that going through it all has given me a serious attack of vertigo.

It's an awful lot of typewriter-banging in an awful lot of different directions considering that at the time this book appears, I will still be on the sunny side of fifty.

Nor, frankly, do I intend to stop

I've got a huge book on Shakespeare in the works, and a history of the Byzantine Empire, and a book on sex for teen-agers (honest!), and a number of other things.

Am I going to be aiming at My Two Hundredth Book now?

Oh, I don't know. No one lives forever, after all. But I can say this—as long as I do live, I intend to keep writing.

Charles Dickens died as he was working on The Mystery of Edwin Drood *with his pen trailing a mark along the page and his head slumped over the manuscript—and that is the only way a writer would want to go.*

APPENDIX
MY HUNDRED
BOOKS

	TITLE	PUBLISHER	DATE
1	Pebble in the Sky	Doubleday	1950
2	I, Robot	Gnome Press	1950
3	The Stars, Like Dust—	Doubleday	1951
4	Foundation	Gnome Press	1951
5	David Starr: Space Ranger	Doubleday	1952
6	Foundation and Empire	Gnome Press	1952
7	The Currents of Space	Doubleday	1952
8	Biochemistry and Human Metabolism	Williams & Wilkins	1952
9	Second Foundation	Gnome Press	1953
10	Lucky Starr and the Pirates of the Asteroids	Doubleday	1953
11	The Caves of Steel	Doubleday	1954
12	Lucky Starr and the Oceans of Venus	Doubleday	1954
13	The Chemicals of Life	Abelard-Schuman	1954
14	The Martian Way and Other Stories	Doubleday	1955
15	The End of Eternity	Doubleday	1955
16	Races and People	Abelard-Schuman	1955
17	Lucky Starr and the Big Sun of Mercury	Doubleday	1956
18	Chemistry and Human Health	McGraw-Hill	1956
19	Inside the Atom	Abelard-Schuman	1956
20	The Naked Sun	Doubleday	1957
21	Lucky Starr and the Moons of Jupiter	Doubleday	1957
22	Building Blocks of the Universe	Abelard-Schuman	1957
23	Earth Is Room Enough	Doubleday	1957
24	Only a Trillion	Abelard-Schuman	1957
25	The World of Carbon	Abelard-Schuman	1958
26	Lucky Starr and the Rings of Saturn	Doubleday	1958
27	The World of Nitrogen	Abelard-Schuman	1958
28	The Death Dealers	Avon	1958

Award-Winning Science Fiction

Magnificent Fantasy From Dell

Each of these novels first appeared in the famous magazine of fantasy, *Unknown*—each is recognized as a landmark in the field—and each is illustrated by the acknowledged master of fantasy art, Edd Cartier.